Also by Shannon Burke

Into the Savage Country

Safelight

Black Flies

The
Brother Years

The
Brother Years

Shannon Burke

 Pantheon Books, New York

Copyright © 2020 by Shannon Burke

All rights reserved. Published in the United States
by Pantheon Books, a division of Penguin Random House LLC,
New York, and distributed in Canada by Penguin
Random House Canada Limited, Toronto.

Pantheon Books and colophon are registered
trademarks of Penguin Random House LLC.

Library of Congress Cataloging-in-Publication Data
Name: Burke, Shannon, author.
Title: The brother years / Shannon Burke.
Description: First edition. New York: Pantheon Books, 2020
Identifiers: LCCN 2019037326 (print). LCCN 2019037327 (ebook). ISBN
9781524748647 (hardcover). ISBN 9781524748654 (ebook).
Subjects: GSAFD: Bildungsromans.
Classification: LCC PS3602.U7555 B76 2020 (print) |
LCC PS3602.U7555 (ebook) | DDC 813/.6—d23
LC record available at lccn.loc.gov/2019037326
LC ebook record available at lccn.loc.gov/2019037327

www.pantheonbooks.com

Jacket photograph: ClassicStock/Alamy
Jacket design by Kelly Blair

Printed in the United States of America
First Edition
2 4 6 8 9 7 5 3 1

To my family

Something long preparing and formless is arrived and form'd in you,
You are henceforth secure, whatever comes or goes.

—Walt Whitman, "To Think of Time"

The
Brother Years

1

The Wager

In later life, we see things with a more practical eye, one we share with the rest of society; but adolescence was the only time when we ever learned anything.

—Marcel Proust

The four of us—the Brennan kids—were a tight-knit, tumultuous, bickering, cohesive mob. Our father was a Southside dreamer full of elaborate plans meant to advance the fortunes of his family. Coyle, the oldest kid, was our drill sergeant, implementing Dad's extreme orders with an iron fist. Brave, exacting, and unrelenting, Coyle had a spartan sensibility. I'll give an example.

One day in the sixth grade my friend Jimmy and I were drawing pictures of tanks and dragons while listening to *Hot Rocks* on a cassette deck. Coyle came into the doorway and stood there with a judgmental scowl, hanging on to the molding, suspicious of the chaotic sounds coming from the cassette player.

"What's this music?" he said.

"Rolling Stones," Jimmy said. "Don't you know it?"

"I don't listen to music," Coyle said. "It's a waste of time."

That was Coyle in a nutshell. Music was a waste of time. Everything was a waste of time except work and school and sports and the marching orders from Dad. As far as I could see, Coyle's whole purpose in life was fulfilling our father's wishes.

I was the second-oldest kid in the family and the one most different from Coyle. I did not fulfill my father's wishes in anything. I was not orderly. I was not diligent. I liked any book with a barbarian or spaceship on the cover. I played Dungeons and Dragons, which Coyle thought was about the lamest thing he could imagine. I had a notebook of poems and little stories and made movies on Dad's video recorder, mustering my younger siblings to act in these productions, all of which Coyle thought, of course, was a waste of time.

Our family was poor. I should get that out of the way at the beginning. Dad was taking classes to get his teacher's certificate, but in the meantime he had about six jobs—paper delivery, painter, roofer, renovator, tennis pro, maintenance. And while Dad was going through his endless rounds of drudgery, and Mom was cooking or cleaning or repairing the old house, Coyle was left in charge of his younger siblings. He liked being in charge. Coyle's natural, domineering temperament flowered when he had subjects to rule over. And there was no one he liked to boss around more than me.

He pointed out that I didn't fold my clothes in the right way. I scattered food when I fed the cats. I missed the corners when I swept floors. To his eye, everything about my methods was idiosyncratic and inefficient. But I didn't care what he thought was the proper way. I wanted to do things my own way, which was endlessly irritating for him. And that was satisfying for me. Irritating Coyle was a side benefit to doing things in the way I wanted.

This pattern of instruction and resistance was the basis of our relationship for our childhood until the year I was twelve and Coyle was thirteen. That year, in the late winter of his eighth grade, my exacting older brother did something that surprised everyone: He refused to get a haircut.

Our mother cut our hair, so it wasn't like we'd make an appointment or anything. Mom just said it was time for a cut and we'd sit on the high chair in the kitchen and she'd take out the scissors and hack away. Up to that point in his life Coyle had been utterly indifferent to his hair. He kept his hair short so it didn't get in the way of his achievement in school and sports, but I don't think he'd ever thought about how it looked. Worrying about your hair was for girls.

But on this day in February 1979, Mom told Coyle to get on the high chair and he said, "I'm not getting my hair cut. I don't want to look like a geek."

"Since when is having normal-length hair looking like a geek?" Mom said.

"Since now," Coyle said.

And that was that. Coyle refused. And once Coyle decided on something it was almost impossible to get him to change his mind. Mom wasn't going to war over a haircut. So she just told me to get on the chair instead.

"You want to be a hippie, I guess," Dad said that night when he came home.

Dad was a swaggering, bustling bull of a man. He had a

thick neck and arms so muscle-filled that they stuck out to the side. Excessive work was Dad's religion. He didn't put up with back talk or resistance to his schemes. But I think Dad was secretly pleased that diligent Coyle finally wanted something other than high grades and a winning baseball season. Coyle, finally, was acting like a normal human being.

So, Coyle was allowed to skip the haircut and that seemed to be the end of it. But a few weeks later Coyle refused to wear the khaki pants Mom laid out for him for school. He put on old, ripped jeans instead and a T-shirt with an emblem of a rooster.

"Collared shirts are for dorks," Coyle said.

A few days later I heard music coming from the basement. I went down and saw Coyle doing sit-ups on the dichromatic gym mat, listening to my cassette copy of *Who's Next*. A while later I heard Coyle lifting weights and listening to Led Zeppelin. No one listened to Led Zeppelin in our house. That was hard rock. It was supposed to be immoral in some undefined way. And it was perfectionist Coyle listening to *Led Zeppelin IV*. That was just weird.

In school that week I noticed that Coyle had migrated from the center lunch table where the studious kids ate and was now sitting at the edge of the cafeteria with some long-haired kids we called "burnouts." The burnouts were considered to be the worst kids in the school. They wore concert T-shirts and hung out with girls that had long bangs and wore black eyeliner and smoked cigarettes and talked in bored monotones. "Freaks," Coyle had called them before. "Loosers." But now perfect, straight-A-student Coyle was sitting with the burnouts. At one point during the lunch period I even saw him get up and stand on his chair and pretend to be Commander Cornelius from *Planet of the Apes,* pointing at the popular kids and saying, "Kill the humans!"

A few more weeks passed, and then I was on the back porch when Coyle appeared around the side of the house riding a Honda 125 on-road/off-road motorcycle. I could see right away that it was a used bike, a Frankenstein-type deal, with metal table legs as monkey bars and with a kid's sparkly banana bicycle seat to sit on. All the paneling and unnecessary framework had been removed. It was light and fast and stripped down and jerry-rigged and there was something undeniably pleasing and just utterly cool about that bike. I was attracted to it immediately.

Our house was the smallest in the neighborhood. We had a long, narrow backyard wedged between larger plots of land with weedy bushes on either side. Coyle rode the bike up into the middle of the yard and came to rest in a patch of dirt that was the pitcher's mound in our backyard ballgames. I jumped off the porch and walked over.

"Where'd you get it?" I asked.

"Farrelly's brother is a mechanic. He helped me find the parts and we've been putting it together bit by bit. I'm going to ride it to school."

Dan Farrelly was one of Coyle's new burnout friends— a skinny kid with straight blond hair, very blue eyes, and a wolfish look. He was the catcher on the baseball team.

"Dad won't let you ride it," I said.

"When I'm sixteen he will. It will save them time so they don't have to drive me around. Until then I can ride it in the backyard and at Deach's Pit."

"You have to ride on the roads to get to Deach's Pit. Dad won't let you."

Coyle didn't bother commenting. He didn't need my approval to do what he wanted to do. He just revved the engine and I walked around the bike, pretending not to be impressed. Our six-person family lived in a two-bedroom house. All our possessions were communal, including our clothes. Everything was worn out or broken or had lost its luster from overuse. That bike was undeniably the coolest thing that anyone in the family had ever owned. And it was diligent Coyle who had it. I was already thinking of ways of convincing Coyle to let me ride it when I heard the screen door slam and turned to see our father walking out.

Dad had a way of moving when he was angry. The Southside street swagger came out. He didn't like surprises.

"It's mine," Coyle said before Dad even got to him. "I got the frame and the engine from Andy Brands. I've been working on it in Farrelly's garage at night. I'm going to start riding it to school when I turn sixteen so you don't have to drive me. It will save you time," Coyle added hopefully.

"You don't get your license for over two years," Dad said.

"I can practice before then in the backyard and at Deach's Pit, where all the other kids ride their dirt bikes."

"You're not other kids" was all Dad said. "Get off. Now."

Coyle knew not to counter Dad directly, particularly when he was in a bad mood. Coyle got off. Dad threw a leg over the bike. He revved the engine a few times, then got off and took the key out and put it in his pocket.

"I need to talk to your mom. Until then, you don't ride."

Coyle let out an exasperated puff of air.

"My friends ride at Deach's Pit every weekend."

"Yeah, well, those friends are not role models," Dad said.

That was the first time I heard Dad acknowledge that he knew what was going on with Coyle and his new group of burnout friends.

"I had the same kind of friends growing up," Dad said. "Smoking. Cutting class. Up to no good. It's why I moved out of the city. To get away from that. If those guys you're hanging out with ride motorcycles, it makes me think you shouldn't do it."

"You don't know them," Coyle said sullenly.

"I can tell what they're like," Dad said.

Next door, in Mrs. Chambers's house, the blinds moved. Seneca, the suburb we lived in, was supposed to be this fancy place. Dad had moved us there so we would have what was supposedly "a better life." All the houses around us were large and fancy, with red tile roofs and manicured lawns and long curving driveways with multiple expensive cars parked in large garages. Our house didn't fit in at all. It was small, squat, and redbrick, with dirt patches in the yard. We had one shower for the six of us. When we got in fights they spilled out into the yard and all the neighbors peeked out to see what was going on with the weird, poor family in that rich neighborhood.

Dad ignored Mrs. Chambers. He held the key up to Coyle.

"Is this the only one?"

Coyle grudgingly took another key out of his pocket. He handed it to my father.

"I'll talk to your mother. Until then this is a lawn ornament," Dad said.

He walked back to the house.

"Lawn ornament," Coyle said when Dad was gone. "Where'd he get that one?"

"I knew he wouldn't let you ride it," I said.

I reached out for the bike, but hesitated to see what Coyle thought of that. He gave me a skeptical look.

"Don't even think of touching it," he said.

Our father delivered five hundred *Chicago Tribunes* every morning of the year, and three days a week the older kids helped. That meant on Tuesdays, Thursdays, and Sundays, Coyle and I woke at three in the morning and drove with my father to the delivery garage, where Coyle and I stood side by side at the binding tables passing rolled papers through machines that mechanically knotted papers with a string. There were stacks of bound *Chicago Tribunes* piled in the corner and the smell of cigarette smoke and fresh ink. Hot, stale air blew constantly from high fans while an old radio played WGN Newsradio 78. Coyle was faster and stronger and more adept at the rolling than me, and since we split the work, every morning we were at the garage he complained that I was too slow and made more work for him.

On that morning, though, the morning after Coyle got his motorcycle, as we stood side by side at the binding tables, there was the normal invective-filled conversation that went back and forth among the other workers and the drone of the radio and the slap of the wooden door on the spring, but Coyle didn't comment on how slow I rolled or how I took too many breaks. It was unusual not to be derided and I noted it.

Once the papers were bound and tossed into a wheeled canvas hamper, we brought the hamper out into the pitch-black and frigid dark at four in the morning and filled the back of the station wagon with the papers. Afterward, I got into my spot in the very back of the car, half buried in *Tribunes*. It was my job to push the papers forward so Coyle, who sat right behind Dad, could transfer the rolled papers to the front seat, where Dad would grab them and toss them out the window in a continuous stream while he blasted classic rock over the station wagon's speakers. "Don't Do Me Like That." "Hungry Heart." "Summer Breeze." Those songs in the backseat with the frigid wind swirling and the aching, queasy nausea of being up before dawn in my gut, and the smell of ink, and the dull, flat, intermittent smack of the paper on cold concrete—that was the delivery part of the mornings, and usually during the delivery Coyle complained that I didn't transfer the papers fast enough to the middle seat. He said that I lay down and closed my eyes and he had to reach over the seat and smack me with a rolled paper to get me to do my job.

But on that morning Coyle did not smack me with the rolled paper when I lay down to rest, even though I did fall behind, and that, also, was unusual.

By six o'clock we were back at home, walking into the lit house, where Mom was cooking bacon and eggs and toast, and Fergus and Maddy, my two younger siblings, were on the living room floor, doing sit-ups, push-ups, and jumping jacks. Every morning, even if we did the paper route, we had an hour of calisthenics before school. Using all of our time for improvement was our father's obsession. We were going to get ahead in life with hard work and diligence, and he had begun to train us from the day we were born in reading and math and also in all athletics. So in the morning we did calisthenics, like we were in boot camp. The exercise routine was listed on an individualized note card, one for each kid in the family, one for each day of the week, kept in a small, metal note card box.

On that day, within a minute of arriving home Coyle and I had flung off our jackets and gotten our exercise card for the day from the metal box and were side by side in the living room, feet beneath the couch, doing sit-ups, while Dad passed through the room, calling out to me, "Aw, you're lagging behind, Willie. Look at your brother. He's faster. Pick it up!"

Usually Coyle would have chimed in with my father's criticisms, but on that morning Coyle did not comment about how I lagged behind during the exercises, and because Coyle had not commented at all that day—not on how slow I rolled papers or transferred papers or did my exercises— I knew Coyle was thinking about ways to get my parents to allow him to ride that bike. He was obsessed with it. The four of us—the kids in the family—worked together with our father every day. We did sports together. We slept together in the same small room on two bunk beds. There were no secrets among us. And I knew that if Coyle was so distracted that he couldn't spare the time to deride me, he must be working out some elaborate plan.

For the next few days Coyle moved around in a daze, wandering out into the backyard and rubbing his motorcycle down with a rag, polishing the seat and gas tank and the chrome exhausts. The neighborhood kids gathered in the grass around the bike and Coyle pointed out his favorite features.

"See, no splash guard. Saves weight. And I switched to a smaller gas tank. Makes it faster. It can jump, too. Look at the shocks. And it's got pegs for a passenger. I'm going to ride it in the backyard until I'm sixteen. Then I'll ride it wherever I want."

I was pretty sure our parents were never going to let Coyle ride that bike. We were already total outcasts there in fancy Seneca. And having a motocross track in the backyard was pretty much the definition of low-class. I thought the only reason my parents hadn't told Coyle right away that he couldn't ride that bike was because Coyle had been so perfect for so long that they didn't know how to tell him that they were going to forbid the one thing he'd ever really wanted. I anticipated a long, festering disagreement, but as it turned out, the whole thing came to a head quickly and simply during our first baseball practice of the year, and inadvertently, I played a small role in the outcome.

Baseball had a special place in my father's heart, as he felt it had saved his life. My father grew up around 55th and Western, the son of Lithuanian and Irish immigrants. As far as he told it, his childhood consisted of haunting the vacant lots and back streets off Western Avenue, playing wall ball during the day, and roaming the streets with gangs at night. By the time he was a teenager our father and his friends had gone from stealing candy to smashing windows and breaking into cars. As he told the story, he was headed for a bad end. But our father had one talent. He was a great baseball pitcher, the best pitcher his age in Illinois, and though he almost failed out of high school, he got a scholarship offer from Northwestern.

So, at the age of eighteen Dad left his street gang and the Southside and moved to the grand, tree-lined campus of Northwestern University. Dad spent five years at Northwestern. He almost failed out twice, but he played ball and attended his classes and he came out the back end with a degree in finance, and wholly infected by the dream of an easy suburban, white-collar life. Forget the streets. Dad wanted to be a business guy, an investment banker, an entrepreneur, someone who made money in an office, not with his hands.

Dad married my mother, and they bought a house in Seneca, Illinois, close to Northwestern, and over the next fifteen years Dad tried to figure out how to pay for that house. He started a restaurant that failed. He worked as a stockbroker but was laid off in the market downturn of 1974. He picked up part-time work and started taking graduate classes in medicine, but the kids started coming and he had to drop out. For a while he worked as a teacher in Chicago, where you didn't need to have completed your state teaching certificate as long as you were working toward getting it, but he got laid off from that job because he failed forty percent of his class.

That's right. As a first-year teacher without a certificate my father failed forty percent of his class.

"I don't pass people who don't know the material," he said.

The principal begged my father to reconsider his grades, but he wouldn't do it. That was our father—absolute, unyielding, and impractical.

By the time I was in middle school Dad had reverted to working whatever job he could pick up to pay the rent, while also taking classes for his teacher's certificate. In the meantime, he concentrated on what he considered to be his real job, which was raising his kids to be "superior human beings."

Like I said, we were woken every morning at five for the calisthenics, except on the days we helped with the paper route, when we woke at three. There was extra math and reading. On the weekends we helped our father with his painting, janitorial, and renovation jobs. I was filling out adult work crews when I was nine years old. By the age of twelve I knew how to professionally clean a bathroom and hang drywall. We were also taught sports, but particularly baseball, and also tennis, which Dad thought was an upper-class sport that we'd "play at the club" when we got older. Every day was crammed with as much work, study, and sports as possible.

My father called this religion of maximum effort The Methods. And for a while The Methods seemed to be utterly effective. We did well in school and were responsible, obedient kids, at least until that day when perfect Coyle showed up with that motorcycle and became obsessed with the idea of riding it in the backyard.

A few days later, we were out at the first baseball practice of the year. I was batting. Coyle was pitching. And I was annoying everyone because I kept whiffing.

"Choke up!" Dad yelled from the outfield.

"I can't get around. He's too fast," I said.

A few patches of snow lined the parking lot. The cold, moist, squishy grass of the playfield stretched out to a cottonwood grove in the distance. Fergus, my younger brother, was in center field. Dad was in short left.

"Cock the bat and bend your knees before he throws!" Dad yelled. "You're not getting the bat around. You have to cock the bat."

"He's too fast!" I yelled.

"You're too slow is the problem," Coyle said.

He wound up and threw again. I missed. He pitched again. I missed.

"You're too far from the plate!" Dad yelled from the outfield. "You can't hit it if you can't reach it. Get in the batter's box."

"I am in it."

"Closer!" Dad yelled.

I got maybe a half-inch closer.

"If I want to bean you, standing away isn't going to help," Coyle said.

"Did you hear that?" I yelled.

Fergus, an athletic, stocky kid two years younger than me with a mop of straight, dark hair and a keen sense of mockery, yelled from the outfield, "What're you, afraid?"

"Yes!" I shouted. "Do you see how hard he's throwing?"

"I'm not going to hit you," Coyle said.

"Get closer!" Dad bellowed.

I inched in closer to the plate. I cocked the bat. I dug in. Coyle wound up and pitched right at my head. I dropped into the dust. The ball whooshed right over.

"You were crowding the plate," Coyle said, laughing. "Brushback."

Dad and Fergus were laughing, too. "Get back up there!" Dad yelled.

I stood back up. I positioned myself about three feet from the plate.

"Stop being a baby," Coyle said.

I inched closer to the plate, but was ready to jump away at any moment. I dug in. Coyle wound up and pitched. Whoosh. The ball was past me before I swung. He pitched again. And again. And again. Finally, I dropped the bat. I took my helmet off.

"I can't hit him," I said. "He's too fast."

Dad was already jogging in from the outfield. He hated when any of us quit. He grabbed the bat from me.

"You gotta cock the bat and step in as he winds up," Dad said.

"You gotta cock!" Fergus yelled from the outfield. "See, Willie, your problem, you gotta *cock*!"

Dad put on the helmet.

"You pitch to me now, tough guy," Dad said to Coyle.

"That's what I figured," Coyle said.

I walked behind the backstop to watch. Dad dug in at the plate. His athletic prime was long past. He spent his days painting and renovating houses, but he was still muscular and relatively trim and fiercely competitive. He lived for those hours on the playfield. He wasn't the sort of father who let us win. None of us had ever beaten him in anything.

Coyle got a ball from the white bucket. He stood poised, lanky, hand in glove, weight on his front foot, studying Dad's stance.

"You can't hit me," Coyle said.

"Are you kidding me?" Dad said. "I hit pitchers who played pro ball."

"Like twenty years ago," Coyle said. "How about this? If I strike you out I can ride my motorcycle whenever I want."

Dad made a guttural, scoffing sound.

"What was that?" Coyle said.

"That was me saying I can hit you," Dad said. "It's just a question of whether I hit it over Fergus's head or not."

"If you're so sure, let's bet. If I strike you out I get the bike."

Dad let the bat fall.

"And what do I get out of it?" Dad asked.

"What do you want?"

Dad thought for a moment.

"If I get a hit, I get to cut your hair. I'll shave that mop off. And you shut up and stop moping about that bike and don't ride it until you're sixteen."

"Ok," Coyle said.

"So you agree?"

"Why not? I'm not getting to ride it now anyway. So is it a deal?"

"You'd really let me shave your head?" Dad said.

"If it means I get a chance to ride the bike."

Dad had never lost to us in anything, but particularly not baseball.

"All right," Dad said. "Deal."

Coyle stepped back on the mound and rubbed the ball.

"When I strike you out you give me the keys," Coyle said.

"And when I get a hit I personally shave your head," Dad said.

Fergus was in left field now, holding his hair back like he was bald. "Krishna, Hare Krishna . . ." he sang.

"Your shaved head's going to look great with your druggie friends," Dad said.

"They aren't druggies," Coyle said.

"Whatever you say," Dad said. "You ready, cue ball?"

I was standing behind the backstop, watching this all play out. Coyle was risking public humiliation to get what he wanted. That was brave, and as much as he annoyed me most of the time, I admired him at that moment.

Dad held the bat up, waving the tip. Coyle looked at Dad's stance, where he was positioned in relation to the plate, how much he was turned. Coyle took a deep breath, then wound up and threw.

Ting.

The ball hit the fence before Dad could swing.

Dad looked behind him where the ball had dropped to rest in the dust. He let the bat fall. He sniffed and dug his feet in and cocked his bat. Coyle pitched again. The ball was just a blur. It dipped as it reached the plate.

Ting. The ball bounced and hit the back fence again. Dad hadn't even swung.

"Thanks for showing us how to do it," Fergus yelled from the outfield.

"I'm pitching to you next," Dad yelled at Fergus. "At your head!"

"Better you than Coyle."

Dad got ready again. Coyle pitched. Dad swung and missed. Coyle pitched again. Dad didn't even get the bat around. He stood there, puzzled.

"You should be pitching from the adult mound. No one could hit this."

"You just gotta cock the bat," I said. "That's the problem."

Dad turned and pointed the bat at me as if to say, *You're dead*.

Fergus sat down in left center.

"You can't hit him anyway. Why should I stand?" Fergus yelled.

Dad cocked the bat again. He swung and missed. Then he missed again. And again. What none of us had realized was that since Coyle had gotten his new burnout friends, since he'd started to wear the clothes that he wanted, and to act in a way that was more natural to him, he had also started to practice pitching on his own, away from all the coaches and also away from our father, who had been hovering over him his whole life, telling him what to do. Dad wanted Coyle to be a perfect little suburban scholar-athlete, and Coyle had gone along and taken Dad's instruction and demands for thirteen years, fulfilling every one of Dad's exacting expectations, but that winter something had changed in Coyle. He'd broken out of the goody-goody mold that he'd been in for his whole life. He'd found new friends and a new way of doing things. There was a joy and an offhand swagger in the way he pitched now, something that had not been taught by our father but was entirely his own. The balls were coming in fast and low and wavering in the air and sinking at the plate. Fergus and I just stood watching as Dad missed again and again. It was impressive, but it was also unnerving. Dad had been one of the best players in the state. If Dad couldn't hit Coyle there was no way the rest of us could. That was the end of our playing pickup ball with Coyle. He was too good. It had happened all at once.

After about fifteen pitches Dad hurled the bat against the fence.

"You can give me the keys when we get home," Coyle said.

"Yep," Dad said. "Let me tell your mom first. Then you get them. Only for the backyard. And only as long as you keep the rules."

"Until I'm sixteen," Coyle said. "Then I ride wherever I want."

Coyle knew not to celebrate too much or to annoy Dad. Not that he didn't have the right to do those things. In our family there was none of this crap about everyone being a winner. You were a winner if you won. And if you won you could celebrate and rub it in to the other person and make them feel miserable. On the other hand, if you lost you had to grit it out and accept the ridicule and go back to work so you could stick it to the other person the next time. Coyle usually took full bragging rights, but he was careful that day with our father, who had a bad temper.

In the car on the way home there was a nervy, uneasy

silence, like someone had done something wrong, but all that had happened was Coyle had beaten our father.

"How was it?" Mom asked when we got home.

"Good," Coyle said.

"Good," Dad said.

Dad motioned to Mom that he needed to talk to her. They went upstairs and Coyle sat at the kitchen table. Maddy came in.

She was the youngest, six years old, a blond-haired beanpole, gawky and eager to please. She'd been cleaning windows and had a soiled rag in her hand.

"What happened?" she asked.

Fergus tossed his mitt onto the table.

"Coyle struck Dad out so he gets to be a badass and ride his motorcycle."

"Really?"

"Yeah, don't you know?" Fergus said. "That's the way it is in this family. If you lose you get kicked in the dirt. But if you win you get whatever you want."

Later that afternoon we all stood on the porch and watched Coyle straddle his bike and kick-start the engine. We watched him ease the bike into gear. We knew what the neighbors must think—a motorcycle in the backyard to go along with our rusting car and the constant sound of bickering coming from our small house. Lovely. But there was nothing to do about it. Coyle had won the bet so he got to ride the bike. Coyle revved the engine, then started around the yard in a circle and then in a figure-eight and then in a circle again, and for the next months we watched Coyle on the bike until he wore a path in the dirt and until he could go fast enough to kick the bike into second and then downshift on the turns. When Coyle was not delivering papers or scraping cabinets or doing exercises or any of the other extra work demanded by our father, he was riding that bike, getting ready for the day when he would take it out on the streets. Coyle's long-haired friends came over and examined the engine. They tinkered with it and pulled their bikes alongside his and compared them and all of them rode in a circle like a gang. I think of that now—Coyle, the perfect student, the blue-collar striver, suddenly breaking from Dad's restrictions and hanging with those new friends, playing ball with them, casting off some of the rules that we'd grown up with, learning to do things in a new way. And anyone who knew Coyle, who knew our whole family, really, and the excessive, combative manner that had been drilled into us for our whole lives, would have known that though Coyle might have at first agreed to stay in the backyard, neither he, nor the rest of us, would be back there forever.

2

Superior Human Beings

Children have never been very good at listening to their elders, but they have never failed to imitate them. They must, they have no other models.

—James Baldwin

Five months after Coyle was given permission to ride his motorcycle in circles in the backyard, I was walking out of the junior high on a hot, dry, windy July afternoon. I was taking an art class in summer school, and that hour in the air-conditioned art room, away from the rigorous striving in the house, away from the bickering with my siblings, was pure pleasure for me. For that hour I drew or sculpted whatever came into my mind and nobody told me I was going too slow because we were the poor family, or that I had to push myself and try harder, which was the normal mantra at home. For an hour, in the art class, I did what I wanted to do.

Afterward, I lingered at school, walking home slowly, reluctantly, crossing the faded white lines of the soccer field, and on this day, as I neared the grove of cottonwoods, I saw a group of kids gathered around a toppled motorcycle in the grass—Coyle's bike—and at the very center of the group, Coyle and a slender, good-looking kid named Robert Dainty were faced off against each other.

I knew Robert. He was one of the high-achieving kids that Coyle had sat with in the lunchroom before Coyle started hanging with the burnouts. He was the snide prince of the preppy kids, and even when Coyle was a part of Robert's crowd he'd never gotten along with Robert. As I walked up I saw that Robert was holding a basketball on his hip and motioning to Coyle's motorcycle.

"Oh, come on," Robert was saying. "If I can't ride it, at least let me sit on it."

"Can't. Sorry," Coyle said. I could tell that Coyle was not sorry at all to refuse this favor. "Willie knows," Coyle said as I walked up. "I can't let other people ride it, right?"

"That's the rule," I said.

"See," Coyle said. "Sorry. Too bad for you."

Coyle gripped the handlebars of the bike and rocked it upright, and when his back was turned, Robert tossed the basketball, bonging it off the back of Coyle's head.

The group of kids laughed nervously. Coyle just stood there, with his back turned, not moving for a moment. Then Coyle lowered his bike down gently, stood still for a minute and whirled and leapt on Robert. The two fell into the grass, thrashing each other, as everyone crowded around and shouted, "Fight! Fight!"

Coyle got on top of Robert, holding an open hand up.

"Do you want this? Do you want this?"

Smack—Coyle brought his hand down and slapped Robert across the face. We all heard it and I was surprised and a little afraid. Smacking us was something Coyle would do from time to time, but I'd never seen him do it to anyone else, and definitely not to a rich kid like Robert Dainty.

Coyle raised his hand again, but a stocky kid named Liam, a friend of Robert's, shoved Coyle and yelled, "Savvy's coming!"

Principal Savitt was a lumbering, curly-haired guy with bad knees, an ex-lineman. He limped his way across the play-field as Coyle picked himself up and Robert brushed his clothes off. Robert's eyes were glassy from the smack and I could tell he was ashamed of this and he kept looking down, trying to hide it.

Robert stepped out to meet Principal Savitt and in a wounded, indignant tone, Robert said, "I did nothing. Literally nothing. And Coyle Brennan attacked me."

"Coyle?" Principal Savitt said. "What's your story?"

"It was definitely me who started it," Coyle said sarcastically.

Coyle lifted his motorcycle. He started wheeling it away.

"Coyle Brennan. Stay here," Savitt called to him.

"You already heard his story," Coyle said over his shoulder. "I just attacked for no reason. Right, Robert? No reason at all."

Coyle wasn't the sort of kid who would plead his case with teachers. He felt pleading was suckass. He wanted his actions to speak for themselves.

Coyle swung his leg over the bike and kick-started the engine.

"Stay here!" Savitt ordered.

Coyle pretended not to hear. He held a hand up.

"Adiós, amigos," he called, and roared away, bouncing over the grass and cutting into the parking lot, weaving among the parked cars, going off in a blaze of defiance.

"See," Robert said. "He's not supposed to be here with that bike. He knows it. And now he's running. Whatta you expect? Total burnout."

Savitt, who'd been a principal for more than ten years and was not easily suckered, knew both Coyle and Robert, and did not seem to believe Robert's story.

"Did anyone else see?" Savitt asked the crowd of kids who were drifting away. "Who else saw? Anyone? Willie Brennan!" he called to me. "Get over here."

Savitt put a hand on my shoulder, and as the group of kids dispersed, I was led back to the school and was asked to tell my version of the story, which I did.

Later, Coyle said that I went with Principal Savitt voluntarily because I wanted to get him in trouble. Even now, years later, I'm not sure what's true. I had lost to Coyle in every contest for my entire life and Coyle was always telling me my methods were flawed. I resented that. Of course I did. But did I linger there on purpose to get him in trouble? I try to go back to that moment to ask myself honestly what I was thinking, but I really don't know. I can only say with certainty that whether I wanted to get Coyle in trouble or not, the telling of that story changed my life, and the life of every person in my family.

———

A few hours after Coyle smacked Robert Dainty in the face, Fergus, Maddy, and I were sitting around the table in the living room. I was sent home with a pink disciplinary slip. I leaned over and read it for the fifth time:

> *"This is to notify the parents of Coyle Brennan that Coyle got in a fight today outside the grounds of Seneca Junior High. As Coyle is no longer a student at the school, and his fight was with another former student, there can be no official reprimand. Nevertheless . . ."*

"Nevertheless!" Fergus mocked, tenting his hands.

"It sucks," Coyle said. "Dad says not to let anyone else ride the motorcycle, and when I tell Robert he can't ride it, he beans me in the head with a basketball. Nothing would have happened, but Willie tattled."

"Not Willie who got the pink slip," Dad said as he lumbered in. He picked up the small slip of pink paper, glanced at it, then tossed it back onto the table. "We have to be better than other people, Coyle. We're not rich—"

"Might as well admit it. We're poor," Fergus said.

"Middle class," Mom said gently as she came in with a steaming mug of tea. "We're middle class."

Mom was slim, with dark hair in a mushroom cut, a serious, patient woman who didn't put up with a lot of nonsense. She was the ice to counter Dad's fire.

"Explain again what happened," Mom said. "Because this notification says you attacked Robert for no reason."

"It does not say that I attacked for no reason," Coyle said.

"It says that Robert's *story* was that I attacked for no reason. *Willie's story.*"

"I just told the truth," I said.

Coyle made a dismissive, puffing sound.

"Willie's mad that I do everything better, so he tried to get me in trouble."

"Not me who beat on Robert Dainty," I said.

"Anyway," Dad said, cutting in. "The point here is that you're out of the yard with that bike. You broke the rules. So you lose your motorcycle privileges."

"For how long?" Coyle said.

"As long as it takes," Mom said. She glanced at our father. "It was a mistake to let you have the bike in the first place. Probably until you're sixteen."

"Until I'm sixteen!" Coyle shouted. "Bullshit!"

"Coyle!" Dad shouted. None of the kids had ever sworn in front of our parents. "There may be a chance to reassess in the future," Dad said. "But first you need to apologize, in writing, to Robert Dainty and to Principal Savitt."

"I'm not doing that," Coyle said.

Dad flicked a pen so it bounced off Coyle's hand.

"Yeah, you will," Dad said. "Write the apology."

Coyle didn't pick up the pen.

"I'm not apologizing to Robert."

"You think I like working eighteen hours a day, waking up at three every morning, and coming home to a pink slip?" Dad said.

"You think I like you telling us to work harder than everyone else and be better than everyone else in everything, then we're taunted by some suckass kid like Robert Dainty? You would have fought, too."

Dad waved a hand dismissively.

"You got in trouble, so write an apology, not because you did something wrong in defending yourself, but because it will be the broad-minded thing to do. You apologize. You eat a little crow—"

"Kiss ass!" Fergus yelled.

Dad pointed a finger at Fergus.

"Be quiet, Fergie. I'm trying to make a point. We don't always fit in in this neighborhood. So sometimes we have to do the broad-minded thing."

Fergus leaned over the table and mouthed the words *kiss ass* to Coyle. Dad gave Fergus a warning look, then turned back to Coyle.

"Write the apologies," he said.

"No," Coyle said. "I was wrong about the bike. I admit that. I understand that I can't take it out of the yard. I'm sorry. See? I apologized. I won't do it again. But I wasn't wrong about fighting Robert Dainty. He's jealous of me because I beat him in grades and in sports. He turned my old friends against me, saying things like, 'Brennan's dad's a paperboy. Brennan's dad cleans toilets.'"

"Well, that is very foolish," Mom said, suddenly flustered.

Dad's face went white for a moment.

"Willie knows it the same as I do," Coyle went on. "These kids in Seneca have never met an adult who wasn't a doctor or a lawyer. Robert makes fun of us because we don't have the right clothes and cars and whatever, but I beat him in everything and so who cares what kind of sneakers I have?

But he's always saying little weaselly things. I ignore it like you tell me to, but then he bounces a basketball off my head. If Willie wasn't a loser he'd've spoken up for me with Savitt."

"He just thought I was lying anyway. I'm your brother—"

"That's why you should have spoken up for me, dick."

Dad smacked his hand on the table.

"That's what I'm talking about. That sullen look. Using bad language. I've seen you out in the field with your new friends, smoking cigarettes."

"I don't smoke cigarettes," Coyle said. "That's for losers."

"Well, your friends do. I pay a lot of money to live here and give you opportunities that neither I nor your mother had. You need to take advantage of those opportunities. Those new friends are the worst crowd to be with. Druggies."

Fergus made horns with his fingers.

"Druggie!" he whispered.

Maddy and I stifled laughter and shrank in our chairs. Fergus liked to bait our father. He knew it was dangerous to do it when Dad was in that mood, but Fergus was a jester, a natural mimic, and he couldn't help himself. He often got away with things the rest of us wouldn't have because he could make us all laugh. But not always. Dad checked Fergus, then turned back to Coyle.

"Write the apology."

"No," Coyle said.

"Just write it," Maddy whispered to Coyle. "Who cares?"

Coyle turned to our father. He took a deep breath. Then he began speaking in a clear, even tone.

"For my whole life I've done whatever you asked. You know I have. In return I just want one single thing—to ride my bike. I might have been wrong to take the bike out of the yard—"

"Write the note," Dad said.

"I'll write to Savitt. Fine. But not to Robert Dainty. He's a little suckass. I'm not apologizing to him. Unless—" Coyle looked down at the table. "If I write the note can I still ride my bike in the backyard?"

Dad glanced at Mom. There was a long silence. I could tell that Dad would have given in here, but Mom said, "This isn't a negotiation. You broke the rules. You lose bike privileges."

"If I can't ride the bike I'm not writing the apology," Coyle said.

He stood from the table. Mom and Dad glanced at each other. No one had ever defied our parents like that. Dad stood up to stop Coyle's departure.

"Write the note," Dad said.

"No," Coyle said, and tried to keep on past our father, but as he did he jostled our father and there was a sudden uncoiling from our father, a blurred motion, like the flap of a bird's wing. Coyle's teeth clacked. His arms went up in the air. He fell back and hit the wall and lay curled on the carpet alongside the table, not moving. Dad had slugged him. It had happened really fast. We all sat silently, stunned.

Coyle lay there alongside the dining room table, sprawled, his head turned away, his eyes knots of skin. After a long moment, in her cool, withering tone, Mom said, "No reason to lie there on the floor making a theater out of it. Get up."

Coyle got up slowly, making little catching sounds.

"Sit back down. Both of you. And act like human beings."

Coyle twisted his neck in an effort to hold back tears. He

hated to cry in front of us. He stepped past Dad and went up the stairway. Dad stood up, too.

"Alex," Mom said, but Dad just kept walking out of the room. I heard the jingle of keys and the door slamming. Dad had gone outside to sit in the station wagon and listen to sports radio. That's what Dad always did to cool down. There was no place in the house for him to be alone, so he'd go out to the car to be by himself.

Maddy was sniffling. Mom put a hand on her knee.

"The boys are just working out a disagreement," she said. Then, to Fergus and me, "You could have helped rather than make a difficult situation worse."

"Like it's our fault Dad beat on Coyle," Fergus said.

"Your father did not beat on anyone. He gave Coyle one hit, which he should not have done, but don't exaggerate. And Willie, you should stick up for your brother."

"So now it's my fault?" I said indignantly, though deep inside I knew I was partly to blame for what had happened.

"I'm not saying it's your fault, but your brother, after being diligent for many years, has decided to take this time to act out. Instead of trying to stir the pot, you might think of how you can help, and not aggravate your brother, or your father, who is not always in control of his emotions."

"Really?" Fergus said. "Dad's not in control of his emotions?"

"Thanks for clueing us in," I said.

"Why don't you two do something useful like clear the table," Mom said.

Ten minutes later the kids were all up in our small bedroom. Coyle slept on the top bunk over me. Maddy slept on the bottom bunk of the other bed, beneath Fergus. There was a rough red carpet in between a desk and two dressers. And that was pretty much it. The bedroom was cramped and cluttered with a single bare bulb in the socket overhead.

As soon as I got in bed Coyle leaned over and hung his fist down.

"All I did was ride my bike out into the park. Robert couldn't stand it that I had something he didn't, so he started a fight. You could have told Savitt that."

"I did tell him!" I said for about the fourth time. "But he didn't listen. Because you're my brother."

"You wanted to get me in trouble," he said.

"It's not my fault!" I shouted, though I knew this wasn't entirely true.

Coyle reached down to grab me, but the front door opened and we were all quiet. We heard Dad's footsteps on the stairs. We knew what would happen. Dad worked too much and he was frustrated with his life. He had wanted to "get into business," but instead he was working as a janitor and reno-vator and paper-delivery guy and taking classes at night. He slept only three or four hours a night and there were constant money worries and so every few weeks Dad had a fist-waving tantrum, sometimes chasing us around the house. Afterward Dad would go outside to cool down and then would come back inside and he'd try to smooth things over.

We could hear Dad's heavy footsteps in the hallway. A moment later Dad appeared at the door of our room. All four of us were quiet, waiting.

"Coyle, you've been a great kid. You work harder than any of your friends. I know that. But you broke the rules and you're going to have to hand over the keys to that bike. And you're going to have to suck it up and apologize to the Daintys and to your principal."

"Ex-principal," Coyle said.

"Whatever," Dad said. "We don't have all the advantages these other families have. But you go to that good school. You'll be paid back in the end. Got it?"

"Yeah," Coyle said almost inaudibly.

"I'm sorry I lost my temper."

"I don't care about that," Coyle said. "I just want to ride my bike."

"Yeah, well, it might be a while before you're allowed," Dad said. "And I'm not going to yell about it, but you have to write that apology."

Coyle paused, then he said faintly, "All right."

Dad looked at the rest of us.

"Willie."

"Yeah."

"You need to stick up for your brother. I know you guys sometimes fight. That's normal. But whatever happens between you and your brother stays in the house. You stand together against everyone else."

"You tell him that, too."

"Same for you, Coyle."

"I do that anyway," Coyle said. "Not that I want to, but I do. If Willie hadn't ratted me out to Savitt none of this would have happened."

Dad didn't seem to disagree. He turned on Fergus.

"Fergie, you need to learn to keep your mouth shut."

"I'm not the only one," Fergus said.

Dad looked like he'd go after Fergus, but in a tired way. Once Dad lost his temper he didn't lose it again for a week or two. It was cyclical.

Maddy was lying in her bunk, the blanket up to her chin, just her eyes and the short-cropped blond hair showing above. She was so skinny she hardly made a lump in the bed. She was timid, like a bird, always skittering away from our fights. trying to stay out of the war zone.

"You ok?" Dad asked her.

"Yeah. I'm ok," she said.

"Nothing bad happened. This is just the way adults discuss things."

There was a burst of laughter from Fergus.

"Shut it," Dad said to him, then walked to the door and flicked the lights off and on. "Go to sleep," he said. "Willie, Coyle, paper route in the morning."

Dad walked out and we all lay there with that blank feeling, sort of laughing about what had happened and sort of not, the whole thing vibrating inside, the gray, simmering feeling after a fight.

Ten minutes later the lights were out and I was lying in the dark, my insides bouncing around. It was nine-forty-five. We had to be up at three-fifteen.

Up till the age of thirteen Coyle was diligent, thorough, responsible, and exacting, but he didn't seem that happy. You could feel a simmering restless dissatisfaction in him. Then Coyle got that bike, and for a brief window of time—about five months—Coyle wasn't just competent, but was joyful. He was filled with a vibrant, jaunty happiness. He acted in a more casual, pleasing manner. That bike was the conduit that connected him to a wider, brighter world.

But that all ended abruptly when he lost his bike privileges. Afterward Coyle became irritable with everyone, but particularly with me.

In those months after Coyle lost his bike privileges Coyle would step on me as he got down from his bunk. He elbowed me when we sat next to each other in the car. He hunted me down at school during his lunch period. We'd fought before. Of course we had. Fighting was in our blood. I think initially our father even encouraged it. He thought it built character. But this was different. It was not a single squabble. It was an unending war. And as I try to parse the threads of what went wrong, I have come to believe that there was something in the excessive, confrontational, competitive nature of our upbringing that spurred us to achieve, but also fostered combativeness. And once things went wrong, they went really wrong, because we had no training in moderation. Through that motorcycle Coyle had caught a glimpse of a bright, vibrant life that was suddenly snatched from him. And with no other outlet, he took his frustration out on me.

I was punched and kicked and pinched and elbowed and tripped and tormented. And I hated this. I was not combative by nature. Just the opposite. I was a dreamy kid—a lover of books and music and poetry. So at first I did everything to avoid fighting. I went through the usual progression of trying to hide, trying to tattle, but none of that stopped Coyle, and I came to the natural understanding that anyone would come to in that situation: Even the weakest in a group, the most frail, the most fearful, the most withdrawing, will see that the only way to keep from getting hit by a more powerful enemy is to hit first and make it hard enough that it's a real deterrent. And if this were true in a normal family, it was doubly true in ours.

"Pull me," Coyle said.

"I can't do it," I said.

"Pull fast."

"Jimmy will pull you," I said. "I'll pull Fergus."

It was December, dusk, the trees heavy and thick and rounded with snow, flakes drifting here or there in the suburban twilight. We were out on the sidewalk playing a game called the gauntlet, named after a Clint Eastwood movie. Like all our games, it involved strength, enduring punishment, and the chance to attack one another. The rules were simple: You stood on a sled and were pulled down the sidewalk while other kids threw snowballs. If you didn't fall off the sled you won. It was Coyle, Fergus, me, and my best friend Jimmy, our neighbor, a good-natured kid, who, like everyone who spent time around Coyle and me that year, was always trying to keep us from fighting.

"I don't care," my friend Jimmy said to Coyle, taking the rope. "I can pull you."

"I don't want you to pull me," Coyle said, jerking the rope back. "Willie should pull me."

"You're too big for me to pull," I said. "I'm pulling Fergus."

"You won't get stronger if you don't try to do hard things," Coyle said.

He was always noticing how frail and skinny and weak I was. It bugged him.

"Why should I do harder things? You can always do them for me," I baited him.

Coyle reached out to grab me, but stopped because a voice from across the street called, *"Hey, losers!"*

It was Robert Dainty. He sauntered over, coming from his big house down the block. Robert had stayed away for a few months after he fought with Coyle, but had then started hanging around again. Coyle and Robert, two alpha dogs, had a sort of negative attraction to each other.

"We're playing a sled game," I called to Robert.

"A sled game," Robert said in his snide tone.

"Yes. Pulling sleds!" I said. "Coyle pulled me. Now I'm supposed to pull him, but he doesn't think I'll do it. Coyle loves the sled game!"

"Is that right, Brennan? Are you a sled fanatic?" Robert said.

Coyle didn't bother answering. He just stepped toward me.

"What?" I said.

"You know what," he said.

Coyle punched me, but my puffy parka softened the blow. He shoved me so I fell, but I landed in a snowdrift. I laughed. Coyle hated that. He got on top of me, flipped me over, and shoved my face down.

"Eat snow, weasel," he said.

There was a moment of burning, icy smothering. Then Coyle let go and I leapt up, wiping the snow and a little blood from my face.

"I'm bleeding!" I bleated.

Coyle got a dismissive look.

"Like one drop. Who cares?"

Jimmy and Fergus laughed. Even Robert Dainty laughed. I must have sounded pathetic. I retreated down the snowy street.

"Idiots!" I yelled.

I arrived at the house. I packed a snowball and waited on the porch to ambush Coyle, but he didn't come back. I could hear them down the block. They were playing the game again. Even Robert was playing.

I went around the house to the backyard. The shape of Coyle's motorcycle with a tarp over it made a stationary lump in the snow. I thought of pushing it over, but I knew Coyle would go crazy if I touched his bike. I didn't dare do it.

I walked back to the front yard. I made the snowball larger. I went inside and held the snowball beneath the faucet until it compressed into ice. I went back to the porch. Coyle still wasn't coming. I packed the ball even tighter. It was heavy and hard as a lump of steel. I put the ice ball in the freezer. I went back to the window. I waited. I knew what I was thinking of doing was wrong. A face-wash in the snow was unpleasant, but an ice ball, frozen solid in the freezer, was a dangerous weapon. I was afraid of what I was doing, but also felt justified in doing it. I was sick of Coyle blaming me for losing his bike privileges and I was sick of taking beatings, and there was a defiant, slippery temptation to get revenge.

I waited at the window. It got dark. Twice I got up from

the window and walked away, thinking I'd just let it go. But then I went back to the window and kept waiting, sitting in that dim room with the dusky blue light, wondering, Should I do it? Will I do it? I'd fought before, but I'd never done anything purposefully brutal.

Maddy came down the stairs dragging one of her dolls by the hair.

"What are you looking at?" she asked.

"Don't worry about it," I said. "Go away."

She went back upstairs without a word. The disruption between Coyle and me, the constant fighting, had filtered through everyone in the family. It was like acid on the fabric of the household. Fergus sided with Coyle to keep from getting hit himself. Mom also sided with Coyle. She thought I was sneaky. Dad didn't want to waste time on squabbles, but I think he was on my side, thinking correctly that I was getting the worst of the beating. Maddy just didn't want to get pulled into the maelstrom. She had started talking to her dolls and punishing them when they were "bad." The fighting affected all of us, but no one more than me. Under that constant assault I had been changing secretly, and now, the flowering of that change: I was waiting at the window with an ice ball in the freezer.

It grew dark. I thought my parents might come home before I did anything. Maybe I even wanted them to come home, to stop me from what I was planning. I knew it was wrong. I didn't care.

After an hour I heard a voice in the gloom. It was Coyle.

I ran to the freezer and got the ice ball. It was heavy and as hard as stone. I propped the interior door open so I would have a straight shot. I waited. I heard Coyle on the steps. I held the frozen ball in my cocked hand. And then there Coyle was, opening the door. I didn't hesitate. I threw as hard as I could from three feet away. The ice ball hit his face with a nasty, fleshy thud. Coyle's head snapped back. He fell on the porch. The ice ball skidded away, not even dented.

"That's what *you* get!" I shouted.

Coyle reached out blindly. I jerked away, but too late. Coyle had me. He pulled me to him. Even with blood pouring from his nose and mouth, he dragged me to him and knocked me to the ground. He began to pummel me blindly. Both of us cursed each other, our blood mixing in snow.

Two hours later Coyle and I sat on opposite ends of the couch. I had what would be bruises on my face from where Coyle had hit my head against the porch. Coyle had the beginnings of two black eyes.

"One of us was supposed to pull him on the sled," I said in a wavering, indignant tone. "Jimmy said he'd do it, because he's stronger than me, and he can pull Coyle faster, but Coyle was being bossy, as usual. He said it had to be me who pulled him and he went crazy when he didn't get his way."

"Did you agree to pull him?" Dad asked me.

"No," I said. "There wasn't a rule that I had to pull Coyle. It was that I had to pull someone. Coyle just decided that I was going to be the one who pulled him and got mad we weren't bowing down to him like slaves."

"You're such a liar," Coyle said. "It's true I wanted him

to pull me. But I shoved his face in the snow because he was being a weasel with Robert Dainty. Robert showed up and Willie yelled, 'We're playing with sleds.'"

"What's wrong with that?" Dad asked.

"They think sleds are passé," Mom said to our father.

"They think it's for poor people," Coyle said.

"Well, that's just stupid," Dad said.

"They don't go sledding. They go skiing in Aspen," Coyle said.

"Proud to be poor!" Fergus yelled from the living room.

"Cut it!" Dad yelled.

Fergus was pretending to do homework nearby, but was really listening in. Maddy was trying not to hear by playing with her tea set and humming. That was another thing she had started to do, humming to block out our voices.

"Willie tried to embarrass me in front of Robert," Coyle was saying. "So I pushed him over. Big deal. Then he hit me in the face with ice."

"After he started it," I said.

"After you embarrassed me," Coyle said.

Dad waved his hands to silence us.

"Coyle, you shouldn't have shoved your brother's face in the snow. And Willie, you overreacted by hitting your brother with ice. Brothers might fight a little, but they don't use weapons. You need to learn to defend yourself with your hands."

"Look at him and look at me," I said. "He's a year older than me and twice my size. How am I supposed to fight back with my hands?"

"Figure it out," Mom said. "And stop making such a

drama about it. Your father and I are both working very hard. When we leave you together we expect you to behave like normal human beings. Not having us come back to a blood-bath. Too much of our time is spent refereeing."

"Because Coyle's a bully," I said. "He thinks everything is my fault."

"Willie's a weasel," Coyle said. "He lost my bike privileges for me and now he's getting me in trouble again."

"Enough!" Dad said. "Shake hands. Then go upstairs."

Coyle and I shook hands without looking at each other. We went up to the bedroom and stood between the two bunk beds, side by side.

"Is he coming?" I said.

"What do you think?" Coyle said. "It's your fault."

"You always have to get your way. And you blame me for everything that you don't like. I'm sick of it."

"You hit me with ice."

"You shoved my face in the snow."

"You went against me in public with Robert Dainty."

"You beat on me in public all the time."

"Because you deserve it," he said.

I started to reply, but then we heard Dad's footsteps on the stairs. The door opened. Dad came in. He shut the door behind him.

"You know the rules," Dad said. "You can't be wasting time fighting with each other. And if you do fight you need to learn that it's worse for both of you."

"We didn't really fight," Coyle murmured.

"Yeah, you did," Dad said.

Dad stepped in front of Coyle and motioned for him to

lower his hands. As he did, really fast, without warning, Dad hit Coyle with the butt of his hand in the temple. Coyle's head jerked to the side. He fell and lay there on the wool carpet, curled in case Dad came at him again. Dad didn't. He stepped in front of me. I looked down. I knew what was coming. I could hear the scrape of a snow shovel on a drive-way down the block. I could hear the clink of Mom doing dishes downstairs. I was thinking of how to get out of it, of inventing something that would make it seem like it was all Coyle's fault. I was good at making things up, thinking of clever arguments. I was smaller and weaker than everyone else, so I had to be clever to get out of things. I started to think up a lie, but there was a blur to the side and a white light flashed in my head and I was sprawled on the carpet between the beds. I was crying a little. I thought I wouldn't cry, but then I did before I knew I was, and I hated that I was. Coyle hadn't cried. He hadn't even let out a sound when he was hit. I was pathetic. I always cried when I got smacked, even when I promised myself I wouldn't. I lay there for a while, chest heaving. Finally I sat up. Coyle was giving me a look that said, *Why be such a baby?* Dad had already left.

"Can't tell them anything or we both get hit," Coyle said.

"Good," I said. "I'll keep telling. At least it's both of us and not just me."

As we walked out, Coyle elbowed me. I shoved him. We weaved from each other and took little jabs and pretended we were just walking down the stairs.

———

There's a story in our family, legend now, about how, when I was six years old, I was asked to eat three peas at the dinner table and I refused. Mom said I'd sit at the table until I ate them. I said I wouldn't eat them. She said I'd sit there until I did eat them. I sat at the table for five hours. In the end I was sent to bed straight from the dinner table, but I never ate the peas. And a lot of what follows makes sense only if you take in the moral of this story. I was the weakest in the family and the least confrontational of the boys. But I had one strength. I was stubborn. I knew my own mind. And as Coyle and I started to fight I fell back on this stubbornness. I decided that whenever Coyle did something to me, I would do something back, no matter what. When Coyle pushed me or tripped me or poked me or biffed me with a raised knuckle, I promised myself I would always get him back. Tit for tat. So he hit me and I stole his notebooks. I hid his baseball glove. I once pushed him down the stairs when he wasn't paying attention. Not that these efforts discouraged Coyle from attacking me. If anything, they spurred him on. Coyle was trained in the same school of relentless effort as I was. We used our excessive training not to conquer the world but to try to destroy each other. And as our battles progressed both of us descended into a maze of adolescent plotting and brawling. Secret scheming and secret pleasure in watching each other suffer. Thorns in shoes, fiberglass on blankets. I acquired a taste for revenge and he acquired a taste for tormenting me. And when I look back on this now I understand that it wasn't just that I was learning to defend myself. It wasn't really that at all. I was learning to enjoy combat. I was becoming a flintier person than I'd been for the first twelve years of my life. And maybe some people thought it was for the best. Maybe they thought toughness was necessary. But being meandering and gentle by nature, I did not have practice in moderating my responses, so this change in temperament was like some illnesses that are worse for adolescents than young children. Learning to defend myself at that relatively late age was a dangerous thing.

Crammed into the station wagon, we were on the way to see Coyle's basketball game. We were late and Mom had forgotten the parking pass.

"If you'd have remembered the pass I'd be able to see the game," Dad said. "But you had to forget it."

"Oh, stop complaining," Mom said. "I'll go back."

"You'd probably crash the car in the snow if you drove," Dad said. "I shouldn't have to worry about it. But you forgot it."

"I did forget it," Mom said coolly. "I apologized. Now get over it."

"Why don't you ask the guy at the gate?" Maddy said. "He might let us park."

"He won't let us in," Dad said in a beleaguered tone. "You need the pass. So I'll go back. Even though it wasn't me who forgot."

"Just pull over," I said. "I'll talk to them."

Coyle made a clicking sound.

"Of course Willie says he'll talk to them. Any chance to suck ass."

"Oh, be quiet," Mom said. "Let Willie try."

"Just don't beg," Coyle said. "Willie the Wheeder."

Dad pulled over in front of the turnoff for the parking lot. I jumped out. It was six o'clock in January. Pitch-black and frigid, and the guy working the lot was dressed up in a heavy parka and boots and thick gloves. I walked over in the headlights.

"My brother's on the team. My mom forgot the parking pass," I said. "Can we still park here?"

"Who's your brother?"

"Coyle Brennan."

The attendant looked over at the old Ford station wagon with the bumper held on with a belt. Everyone knew Coyle. The varsity baseball coaches were already talking about the blue-collar kid who pitched eighty miles an hour and also played good defense in basketball.

"All right," he said. "But remember the pass next time."

"We will. Thanks."

I walked back to the car, swinging my arms. I got inside.

"We can park," I said.

"See," Mom said to Dad. "After all that."

"Doesn't mean you shouldn't have remembered it," Dad grumbled.

"Oh, please," Mom said. "After all your groaning."

Dad pulled into the parking spot and Coyle opened his door and jogged toward the lit gymnasium. It was about ten degrees out, but he was just in his parka and shorts. He liked to show he didn't care about the cold.

Dad turned in his seat, grinning.

"Guys, there's a lesson here. I said not to ask for help, but I was wrong. See," he said, turning to our mother. "I can admit I was wrong." Then, to us, "I never learned how to talk to people. That's one of the reasons I moved here. You live around the good people and you learn how to get along with them and your lives will be easier than mine. That's why we spend all the money to live in Seneca. Good job, Willie."

I held a fist up.

"The winner," I said.

"It was the right thing," Mom said.

Dad opened his door and a blast of icy wind swirled. We all got out and started across the parking lot toward the gymnasium and went up the snowy steps and as we entered the lobby I noticed the other parents glance over to see who'd come in and there was that familiar feeling of knowing there was something wrong with us. Other adults wore trench coats and leather gloves and black leather shoes. Mom and Dad wore old parkas and sneakers. And there was also something wrong with the way we acted, some indefinable flaw in our expressions or maybe the defiant posture we took when we came into a room, but whatever it was, adults seemed to pick up on it instantly. When I was a kid I hadn't noticed it, but that year I turned thirteen, the same year our battles blossomed, I had begun to understand that people who didn't even know us only had to glance at us to see that there was something different about us and we didn't belong in the fancy suburbs.

Inside the lobby, Fergus bent to pet a leashed collie that had been tied off to one of the doors. Fergus ran his hand along the dog and Dad stood over Fergus and felt the same thing I did—discomfort around the well-dressed adults with their silent disapproval, and defiance about our way of acting. So Dad did what he always did when he felt uncomfortable. He put on a big show of not caring, and made it worse.

"Is that dog smelling you?" Dad said loudly. He looked around to see if anyone had heard his joke. "Hey, Fergus. I think that dog's smelling you."

A few parents pointedly turned away. Mom blanched.

"Let's go inside," Mom said.

Fergus stood from the dog and we walked into the gymnasium with the whomp of basketballs and the teammates calling to each other. My friend Jimmy stood inside the doorway, waiting for me.

"Are you ready, soldier?" Jimmy said.

"All set, commander," I said, and Jimmy and I started off together, not toward the basketball stands, but going along the basketball court and out the far door of the gymnasium and into the main body of the high school, all the while acting as if we were on a top-secret mission. We were both in the eighth grade. We'd go to that high school the following year, and in my mind there was an aura to the school, almost like a church. New Trier! The celebrated high school with dozens of world-famous alums. The best high school in Illinois! My father had bought the hype completely. New Trier was the focus of my father's dreams, and was meant to be the lever to raise us up from our blue-collar drudgery.

Jimmy and I wandered off from the gymnasium. The school had been built in many stages and had a pleasing, unsymmetrical feel. It was more like a compound than a single building. There were narrow hallways with rounded ceilings, low passageways, and mezzanine levels. The lights were off, so it was shadowy and eerie in the quiet hallways, like going into an old castle at night. It took us awhile to get our bearings, but eventually we found the main stairway and went up to the second floor and, meandering, found locker 254.

"Target in sight, commander," I said.

I checked a series of numbers I had on a sheet of paper and then tried the locker combination once. It didn't work. I tried it again and the second time the latch lifted and I pulled the handle up to reveal a perfectly organized locker with stacked books and a hung sweatshirt. Of course Coyle kept his locker perfectly.

On the top shelf I saw the edge of a large picture book. I pulled it out to reveal a drawing of a dragon on the cover— *Other Worlds.*

"Success," I said.

I opened the book to see if it was defaced in any way. I paged through the artwork of barbarians and wizards and giant insects and warriors with swords and lasers. It was undamaged. I breathed a sigh of relief. I loved that book.

"Why'd he take it?" Jimmy asked.

"To be a dick," I said. "He thinks everything wrong in his life is my fault."

"You could take something of his," Jimmy said.

His baseball glove hung temptingly on a hook. A few months later I probably would have taken his glove, but at that time I was still trying to be evenhanded in my revenge.

"He'll just go crazy if I do that," I said.

I shut the door to the locker, and Jimmy and I walked

back through the dim, quiet hallways and on to the gym
with its caged lights and the crowded stands. The game had
already started when we arrived. It was the biggest game of
the year—New Trier versus Evanston. The freshman team
was undefeated because of Coyle and a guy named Lanny
Prophet, who played point guard and was a great passer.

Jimmy and I walked all the way up the steep stairway to
the empty seats at the very top of the stands. I sat back and
began paging through my book. I glanced up now and then
to see the teams running back and forth, but I didn't pay
attention. I never watched Coyle playing. I pointedly wanted
to show I didn't care.

"They're not passing to Coyle," Jimmy said after awhile.

"What?"

"They haven't passed to him the whole game."

I began to watch. Coyle sprinted up and down the court
and played defense and scrambled for loose balls, but Jimmy
was right. The guards weren't getting the ball inside to Coyle.
At first I thought it was because Coyle was being guarded
closely, but he kept getting open and calling for the ball, waving his arms.

"He was just totally wide. And they missed it!" Jimmy
said.

"He probably pissed them off," I said.

Jimmy walked down the aisle and talked to some kids
below us. When he came back up, he said, "The other guys
on the team all know each other. The second-string center
is their friend. They want him to start. So they're not passing
to Coyle."

When Coyle came out to rest, the second-string center went in and the guards immediately began passing to him on almost every play. He scored a few baskets. Then Coyle went back in and no one passed to him. It was obvious what was going on.

Coyle was not a complainer. Maximum effort was in the DNA of our upbringing. So Coyle fought for rebounds and loose balls and played good defense. But no one passed to him for the whole game.

I could see Dad below in the stands watching the game. At first he was raising his fist and yelling, "Fight, fight, fight," but then slowly, as the game went on, he fell silent. By the end of the game Dad had settled back and was watching with a fixed grimace. New Trier lost by twenty points.

As I walked past the bench I heard the coach talking to some other adults who wore black trench coats and had black leather shoes. He was a young coach and I could tell he was intimidated by the well-dressed parents.

"I just do it based on statistics," I heard the coach say. "I'll have to run the numbers and then I'll make my decision."

I knew that Coyle would not be starting after that.

A few minutes later we all walked out to the car, and as we did I saw the point guard from New Trier walking with his mother.

"You played so well," I heard his mother say. "I don't think anyone played as well as you. All of you are so talented."

"Not all of us," the guard said loudly. "If other people scored, we'd have won. But not everyone played well. Some of us broke under pressure."

We were meant to hear this. We all walked on in silence. We all got in the car. Dad slammed the door and said, "Well, you lost."

"Yep," Coyle said.

"Wasn't your best game," Dad said.

"I would have done better if they'd passed it to me," Coyle said.

Dad grimaced and gripped the wheel.

"Don't blame anyone else," Dad said. "You lost. Blame yourself."

"I do."

"Good," Dad said. "If you lose it's your fault. No excuses."

Mom turned in her seat.

"But you played very well. No shame in that."

Dad put the car in drive. Coyle looked out the window with a bitter expression, then glanced over and saw I was holding *Other Worlds*. He grabbed for the book.

"Stop!" I yelled.

"Cut it," Dad said.

Coyle gave me a murderous look.

"You're dead," he mouthed.

He reached over to grip my leg. I squirmed away.

"What is going on now?" Mom said.

"Willie has something of mine," Coyle said.

"It's not his," I said. "Coyle tried to hide it from me."

"Cut it," Dad said again. "You lost. No complaining."

Coyle glanced over at me like he'd go at me right there. Maddy cringed, waiting for Coyle to leap over her to get at me. Fergus mimicked Dad, saying, "Cut it." Dad went on driving, the muscle on the side of his cheek tight, a simmering, tense misery bouncing between all of us, the large, bare trees and snow-covered lawns passing by outside the windows.

I think our parents imagined our battles would fade but they were wrong about that. Over that winter Coyle drooled into my food. He held my head underwater in the bathtub. He wrapped a power cord around my neck and said he'd kill me. Twice Coyle hit me hard enough that I was knocked out. In return I put tacks on the ladder to Coyle's bunk bed. I tore his homework. I hid his textbooks. I once smashed his art project in front of him and just curled up, waiting to be beaten. Mom and Dad tried to rein us in. But they were working all the time, and what can you do when two people living in the same room want to kill each other? Our fights went through half-truces and secret plots of revenge, and then one day in late winter, about a year after Coyle refused to get a haircut, I went up to Dad's bedroom and opened the cabinet where Dad kept a loaded .22 revolver. We weren't allowed to touch it, but I knew where it was. I took the gun out. I held it in my hand. I felt its weight. I just sat there looking at it for a while before I put it back.

"Let's scare her," Jimmy said.

"Just have Bennie walk out there. That'll do it," Roscoe said.

"Ha. Ha," Bennie said.

I was with Jimmy, Bennie, and Roscoe, my three friends, out in a forest preserve around the backed-up North Branch of the Chicago River. Jimmy, like I said, was our neighbor. Bennie was a gawky, awkward dork who was good in math and was the one who was most protective of our "group." Roscoe was a good-looking kid who wore a gold chain, had dyslexia, and was pretty much always high, even in the eighth grade. It was a warm day in early spring and we were looking through shrubbery into a clearing where a girl we knew— Harriet Schack—was sitting on a log, holding a cigarette up near her mouth with two upraised fingers.

"We'll scare her," Roscoe said. "And then we'll try to get her to come with us."

We crept forward and two other girls came into view. One was Megan Tivoli, who had a Pat Benatar haircut and whose parents were journalists. The third girl had sandy hair and freckled skin. None of us had ever seen her before.

"Who's that?" Bennie asked.

"We'll find out," Roscoe said.

He held up his fingers.

"One, two, three . . ."

We burst through the shrubs and jumped into the middle of the dirt clearing. Harriet gave a shriek.

"Oh my God. I thought you were my father."

"Hello, Mr. Schack. This is Roscoe Schwartz. Friend of your daughter's. I was just wondering if she's allowed to smoke cigarettes."

"I would die," Harriet said.

"Is that even a cigarette?" I asked.

"Clove," Harriet said.

"Oh. Cloves. Sophisticated," Roscoe said.

Roscoe was slicker than the rest of us. He knew how to talk to girls.

"So, who's your friend?" Roscoe said.

"Angela," Harriet said, introducing the third girl.

She had green eyes and a flat nose.

"Hey," we all said.

"We have a fort near the water," Bennie said to Harriet. "Do you want to come?"

"Only if you beg," Harriet said.

Roscoe put his hands up like he was a dog, begging, and then let his hands drop, and in a laconic tone, said, "Come if you want. We have a boat."

"Sure, we'll come," Megan said. "As long as Bennie doesn't get weird about it."

"No chance of that not happening," Jimmy said. Bennie's ineptness with girls was a joke for the entire grade.

We started off for the fort, the seven of us, walking on the dirt path, down the embankment of a dry creek bed and back up the other side to our fort, which was a piece of plywood over two rocks with a tarp over it. An old wooden dingy with brass eyelets rested in shrubbery. Roscoe and I turned the boat over and dragged it down the dirt embankment and dipped the nose into the water.

"I like the yacht," Megan said.

"Don't get in it if you don't like it," Bennie said indignantly.

"Try to be cool," Roscoe said to Bennie.

I was standing close to Angela, the new girl.

"Do you want to go?" I asked her.

"Ok," she said.

Bennie and Jimmy glanced at each other. I'd just asked a girl I didn't know to go on the boat with me. I had never done anything like that in my life.

"We'll push you out," Roscoe said.

Angela clambered into the boat. I dropped the paddles in the back and pushed so only the back tip was in the water. I climbed in and Roscoe shoved us off and there was a moment where we broke free from the ground and drifted slowly, slowly, through the green water. I fit the oars into the eyelets. I leaned forward, pulling with my whole body, and then pulling again. Within a minute we were far out on the lagoon among the trees and birds. The inlet curved so when we looked back we just saw the stirred trail of water going around the bend. There were no other people in sight.

"Do you want to try to paddle?" I asked.

"I don't know how," Angela said.

She had a gentle, measured manner.

"It's not hard. You lean forward, cross your arms, then use your back to pull. See?" I showed her a few times and then I said, "You try."

We switched places, the boat rocking crazily. I sat facing her.

"Cross your arms. Use your back," I said.

She began to paddle. She picked it up quickly. She went on for a while.

"You're good at this," I said.

"I like being on a boat," she said. "It's away from everything."

She stopped paddling and we drifted. It was quiet. Leaves rustled.

"You're in the eighth grade?" she asked.

"I go to Seneca. Where do you go?"

"Saint Joe," she said.

That was the Catholic junior high.

"Will you go to New Trier?"

"Regina," she said, which was the girls' school. "My mom thinks I'm shy and need to be at a small school."

"Are you shy?"

"No," she said, indignant. "She thinks because I'm quiet that I'm shy. It's not the same thing. Obviously."

"Did you tell her you're not shy?"

"She doesn't believe me. She just thinks I am."

"My brother thinks because I don't do everything exactly the way he says that I'm bad. He blames me for everything in his life."

"That's the way people are. If you aren't exactly like them they think there's something wrong with you. My mom thinks that because I don't talk all the time like her that I'm weird. But I think she's the one who has the problem."

"It's the same way with my brother," I said. "He thinks because I don't do everything his way that there's something wrong with me. But he's a bully. If he doesn't get his way he just goes crazy."

We went on like that, talking about our families, complaining about them. I told her a little more about Coyle, and she told me a little more about her mother and sister, who ganged up on her. Angela said that she didn't fit in with her family and I said it was the same with me. Then Angela started up paddling again, turning us back along the bend in the inlet. We began to hear the sound of the others' talking. Angela ran up onto the mud bank and we joined the others who were shooting a BB gun at an old pie tin nailed to a tree. We'd only been gone half an hour, but it seemed in that time I'd gotten to know Angela and we had a secret understanding with each other. We clambered off the boat and a minute later the girls walked off on the dirt path, talking low to one another.

"See you never," they called.

That was on a Monday. We met the girls in the lagoon again on Wednesday and then again on the following Saturday. We became after-school friends for that spring. We met in the afternoons in the lagoon in the time after I got out of sports and before dinner. In that group, Angela and I were special friends. Sometimes we walked along the shore together, just the two of us, and she'd tell me about her sister or her mother and how they were loud, abrasive people, and how they thought she was shy and needed special treatment. I told her more about my family, how my father had all those jobs and was trying to get his teaching certificate, and how he was from the Southside and had been in a street gang growing up and how sports and hard work had saved him. I told her how he responded to every obstacle by making lists, by trying to eke out every free moment for self-improvement, and how he'd given up on his own success and put all his hopes in us, his kids. I told about how Coyle had been the perfect kid until one day he came home with a motorcycle and it started a cascade of events that ended with us wanting to kill each other. I made the whole thing into a story, and when I told this story to Angela it seemed to make much more sense than it did in real life, where it was just a vast landscape of mindless drudgery punctuated with violence. It was the beginning of my understanding that these fights with Coyle, my parents' struggle to live in Seneca, and the feeling of being "the poor kid" in a rich area were the story of my life, and it was what would seem important later.

I saw Angela eight or ten times that spring. We didn't go out. We didn't kiss. I never held her hand. I was way too self-conscious for anything like that. But we were friends. And telling those stories to her clarified them in my mind and elevated the growing feeling of defiance inside me. It made it less likely that I'd accept Coyle's demands. Whatever happened, I knew I wouldn't go on taking it.

In May of 1980, three months before I started high school, on a clear, warm, spring day, I was raking in the backyard, gathering the cut grass into lumpy piles. We didn't have a bag for our mower, so after our father cut the grass, Coyle and I had to rake up. Coyle was annoyed at the inept way I raked, thinking he went faster than me and was doing more work, which was true. He shoved me, saying, "Rake faster." I did speed up, but raked near his motorcycle to show that if I went faster I might scratch his bike.

"Don't touch my bike with the rake," Coyle said. And because he said that, I raked even closer to his bike and one of the tines of the rake grazed the tire of his bike. Coyle was waiting for this act of defiance, and as soon as the rake grazed the rubber, Coyle stepped over and pushed me from behind. I scrambled up and pushed his bike, which tottered, then fell over, the side mirror shattering as it hit the brick edge of the garden. For a moment we stood there, stunned.

"You broke it."

"It's just the mirror," I said, backing up.

"You hurt my bike," Coyle said.

And then Coyle was on me, gripping me in two shaking fists. He flung me to the side. I landed, rolling, and was trying to scramble up when there was a white explosion in my chest, a blossoming of blinding pain. I'd been kicked.

"Don't."

He kicked me again.

"Touch."

He kicked again.

"My bike."

Coyle pulled his foot back again but I crawled free, gasping. I got up. I staggered to the rake. I turned, swinging. Coyle blocked the rake with his one hand and held his other hand high. He smacked me, hard, across the face. A part of my mind was knocked far away, a kind of narrowing stillness spreading inside. Distantly, I heard myself screaming, but inside a part of me was calm and certain. We had been coming to that point for a long time and I knew what I would do.

Coyle held his hand up and—smack, smack—he hit me twice. Then he stood away. I fell. I got up and limped across the grass with him walking after me, laughing.

"Can't get away," he called.

I got into the house and shut the back door. I locked it, but Coyle was already going around to the side. He knew

I couldn't lock all the doors before he got in. I ran up the stairs to Mom and Dad's room and jerked Dad's cabinet open, breaking the lock. I could see the .22 pistol at the back. I grabbed it. Coyle was coming up the stairs. I took the pistol and hid behind the open door to Dad's bedroom. Coyle went into our bedroom, thinking I'd hidden in there. I slipped out behind him and ran down the stairs, holding the gun. Coyle came after me.

"Can't get away," he called again.

I burst out the back door and jumped down the porch stairs. Coyle was right behind me. I curved off into the Chambers' yard. Coyle grabbed my shirt and I turned, swinging with the gun, pulling the trigger. The gun hit Coyle's head and fired. Coyle's head jerked to the side in a crazy way. He fell and lay motionless in the grass. There was a little blood near his head, not that much at first. I waited for Coyle to get up. He didn't. I could hear a lawnmower somewhere far away. I could smell cut grass. I could smell gunpowder. The sound of the shot was loud in my ears. I waited for Coyle to get up. His right leg was folded beneath his body. He still wasn't moving.

The neighbors' back door opened. Mrs. Chambers came out. She was wearing a white tennis outfit.

"I called an ambulance!" she said.

"What for?" I said nervously.

"You've killed your brother and you say what for? He says what's the ambulance for!" she shouted to the neighbors. "They've finally done it. One of them's dead. He shot his brother. Dead!" She danced around in her tennis outfit, screaming. "Now he's dead! They've killed each other! Dead!

In my yard!" She threw her tennis racket out into the grass. "Dead!" she shrieked, doing a hysterical dance over Coyle.

"He's waking up," I said.

Coyle had started groaning weakly. I backed up.

"You could help instead of going crazy," I said.

"He says *I'm* going crazy. *I* am. And he just killed his brother. There he is. Dead!"

The gun was resting in the grass. I picked it up and walked slowly back into our yard. I stopped once I was on our property. I looked back. Then I walked to our porch and sat. I set the gun down beside me on the wooden step. I pretended I had nothing to do with what was going on over in Mrs. Chambers' yard.

I saw Coyle's legs move. Then he sat up slowly with wide, dazed eyes. Blood streamed down his face. Mrs. Chambers bent to him. He pushed her away.

"Oh my God! I'm being assaulted in my own yard!"

Coyle sat in the grass, gazing off at nothing. His eyes looked big and wide and puzzled. The blood was very red against his pale skin. His blondish-brown hair was soaking up the blood. The tips of his hair dripped blood. There were sirens far away, then close, then they stopped. I heard men calling to one another. I just sat on the porch, watching. Firemen in uniforms hurried past me. After a moment the screen door opened and smacked shut. Fergus walked out. He'd just gotten home with Mom. He didn't know what the firemen were there for, but he figured it must be some entertaining fuckup. He was grinning until he saw Coyle.

"What happened?"

"I hit Coyle with Dad's gun. It went off."

The blood was flowing from the side of Coyle's head. His hair was clotted with it. Maddy had come up behind Fergus at the screen door.

"What happened to Coyle?" she said in a quavering voice.

"Nothing. He's fine," I said.

"Yeah, he's fine," Fergus said. "Willie shot him and that's fine with Willie."

Mom had come up to the screen door as Fergus spoke. She saw the firemen. She saw Coyle in the grass with blood down his shirt and me with that gun.

"Willie shot Coyle," Fergus said cheerfully.

"Oh my God!" Mom shrieked.

She ran into the backyard. One of the firemen hurried out to her, waving his arms. She listened to what the fireman had to say and I saw her expression change. Coyle was trying to stand up now. She turned and glared at Fergus.

"Gotcha," he yelled, but I'm not sure he knew what was happening, either.

The gun was still on the porch step. Fergus gave me a look like I was an idiot. He took the gun and slid it under the porch.

"Go somewhere else," Fergus said to me.

I stood to go inside but two policemen had arrived. One of the cops looked back at us and walked over. I sat back down.

"Are you the brother?" the cop asked me.

"Yeah," I said.

"He's the bad brother," Fergus said.

"Get up," the cop said.

I got up. The cop took me behind the neck and led me away.

I still have a copy of my mug shot. I was fourteen years old, five-foot-three, and under a hundred pounds. I look like I'm about ten years old in that photograph, but my expression is absolutely defiant and unrepentant. In my mind, Coyle had been beating on me a few times a day for more than a year and however I protected myself was justified.

At the station, the police did not put me inside a cell, but handcuffed me to a bar along the wall. I sat on a bench, leaning my head against the wall, not impatient, not even that unhappy. Even if I went to prison, I thought, it couldn't be any worse than what I'd been living through. And I was glad for what I'd done.

After a while a detective came over and sat next to me. I told him that Coyle was coming after me and I took the gun to protect myself. I said that the gun went off accidentally when it hit his head. There was no way they could prove that wasn't true. I said Coyle and I had never gotten along. I said I thought Coyle was going to kill me. The detective didn't believe this last part, but when I pulled my shirt up he saw bruises all over my body. When he raised his hand I flinched instinctively. All of this changed the way the officers treated me. I was still arrested, but they were gentler after that. They never put me in a cell. They had a long talk with my mother and father that afternoon at the station.

Hours later, when I heard that the gun had only gone off alongside Coyle's head and added force to the blow, giving him a concussion, but that I hadn't actually shot him, I was charged with battery and released on two hundred dollars' bail until my court date, when my official punishment would be decided. My unofficial punishment, what I thought of as my real one, was decided the next day in the kitchen with my mother.

Our father was the domineering, churning, chaotic engine of our lives, but Mom was the one who kept the house running and was also the one who, if not deciding the punishments, was definitely the one implementing them. If Dad grounded us for a month in a moment of anger, it was Mom who made sure we stayed inside. If Dad said no dessert for two weeks, it was Mom who refused to serve the dessert. Dad was the one with the temper. Mom was the one with steadiness and grit.

Mom had grown up on the seventeenth hole of the Kenwood Country Club in Cincinnati. Her own mother, a Finn from Astoria, was a flirty, gossipy, middle-class socialite and a bad drunk who pretty much hit rock bottom when Mom entered her teens. Mom's father was a traveling salesman for Procter & Gamble who was away a lot of the time, and so when her mother went on her five-year drinking binge it was our mother who took over the duties of the house and cooked and cleaned for her two brothers while still getting A's at the convent school. This experience of essentially becoming a mother as a teenager burnt some of the joy out of her and taught her early on that life was a series of trials and hardships and the only lessons that really mattered were those that taught endurance and discipline.

When Mom turned eighteen she escaped to Northwestern and met my father, a confident, swaggering, ball-playing city kid on scholarship, an upbeat dreamer who thought that hard work could accomplish anything. Dad's optimism and exuberance, his boisterousness and athleticism, must have been a bright light shining on Mom's bleak, alcohol-soaked childhood. But Mom didn't yet know about Dad's baseline impracticality about money, or his temper, and at some point in our youth she must have understood that she'd traded being a mother at the age of fifteen, while her own mother lolled drunk in her bathrobe, for keeping house for an impractical workaholic with a bad temper and a dreamy sense of finances. But by the time she understood this she had four kids and hopeless debt and lived in a tiny rented house in a fancy suburb they couldn't afford and the only way out of the situation was through it.

At the police station, when she came to pick me up, Mom signed the forms without looking at me. It wasn't until we were back home in the kitchen that Mom said, "Sit. We need to talk, Willie."

The kitchen was a small room with the refrigerator in a nook near the back door and an old gas stove with black knobs. The table had a bench on one side, which I sat on. Mom rinsed a plate and set it in the dishwasher. She leaned against the sink and began to dry her hands slowly with a dish towel.

"You understand that you can't ever use a weapon against your brother again, don't you?" she said.

"I'll use a weapon again if I think he's going to kill me," I said. I was determined not to give an inch. "Have you seen the bruises on my body?" I said.

"I saw your bruises. And his."

"He kicked me as hard as he could three times."

"And you damaged his motorcycle, which you know he's very protective of."

"He was trying to kill me."

Mom gave me a skeptical look.

"If you had those worries you should have come to us."

"I did!" I said. "A lot of times. And you said to shut up and stop complaining. And Dad said to learn to defend myself, which I did, so you should be happy."

"Your father did not tell you to pick up a weapon against your brother. He explicitly forbid it. You know that. No weapons. You understand that, right?"

"I guess," I said faintly.

"Good. That's settled. No weapons." She paused for a moment, then added, "But I also want you to understand that your father and I see your side of this."

I was surprised. I waited.

"Your brother has a very determined personality and has begun to associate with an unfortunate group of friends. Coyle is larger and stronger than you and he takes his frustration out on you. Don't think we don't see this."

I was quiet.

"We don't know how it's gotten to the point it's at now,

but we want you to know that we are taking care of the situation. The violence in this house is going to stop. On his side, and on yours. If you have a problem with your brother from now on, you will talk to us."

I was momentarily flooded with relief, but then something else rose up inside, something dark and defiant. I let out a disparaging puff of air.

"As if talking's going to help. I wake up in the morning and I get beaten on. I come home from school and he hits me. And if I bring it up I'm beaten on even more. By Coyle and by Dad."

"Your father does not hit you," Mom said in a wounded, piping tone.

I heard Fergus laugh loudly from the other room.

"Fergus. Go away!" Mom yelled.

Fergus might have moved a little, but not so far that he couldn't hear. That fight with the gun was the most exciting thing to happen in the house in years.

"What's going to happen if I tell on Coyle every time he hits me?" I said. "You'll get sick of it. You'll just say it's both our faults and that I need to do my work and as soon as we're alone Coyle will beat on me again. That's why I picked up a gun in the first place. It was the only way to get you to take it seriously."

"We are taking this seriously because of an accumulation of evidence."

"You're taking this seriously because I pulled a gun and embarrassed everyone."

Mom took a deep breath and spoke in a tense, cold, utterly patient manner.

"I brought you in here because I want you to know that if you are articulate about a problem, words are more effective than violence."

I laughed derisively.

"Words *and* violence maybe," I said. "I know the truth. You speak up in our family and you get beaten on. You speak up, you get called a complainer and an exaggerator and told you have to shut up until sometime in the future when everything is supposedly going to be perfect. That's what we've been told all our lives: Shut up and be good because we're lucky to be here in glorious Seneca. I tried to tell you before that I was getting beaten on. But you didn't want to hear it."

"What you say is a warped version of the events."

"It's the only real version," I said. "Coyle blames me for things that are his own fault. And you and Dad are so worked up about making us 'superior human beings' that you don't stop to consider what it's like in the house."

"Untrue," Mom said in a faint, quavery voice. "I do consider it. Your father and I spend hours considering every aspect of your upbringing. We are committed to working so you children grow up in a different way than we did. Whatever happens next month in court, take your punishment, but know there has been a resolution here, because we are talking this over together and are living in a safe house."

"Yeah. Thanks for telling me."

She had spoken earnestly. That stung her.

"Sarcasm is not helpful," she said.

"Nothing is helpful except threats and violence," I said. "Just like you learned growing up that lazy people take advantage of everyone else, I've learned that violence is necessary against bullies. That's the main lesson of my life. Whatever you say, I know I'll be hit again. I know Coyle will blame me for everything that goes wrong with him. And I know you can't protect me and I'll never be safe until I'm away from Coyle and this house. Sarcasm may not be helpful. But at least with sarcasm I'm saying what's true."

"You've always had the right to speak up," she said.

"Yeah, sure," I said. "Why don't you call me a complainer for saying this now?"

Mom stood with her lips trembling. I suppose she thought she'd given us a happy childhood. All her work to live in the safe suburbs, with the good schools, all her cooking and cleaning and slaving away eighteen hours a day, like her drunken mother had never done for her. She had thought she'd call me in there and I'd acknowledge her contribution and be grateful for the measured way we were discussing the situation, but instead of grateful recognition she had a spiteful monster snapping at her from across the kitchen table. It was hard to trace back how it had come to that, how their dreams of self-improvement had devolved to that point of utter acrimony, but the damage was done. I had gotten beaten too many times and no half-hour conversation was going to change that. She had good intentions, but her intentions didn't matter to me. I was caught in a system where I got the shit kicked out of me and she was part of that system and she hadn't protected me.

Mom turned to the sink like she'd wash dishes. Her back was shaking and I realized she was crying.

I just stood there watching her back shake. Mom never cried. Mom lectured and gave us withering looks. I had a momentary feeling of uneasiness. I had broken her. But that uneasiness faded quickly into defiance.

Look at her, crying, I thought. Not even hit and she's losing it. Try getting beaten on five hundred times. See how you feel then.

She stood there struggling to hold back tears, understanding the extent of the damage only then, long after it had become permanent. No easy assurances from her were going to melt the ice inside.

I lingered a minute, watching dispassionately, then walked past her and went out. There was a blue medical glove near the porch, left from the ambulance the day before. I could see two compressed lines in the grass from the wheels of the stretcher. I decided I felt pretty good about what had happened. I had hit Coyle with a gun and maybe even tried to shoot him and I had more or less gotten away with it. I decided it was because they were afraid of me. I decided I wanted them to keep being afraid. I decided I was happy.

A day later Coyle came back from the hospital. His head was bandaged and his face was purple and swollen on the side that I'd hit. I said I was sorry in a casual way that made it obvious that I wasn't sorry at all. He didn't expect anything less from me. He murmured that he was sorry, too, but I knew he didn't mean it, either.

The next day Coyle went away on a baseball trip, and while he was gone Dad forked out fifteen hundred dollars

for a criminal lawyer. We plea-bargained my offense down
to a misdemeanor and I was sentenced to a month in a halfway house for violent juveniles. I would have gotten super-
vision, but Mrs. Chambers, our neighbor, was friends with
the police chief and the chief was friends with the judge and
they wanted to show us that that sort of fighting would not
be tolerated in Seneca.

The juvenile house was in Wauconda, a town near the
Wisconsin border. It was run by this hippie guy named Martin Blossom who had a blond beard and wore a friendship
bracelet. He took only six kids at a time. I was the only white
kid and the only kid from the suburbs, and on the first day
Martin grabbed my shoulder and shook a finger in my face
so no one would think he was showing preferences. Not that
it mattered. It was an easy life, much easier than life at home.
We had three or four hours of work on the "farm," which
was really an apple orchard with a large garden. The rest of
the time the other kids watched TV. I decided they were
total cows—illiterate, bored, and uninteresting. I never joined
them in their discussions and was always reading books like
Lord of the Flies and *The Outsiders* to show them that I was
different. Martin, the director, thought I was a stuck-up little
twit and swore he'd never take another kid from Seneca. I
swore I'd never go back. That was my main lesson. I wouldn't
end up in that position again. At the end of the month I left
without saying goodbye.

When I got home Coyle was circling the backyard on his
motorcycle. His reward for getting smacked with a gun was
that he was allowed to ride his bike again. I'm sure he saw
that as a fair trade. He was also allowed to move his mattress

down to a musty storage room in the basement. That room was small, with concrete walls, and stayed about fifty-five degrees all year round, but it had a door with a lock, and that was a luxury in our house. Coyle put a desk and bookshelf down there and it became his bedroom, and after that it was understood that it was better if I stayed upstairs and he stayed downstairs. For a long time after that we pretty much ignored each other. I thought at first it was a temporary reprieve from our battles, but it was more than that. Our physical fights were over. We'd come to an impasse. I'd scared Coyle the way he scared me.

It was the end of the first great struggle of my life.

3

Submission

If animals such as crickets are kept together in a closed group for a time, a kind of dominance hierarchy develops. Individuals that are accustomed to winning their battles become even more likely to win, while individuals who are accustomed to losing become steadily more likely to lose. This is true of crickets and it is true of any species that has a memory of conflicts, including, and I would say, particularly humans, making the label loser, at times, not merely a pejorative term.

—Richard Dawkins

It was a week after I got out of juvie, a few days before I started at New Trier, and I was standing in the hallway of our little house with a torn envelope at my feet and a folded computer printout in my hands. I had just received my New Trier High School introductory packet. I tossed all the flyers and announcements aside. Those were unimportant. I was holding the one thing that really mattered—the dot matrix, perforated-edged, printed sheet with my level placements.

The classes at New Trier were divided between 1 and 4 level, 4 being the best and 1 the worst. The placements were based on standardized tests, grades, and teacher recommendations. Coyle had been placed in the elevated 4 levels his freshman year and I just assumed I would be, too. I knew Coyle thought I was lazy and he was waiting for those level placements to prove that my methods were insufficient. In a vague way I thought my general intelligence would pull me through. It hadn't.

I ran down the list of classes and saw I had been placed in all 3 levels. Every class, just like Coyle had predicted. About three seconds after I saw my placements I walked into the kitchen carrying the printed sheet. My father was at the refrigerator with his paintbrushes, which he covered with tinfoil and froze between painting sessions so he didn't have to waste time washing them. I said, "I just got my levels. I've been put in all 3 level. It's a mistake."

"It's not a mistake. If you wanted to be in the 4 levels you should have studied instead of spending your time fighting with Coyle and reading dragon books."

"I didn't test well," I said.

"You also didn't study."

"I did study. But I wake at three in the morning three days a week to work for you. We're painting every weekend. Other kids have tutors and Ivy League students doing their homework for them. That's why I didn't get the best grades."

"Now you're blaming me for your mediocre results? What a complainer."

"I'm not blaming you. But waking up at three in the morning during the school year does not help with my grades."

"Coyle didn't have a problem with it. We'll see how you do this year. If you do well, you can move up."

"If I wait it's too late. Then a quarter of my transcript is on the lower levels. Are you trying to screw me to make Coyle seem better?"

Whenever I really wanted something I accused Dad of favoritism to Coyle, which struck a chord with him, because he did admire Coyle more than the rest of us. Despite dressing like a hoodlum and spending all his free time on his motorcycle, Coyle had been valedictorian of the junior high. He made the varsity baseball team as a freshman while working adult jobs with my father. Coyle's achievements were always held up to us to show us what was possible. But I knew Dad felt guilty about admiring Coyle, and accusing Dad of favoritism was a trump card that could be used in decisive moments.

"Talk to your mother," Dad said. "See what she says."

"And if she says it's ok, then I can move up?"

He pried the tinfoil from the frozen brush.

"Yeah, if you can get her to agree to sign the form, fine. But I doubt she'll agree."

Mom was out in the vegetable garden, jabbing at the ground with a hoe. I told her I wanted her to sign the petition to move up.

"If you go into 4 level you'll have to work harder," Mom said. "And if you move up and fail it will be worse than if you never went up."

"I don't care about that, because I know I won't fail," I said. "Coyle's in the 4 level. I want to be, too. You can either help me or make it so I go to a worse college."

She leaned the muddy hoe against the fence.

"I'll sign it," she said. "But you still have to get Dean Wilkins to agree."

"Ok," I said. "I'll get him to agree."

"We'll see," she said.

She signed the form.

Ten minutes later I was on my bike, pedaling to New Trier.

I arrived at school. I parked my bike, locked it, and walked in the front door and wandered around until I found the dean's office. The notifications for level placement had gone out that week and there were a lot of other people doing the same thing as me, trying to get into higher levels. There was a line out the door of the dean's office.

I stood at the end of the line and heard the dean in his office, saying, "These are your scores. I'm sorry, but we have to maintain our regulations. Superior students are given the chance to move up after a year. But be warned, the classes in the higher levels are more competitive. Often, it's better to stay in the original level."

I noticed all the other students were with their parents, and by their manners, by their jewelry, by their clothing, and particularly by their voices, I could tell they were in a different social class than our family. That was to be expected. Everyone at New Trier was in a different class than us. They spoke in complete sentences. They ate with their mouths closed. They didn't yell at one another in public. An air of certainty and complacency oozed from them.

A few of the parents glanced at me and then turned away. I was wearing my paint-spattered cutoffs and an Adidas T-shirt. My hair was not cut by a barber and hung into my eyes. I knew I looked different from the other kids. I didn't care. I'd even started to feel a defiant pride in looking like a blue-collar misfit.

I waited an hour. Three different petitioners were rejected over that hour. Then it was my turn.

"Come in. Shut the door," I heard Dean Wilkins say.

Dean Wilkins was a big guy, a weight lifter, with rippled muscles beneath his suit. He carried keys on his belt loop with a carabiner. He had a straightforward gruffness that reminded me of my father. I told him who I was.

"Are your parents with you?"

"No. But I have the signed form."

I handed the form over. He glanced at it.

"So you want to move into the 4 level?"

"Yes."

"You know these levels are calibrated based on your ability and achievement?"

"Yeah," I said. "But I think my ability has been underrated."

"You and everyone else," he said under his breath.

I figured I might as well tell him the truth.

"I need to be in the 4 level," I said. "My brother's in the 4 level. I should be, too."

"Your brother's Coyle Brennan?"

"Yes."

"Well, your brother is an exceptional case," he said.

Dean Wilkins looked at my application.

"You're working for Lucious Ward this year?"

"Yeah," I said. "I start in a week."

Mr. Ward was the building manager at New Trier. I'd

figured it was easier to work for the school and get paid than work for my father for free.

"Working for the school won't interfere with my homework," I said. "I'll just work during my free periods."

"Working through school is admirable," Dean Wilkins said. "It can be difficult, but it can also teach time management, and you learn about the real world, something I wish more of these students here understood. Like I said, admirable."

"I hope it isn't held against me," I said.

For a moment I thought I'd gone too far, but then Wilkins tossed his keys on the desk with a clatter.

"All right. Four level it is. You do well, you stay up. But if you don't, you move back down. And no favoritism because you're an employee."

"Definitely not. I'll do well. Thank you," I said.

Wilkins signed his part of the form. And that was it. I was in the 4 level.

As I walked out I understood that it was in my favor that I'd come alone. It was in my favor that I was Coyle's brother. It was hugely in my favor that Dean Wilkins did not know what had happened to me that summer.

I walked over to the admin offices and got my schedule changed and that was that. Later I realized that the classes in 3 and 4 level really weren't that different from each other. The classes were segregated based on talent, but also on ambition and connections. And once I was in the 4 level no one questioned why I was there. They just thought I was a smart kid. Even the teachers thought this. And it taught me something.

You had to fight your way to the top, but once you were there it didn't matter how you'd gotten there. Everyone just assumed you belonged.

I came home with my new schedule. Coyle was at the dining room table pretending he didn't care what happened, but I knew he did.

I sat down. He said nothing at first. But he couldn't help himself. He wanted to know.

"So what levels?" he asked.

"Fourth. I got moved up."

He nodded, mouth a tight slit.

It had taken Coyle three years of consistent work to be put in the 4 levels. It took me an afternoon of wheedling.

New Trier was more like a small college than a high school. There were almost five thousand students in the school at the time and it had a reputation as being one of the best and hardest schools in the country. I think most freshmen were intimidated by the school. I wasn't. Whatever my father's initial intentions when he implemented his "methods" of childrearing—waking us up before dawn, working adult jobs at a young age, using every free moment for self-improvement—the result for me, after my battles with Coyle, was that I became fanatically focused on surpassing Coyle, and that blinded me to everything else, including intimidation.

On that first day of high school I walked into the cafeteria to see long aisles of jabbering, gesticulating students. Coyle sat at the far end with a contingent of scruffy, defiant guys from the baseball team who all wore their New Trier baseball caps backward and sat hunched over, talking to one another in low voices. On the other end of the cafeteria, midway down the aisle, I saw Robert Dainty and his blithe, preppy crowd. These were the kids who belonged to country clubs and were forced to take ballroom dancing classes so they'd know what to do at their cotillions. They wore untucked oxford shirts, wrinkled khakis, and red Converse high-tops. An air of utter satisfaction hung over these kids, like mist over a swamp.

Robert's preppy crowd and Coyle's burnout crowd were the extremes of the social world at New Trier. There were about twenty other groups that fell somewhere between them—theater kids, band members, swimmers, math-clubbers, jocks, the radio-station crowd—but Coyle and Robert were the two ends of the spectrum, and right away I thought that if Coyle was at one end of the social scale, I wanted to be at the other. As I walked up the aisle that day I slowed as I neared Robert's table.

"Hey, Little Brennan," Robert said. Then, to the others at the table, "This is Coyle Brennan's younger brother."

"Is it true you shot your brother?" Liam called out.

He was the kid who'd been at the fight on the playfield. He knew Coyle.

"I was provoked," I said.

That started all of them jeering.

"I was provoked the same way last summer," Robert said. "You remember how he provoked me?"

"You wanted to touch his motorcycle and he went crazy," Liam said.

"That's what happened to me, too," I said. "I just touched his front tire with a rake and he kicked me three times."

"What'd I tell you?" Robert said to the others at the table. "Brennan's wild about that bike. You just look at it and he loses his mind. His brother here had to shoot him."

Liam glanced down the aisle at Coyle.

"Doesn't look hurt to me," Liam said.

"I missed," I said, laughing.

We bantered back and forth for about a minute, and then I said, "Later," and some of the other guys said, "Later," and that was it. I went on to the table where my three friends Jimmy, Bennie, and Roscoe were waiting.

I tried to pretend it was no big deal, me standing there at Robert Dainty's table, but I was brimming with satisfaction. Robert was like royalty in the school. Everyone knew him. And everyone, including my brother, had seen me talking with him.

Robert Dainty lived in the biggest house in our neighborhood and was one of these overscheduled, competitive, high-achieving rich kids who are trained and coached by professionals from a young age. Robert was all-state soccer. He was ranked in tennis. He spoke French fluently. And he had a domineering personality, not that much different from Coyle. If Robert was walking to a car with his friends he would just naturally get in the front seat. If there was one cookie left Robert took it and felt it was his right to take it. If there was a video game, Robert always played first. And unlike Coyle, he was socially savvy. Robert could make or break your social life in school and everyone knew it. I once saw Robert say to a girl named Lizzie Denton, "That sweater's hideous, Lizzie. Take it off. I'm sick of looking at it." And she did take it off. He had that kind of power.

There were people who complained about Robert, saying that he was a poor sport, that he always had to get his way, and all of this was true, but I saw quickly that no one at New Trier would go against him publicly. As far as I could tell, Coyle was the only person who ever stood up to Robert, but Coyle could do it because he was already an outcast, which maybe was the point of joining the burnouts in the first place.

Even in those first weeks at New Trier I knew that if I succeeded in joining Robert's crowd Coyle would see that as a victory for me. But it wasn't so easy to join. Robert's snide, picky friends all sat in judgment of anyone who tried to get close, and I knew they saw me as some weird blue-collar loser. But I had one card in my favor: Robert was competitive with Coyle, and befriending me would bug Coyle, so I lingered around Robert's table in the first week, hoping that he'd banter with me again, but it didn't happen. After that first day he seemed annoyed when I lingered, and after awhile I gave it up.

"They slip the orders through here," Deanny said. "Ten sheets of carbon. A box of number-two pencils. A ream of mimeo. That's five hundred sheets."

I was down in storeroom B, of New Trier, in the basement

starting my job for the building manager. I was being shown the ropes by a student named Teddy Deane, or "Deanny." He'd done the job for three years. Now I was taking over.

Deanny was a muscular, athletic kid with wavy brown hair, a wrestler, with veins that stuck up on his forearms.

"This is the best job in the school," Deanny said. "In the bookstore you have Miss Winters and Miss Schock pecking away at you. The old hags. In the file office it's just so boring. But down here, no one bothers you."

Deanny picked out office supplies casually, tossing them into a cardboard box, talking the whole time, explaining the job.

"Keep the old boxes. Use them as containers. Label the box with the teacher's name and room number. Put the yellow carbon in the box for verification. Then leave the order here, on the cart, for delivery."

There were four aisles, with black metal shelves stocked with office supplies. There was no one else in there—just the two of us.

"You do the next one. Only way to learn."

Deanny sat against the wall with a copy of *Candide,* in French, and I started on the next order, searching through the aisles for number-two pencils, mimeograph paper, a three-hole punch. I was slow because I didn't know where anything was, but I made sure to be accurate. A part of me was thrilled. I had my first paying job. And it was in school. I got paid to go to school! But there was another side to it. I worked in the storeroom like a janitor, and I knew that was an embarrassment. I had learned from my peers that manual labor was shameful. "Normal" people worked as doctors and lawyers and businessmen. If you had to use your hands for the job, it was not something to be proud of. This attitude was all around me, in the air I breathed.

We'd been working about twenty minutes when there was a knock on the door.

"We're being hailed," Deanny said, and, reaching over, opened the door to see a pretty, dark-haired girl named Renata. A cheerleader and field hockey player.

"Hey, Deanny," she said in a singsong tone.

"Welcome to my lair," Deanny said. "What can I do for you, RJ?"

"I can't get into my locker."

"Is that so?"

"The dial won't turn. They said you can fix it."

"If I feel like it," Deanny said.

He checked her combination in a book and then the three of us started out into the basement hallway of the school, Deanny carrying a steel toolbox, me carrying spare parts for the lock. As we walked I noticed Deanny was constantly saying "Hey" or "What's up?" or giving the cool nod to other students. He didn't seem to be embarrassed at all to be out in the open with his tools. He walked with a swagger. He was "The Deanny." In everything he did he exuded a casual confidence. No one was going to make him feel small.

When we arrived at Renata's locker, Deanny found it was not just jammed, but broken, the dial not turning at all. Deanny immediately went at it with a little screwdriver, removing the dial from the locker, taking the lock apart right there in the hallway, laying the pieces out on the tile floor.

"I'll teach you how to do this. It's like a puzzle. It's fun," he said.

Deanny explained the basics of how those locks were put
together—the tumbler, the various dials and gears and bars—
and while he talked his hands moved in a practiced blur. I
stood over him, watching closely. And the whole time he
was working and I was trying to follow his instruction, other
students wandered past and stopped to watch. Deanny made
casual, jaunty comments to them, and they seemed impressed
and interested in what he was doing. And I took this all in.

And when I look back on this interaction now, I understand that watching Deanny was deeply instructive for me.
As a younger kid I had thought that knowing how to hang
drywall or deliver papers made me special. I knew something
other kids didn't. But bit by bit as I got into junior high I
understood by the sneering of other students, by consistent
derisive comments, that manual labor was inherently shameful, and I had started to hide the work I did for my father.

But now, observing Deanny, this competent, intelligent,
popular guy, striding through the hallways with his tools, setting up a workshop in the middle of the hallway, I saw a
different way of being. Deanny's whole manner was a counter-
argument to what I had learned about certain kinds of work
being shameful.

Afterward, as we walked back to the storeroom, an angu-
lar soccer player named Jack Renn, an unpleasant kid, said,
"You still cleaning up our messes, Deanny?"

"Only if I feel like it," Deanny said, and we kept walking.

Back at the storeroom, Deanny set the toolbox in its spot
and said, "Forget losers like Renn. It's only weird if you let
them make it weird."

I always remembered him saying that.

September, I'd been at New Trier for about a month when I walked into the back hallway of the field house and found Coach Schneider with his cowboy boots on a desk, grading driver's ed tests and listening to country music.

Coach Schneider was a straight-backed, ex-military guy from West Texas who was the basketball and tennis coach. His no-bullshit manner reminded me of Bobby Knight. I stood in the doorway of his office.

"I'm Willie Brennan," I said. "I think you're the varsity tennis coach."

"As far as I know I am," he said. "Unless you know something I don't."

That was the way Schneider talked. Everything was a little sarcastic.

"I'm a freshman," I said.

"You don't say," he said.

"I play tennis. I want to be on the varsity. My brother made varsity baseball as a freshman. I'm too small to play baseball, so I play tennis. I want to make a varsity sport, too, just like my brother."

"Sibling rivalry. No better incentive," he said. "Is your brother Coyle Brennan?"

"Yeah."

"Well, I know your brother. Good athlete. I also know your father." He held his fist up. "Strong disciplinarian. I like that. I wish there were more fathers like him at this school. It would make my job easier."

He looked me up and down.

"You know we won state last year and are expecting to do well again this year. Normally, some freshman comes in here, says he wants to make the varsity, I'd say, 'Yeah, good luck with that, Chief.' But if you're anything like your brother maybe you can do it. Do you know how the team's organized?"

"Six people make it, right?"

"Yeah. Six, and one alternate. But four of those spots are already taken. There are two spots left. They'll be filled by high-level state players. If you aren't good already you won't make it."

"I am good," I said.

It wasn't a complete lie. Dad had made sure we all concentrated on one sport, and I had chosen tennis because it was a sport where you didn't get knocked around.

"You'll have to start playing doubles," Schneider said. "Have you played doubles?"

"Sure."

"It's a whole different beast. Some of the better JV players get together three or four days a week during the winter. If you could get in with them it would help."

"Who are the players?"

"Well, the guy who runs the court is named Robert Dainty. Do you know him?"

I looked away, biting my lip.

"Yeah, I know him. He lives close to me. Coyle got in a fight with him."

"Who won?"

"Coyle," I said.

Schneider looked pleased.

"Well, whatever happened, I'm sure Dainty deserved it. He's a real piece of work, that kid. But the Daintys have this court reserved three times a week and the kids all play together. Robert thinks he'll be the fifth man. Maybe he will be. That's to be determined. Get in with them. That will help."

I said I would and Schneider put his boots back on his desk and picked up a test.

"What'd you say your name was?"

"Willie Brennan."

"Yeah, well, good luck, Willie. See you in the spring."

There was a signup sheet for the pickup tennis outside the Tri-Ship Club, which was like a fraternity in the high school. When I checked the list there were already about twenty names on it. I put my name down, but that didn't mean they'd call me. Only a select few got chosen. Over the next few days I said hey to Robert in the hallway and gave him the cool nod in the cafeteria but I didn't get the call for their after-school tennis club, and Robert didn't bother to talk to me again, either. Just the opposite, really. Signing up for tennis seemed to assure that he'd keep his distance, though he was good-natured about it. Robert seemed pleased to be completely friendly to me and to also completely ignore my request to play with them. He genuinely seemed to enjoy my discomfort. I didn't hear anything more about it, except that a few of Robert's friends whispered to one another when I walked past and when I stopped by their table at lunch a kid named Tom Corley tossed a bit of hamburger at my feet and said, "Coo coo, pigeon." I didn't stop by again. A few more weeks went by. Nothing happened, and I figured nothing would. Being a large public school, New Trier was often seen as being a meritocracy, but to get in the clubs or on the sports teams, you had to be either part of the crowd of people who ran the school or just be undeniably better than the other kids. I was ready to do what I had to do, but if I wasn't allowed to even practice with the guys from the team, I had no chance. A few more days passed and my dreams of making the varsity tennis team and showing up Coyle began to fade.

Then it was the last day of September. I was at my locker and suddenly Robert was standing there.

"Willie," he said in an unnaturally upbeat tone. "How you doing?"

He'd never acted so pleased to see me. I figured he must want something.

"What's up?" I said.

"I got a question. Did you get moved up in levels?"

"Why do you ask that?"

"Because I heard you did."

It wasn't something I publicized. I wanted people to think I'd tested into the 4 levels on my own, not that I'd weaseled my way in.

"Who told you?"

"Your brother."

"You talk to him?"

"You know, in between beating on each other, yeah, sometimes we talk. We're in all the same classes, except I'm in 3 level Latin. I was complaining about it and he said I obviously wasn't as persuasive as you were, because you'd talked your way up in all your classes. Is that true?"

"Sort of."

"What does that mean?"

"It means, yeah, I did."

"So, in every class?"

"Yeah."

He opened his eyes wide.

"Do you realize how lucky you are? I know like eight people who tried to get moved up and it didn't work for any of them. Your parents must have done something. Did they pay money?"

I laughed.

"My parents said if I wanted to get moved up I should ask myself," I said.

"So you just showed up on your own without your parents?"

"Yeah."

He considered this silently for a moment.

"And what'd you say?"

"I just told Wilkins I wanted to move up."

"That's it?"

"I mentioned that I was working for the school."

"Did he like that? That you were working?"

"He might have."

"And what'd you wear?"

"Just my normal clothes."

"You mean like jeans and a sweatshirt?"

"It was summer. I actually think the shorts I wore had paint on them. I didn't dress up, if that's what you're asking."

Robert took this in.

"Thanks," he said. "I get it."

He walked off and that night I saw Coyle in the basement, lifting weights.

"Did you tell Robert I got moved up in levels?" I asked.

"His mother knows someone in the admin offices," Coyle said. "He already knew. Did he ask you for advice on how to weasel with Wilkins?"

"Yeah."

"Did you give it?"

"Yeah," I said.

"That was stupid," he said.

"Why's it matter?"

"Extra competition."

"He's not in my grade. And maybe he'll help me someday," I said.

Coyle smiled knowingly. It was irritating.

"Robert Dainty is never going to help you. That guy will pretend he's your friend and then stab you in the back when it's time for him to help."

"Maybe that's just what he does to you," I said. "Because you're such a pleasant person."

Coyle sat up from the bench press. I backed away, starting up the stairs.

"Good luck getting in with the cool kids," Coyle called after me.

"Good luck fighting with everyone for your whole life," I said.

Nothing happened for a few more days. I forgot about it. Then Robert showed back up at my locker, brimming with self-satisfaction. He tossed a Super Ball at me—a translucent dusty thing with a twisted red ribbon inside.

"Keep it," he said. "Reward. For helping me. I talked to Wilkins. I did just what you said. I showed up alone. I didn't dress up like I was going to church. I told him I was working part-time at The French Baker."

"Are you?"

"Of course not. My dad would probably die from embarrassment if his friends at his office heard that I had to work. No. I just said I did because Wilkins likes kids who work, apparently. Thanks. You saved my GPA."

"I aim to please," I said.

He walked off, holding a fist up.

"Willie Fucking Brennan!" he shouted, when he was halfway down the hall.

A few days later I was unlocking my bike when Robert's BMW pulled up to the curb and stopped. The window rolled down.

"Hey, Little Brennan," Robert called. "Get in. We're on patrol."

"Patrol?" I said.

"Don't worry about it," Tom Corley said. He was riding shotgun. "Just get in."

Tom was the guy who'd said "coo coo pigeon" to me. Tom was territorial about their group and had noticed me lingering. He didn't like it.

"Patrol for girls," Robert said. "Put the bike in the back. I'll drop you off later."

Robert popped the trunk and I put my bike in the back and hooked the trunk with a bungee cord. When I got in the backseat Tom turned with exaggerated disapproval.

"You took your time getting in," he said.

"Was I supposed to hurry?" I said.

Tom let out a puff of air, like that was just beyond everything. He turned back to Robert and gestured laconically to two girls passing.

"She's PP," Tom said to Robert.

"Possible pussy," Robert said back to me. "Tom swooped on her younger sister. What's her name? Sheri the Cherry?"

"Shut up," Tom said.

"Not 'the Cherry' anymore," Robert said.

I thought I was supposed to laugh, so I did. Tom turned again, scowling.

"Shut up, freshman. Not like you've ever gotten any."

"How would you know?" I said, though he was right.

Tom gave me an appraising look and, reaching out, fingered the cuff of my jacket.

"Isn't that Jay Ellison's jacket?"

I realized Jay's mother must have donated the jacket to the Salvation Army, where Mom got all our clothes.

"Jay's mom gave it to my mom," I lied. "It didn't fit him anymore."

"Well, you need other hand-me-downs, let me know. I got some old underwear and shit you could probably have." Then, turning to Robert, "Can you believe he's wearing Jay's jacket? You always go around begging?"

"It didn't fit Jay anymore," I said. "And I didn't beg for it. What? Are you jealous? I'll let you wear it if you like it."

"Kid's a smartass," Tom said to Robert. "He's trying to pretend he's like Jay Ellison." Then, to me, "You're not even close to being as cool as Jay. He was totally classic, that guy."

"I'm just wearing the jacket," I said.

"Don't think it means you're as cool as Jay. That's all I'm saying," Tom said.

"And all I'm saying is it's just a jacket."

Robert raised his eyebrows and looked at Tom. I could see he agreed with me. It wasn't a big deal.

Robert turned right on Church, which was not the way home for me.

"Where're we going?" I said.

"He already told you," Tom said. "On patrol. And I told you not to ask questions. What're you, like, Mr. Interrogator?"

"We'll drop you off later," Robert said.

"After we're done with you," Tom said ominously. "You can't get away now."

My eyes went to Robert's in the mirror. He looked away, embarrassed, and I knew something unpleasant was about to happen. I'd thought they'd picked me up to hang out, because I'd helped Robert, and maybe even because we were becoming friends, but now I understood it was for casual tormenting because I was a freshman and I'd put my name on the list for the tennis group.

Tom was rattling through the tapes in the glove compartment. He found a cassette and slid it into the deck. The sound of a saxophone blasted out.

"Do you know this?" Robert said, glancing at me in the mirror.

"It's Madness," I said. "I love this song."

"I knew that band sucked," Tom said. "It's for freshman losers."

Tom ejected the tape and tossed it out the window.

"Asshole," Robert said, laughing.

"I was sick of that tape," Tom said.

Tom adjusted the radio, finding WXRT. Then turned back, and, with a haughty look, said, "What're you, Helen Keller? Join in the conversation."

"You weren't talking, either," I said.

"He's got a point," Robert said. "None of us were talking, including you."

"I was listening to the radio," Tom said.

"I was listening to it, too," I said.

"Don't talk back," Tom said.

"You just said I was Helen Keller. Now you're saying not to talk."

Robert laughed and Tom gave Robert an exasperated look, as if to say, "Whose side are you on?" Then, to me, "You got a big mouth for a freshman. Lean forward."

"What?"

"Just lean forward. I gotta tell you a secret."

Robert watched in the mirror. Something was about to happen. I could feel that it was, and I was pretty sure it was something bad.

"Come on," Tom said. "Just for a second. Lean forward. What? Are you afraid?"

"No."

"Then do it. Lean forward."

I leaned forward just a little. Tom grabbed my head. I jerked to get away. We knocked into Robert and the car swerved, hit the curb, and jolted. Tom stretched something over my head.

"Jock head!" he said, laughing loudly. "Jock head! Jock head! Look at him!"

I tore the elastic band off my head. Robert swerved back to the street.

"Idiots," he said.

Tom reached back and grabbed me again and got the jockstrap on my head.

"Oh my God! Jock head!"

"Don't knock into me while I'm driving," Robert said. "If I crash this car my dad will kill me."

I got the jockstrap off my head. Tom's leather backpack was at my feet. I rolled my window down, lifted the backpack, and shoved it out the window. The backpack hit the pavement and tumbled. A flurry of papers spread behind us.

"Stop the car!" Tom yelled.

Robert screeched to a halt. Tom turned to me.

"You are so fucking dead."

Tom tried to grab my backpack but I jerked it from him. He reached out to hit me and I punched him, hard, in the chin. I'd been in so many fights with Coyle that it just came naturally. I didn't even know I was going to do it. After a moment I leaned forward and punched Tom in the throat. He made a gargling sound. I moved forward to hit a third time but Tom opened the car door and fell out, trying to get away from me. I got out to go after him but Tom was scrambling from the car.

"Dead," Tom croaked. "You are so dead."

But I could see he was afraid. He ran off to where his backpack and papers were spread across the street. His hand kept going to his neck. Cars were stopped and waiting while he picked up the papers. He was crying a little, turning his head so we wouldn't see. I got in the front seat.

"Drive," I said.

"What?"

"We'll just keep fighting if we're both here. Drive."

Robert and Tom were good friends. I'd just thrown Tom's backpack out the window and punched Tom in the throat. There was no reason to think Robert would do anything except resent me. But Robert was a cocky kid who appreciated a bold gesture, particularly if it had an element of casual malevolence.

Robert hit the gas, leaving Tom behind.

"I thought you were supposed to be the nice Brennan," he said.

"I am the nice one, comparatively," I said. "Tom started it."

"Sort of," Robert said. Then, "Is that how you fought with Coyle?"

"Are you kidding? If I did that to Coyle I'd be getting skewered right now."

"I believe that," he said. "Your brother's a total beast. I had a bruise for three weeks after I fought with him."

"I don't think I've been without a bruise since I was like three years old."

Robert punched his hand into his fist.

"That's a good older brother, teaching you how to act."

He paused, and seemed to consider how to tell me something.

"You know we do that to everyone," he said.

"Do what?"

"Put a jock on their head. It's like an initiation. I had it done to me last year. I was so annoying they did it a few times, actually. We hang out third period. And we play tennis after school. I saw you'd signed up. I know people say I'm an asshole, but I know how to be grateful. You helped me. I was going to invite you to play. That's the normal initiation. It's Chip Bazinski's jock from like eight years ago when they didn't lose a match all year. It's a tradition."

I was quiet, considering this.

"So, everyone has that done to them?"

"Everyone who plays in the tennis group. Yeah."

"What do the other kids do when you put the jock on them?"

"Most kids are glad when it happens. They know what it means. They're being invited to play. But typical Brennan. Just like your brother. We try to invite you and be nice and just treat you like anyone else and you get all touchy and crazy."

"I didn't get crazy."

"You punched Tom in the throat. How much more crazy could you get?"

"He was attacking me."

"He was trying to invite you to our club!" Robert said, laughing. "But typical Brennan. You guys are all so fucking wild."

Robert actually seemed to consider this a compliment.

We arrived at my house. He put the car in park.

"Listen, I'll straighten it out with Corley. Come by the student lounge third period. You can meet everyone else. And you should bring your racket to school. We play at the Nielsen courts on Mondays, Wednesdays, and Fridays. You still want to play?"

"Definitely," I said. "But what about Tom?"

"Are you kidding? Tom sucks in tennis. He just picks on kids who want to be in our group because he knows they'll beat him. He's going to be scared of you."

"Tell him I'm sorry."

"I'm not telling him that. I'll tell him if he's not cool about it you're going to kick his ass again." Then, "I can't wait to tell Liam and Doug about this. They are going to flip when they hear you beat up Corley for trying to put Bazinski's jock on your head. Total Brennan move. High five, Willie."

Bewildered, I gave Robert a high five.

"Thanks for the ride," I said.

"Thanks for beating up my friend," Robert said.

I got out of the car and as soon as I shut the door Robert made a U-turn and pulled away, accelerating. I could see him laughing inside the car.

I turned to the house. Coyle was sitting in the window. He'd seen who dropped me off. I walked inside. I waited for him to say something about Robert Dainty so I could tell him I would be playing tennis on Robert's court. He didn't ask, and I was thinking I might just have to bring it up myself, but then there were footsteps on the stairs and Dad came clomping down. He'd seen that someone in a BMW had dropped me off. To Coyle's annoyance, Dad had an exultant expression.

"What are you standing there for?" Dad said. "You think you get to be lazy because you have a friend with a BMW? You keep hanging out with kids like that, you'll have your own BMW someday. Time for studying. Start up!"

I smiled in a way meant to irritate Coyle. I walked on up the stairs.

All that fall and into the winter I played tennis in Robert Dainty's after-school tennis group. The other kids in that group were country-club players with expensive sweat suits and special tennis duffels and multiple rackets, but I found out soon enough that they weren't any better at tennis than I was. In a lot of cases they were worse. A few of the kids— Tom Corley in particular—made fun of my gray sweatpants or that I filled a tennis-ball can with water instead of getting a water bottle, but I'd been living in Seneca all my life with kids like Tom Corley and I knew how to act with them. By that I mean I knew not to make a big deal about his snarky comments or appear shamed by my relative poverty. I just laughed and said, "Who cares what kind of sweatpants I wear? Let's see who wins." I knew that if I played well and held myself steady against the kids like Tom that I'd have a chance of making the team. I understood quickly enough that Robert didn't care how I looked. He just wanted to win. And I tried to be accommodating when we were partners. I let Robert take the forehand side. I let him hit the overheads. I always acted as if he had played better than me, even when he hadn't. And my consistent play complimented his more aggressive style. Bit by bit Robert and I started playing together and hanging out not just after tennis, but sometimes on the weekends, too. I was a freshman, but suddenly I was riding around in Robert's car, getting invited to upperclassmen parties with the cool kids. I didn't ditch my old friends. I knew they were my real friends. But I started spending a lot of time in that world of big houses with game rooms and large backyards with pools, and all the while, as I was settling into Robert's group, I could feel Coyle watching, and I was sure at the time that he was envious, though later I considered the possibility that I thought Coyle was envious only because I couldn't imagine anyone not wanting to be in Robert's crowd. The social world at New Trier was complex, hermetic, and nuanced, and even now I'm not sure if Coyle thought I was a suckass or wished he could join me.

Mid-January, and Coyle and I were at an office building on Sherman Street in Evanston. Along with the paper route, and work as a janitor, our father had the contract to renovate a four-story office building. It literally took years for us to do the whole job. We moved through the building, floor by floor, room by room. Our job that day was to tear up the linoleum from a four-room office.

Coyle and I spent the morning gouging and pulling at the linoleum and tearing it up, and tossing the scraps onto a tarp in the corner. Later, Coyle and I dragged the pile of torn lino-leum down the third-floor hallway to a large garbage can at the back near the stairway. Normally we would have brought that linoleum straight out to the Dumpster, but there was a girl named Nettie Plumb in the backseat of a car in the parking lot. Nettie's father had an office in that building and neither of us wanted her to see us hauling trash. It would just be an embar-rassment. So we'd carried the garbage can up to the third floor and we were back there, tossing the linoleum into the can, when Coyle paused in his work and asked a strange question.

"Do you pick up the balls for Robert when you play after school with him?"

"Who told you that?" I asked.

"I just . . . I heard you did."

"I *help* to pick up the balls," I said. "But I don't pick up all of them and I don't do it like I'm a slave and I have to do it."

"Does everyone help?"

"Not always," I said after a moment.

"But you always do?"

"Yes."

"Why?"

"I do it cause the balls are just sitting there. Someone has to pick them up. You would do the same thing."

"No, I wouldn't," Coyle said.

"Yeah, you would," I said. "It just makes sense. There are six spots on the team. Those last two spots are a doubles team. Robert will probably be the fifth man. If he picks me as his partner, I'll be the sixth man."

"So you think he'll choose you because you pick up balls?"

"No. He'll choose me because I win. But it doesn't hurt to get along. Even you know that's true. Robert's father pays for the court. I don't put in any money. What's it hurt to help pick up a few balls?"

"If you pick up after them they'll treat you like you're their servant."

"If I don't I'll look like I'm getting all weird about it. And I don't care. It's just a few balls. And I'm not the only one who picks up."

Coyle looked skeptical.

"Do other people put in money for the court?"

"I don't think so. But no one cares. The only reason you heard about the ball thing is that Tom Corley's been saying I get chosen to play because I'm Robert's suckass. But that's crap. Do you really think that Robert would choose me because I pick up? Tom's just jealous because we keep beating him."

"And because you punched him in the face."

I looked away and bit my lip. I didn't know he knew about that.

"I punched him in the throat, not the face," I said.

"Well, I'm sure he deserved it," Coyle said. "That guy's a bigger weasel than Robert. He's even a bigger weasel than you."

"And that's saying something," I said jauntily.

Coyle reached down and picked up a stray scrap of linoleum. He tapped me with the pointy end of it.

"Just don't be a suckass," he said.

"I'm not," I said. "I pick up because there's work to be done and why not do it. And, anyway, when we played tennis you made me pick up after you."

This was true. When we played tennis together Coyle always made me pick up after him. He said the loser picked up. I always lost.

Coyle was quiet for a moment. I don't think he'd ever considered this.

"It's different," he said finally.

"Why?"

"Because I'm your brother. I was trying to help you learn."

"Maybe Robert's trying to help me learn, too."

Coyle gave a derisive laugh.

"Robert's the greediest person I've ever met. He's not trying to help anyone but himself. Just don't be a suckass. Because if you are, they'll know it, and it won't help."

And that was the end of the conversation, but in the days afterward I mulled it over and I decided Coyle thought one of two things: Either he didn't believe I wasn't sucking ass or he didn't believe it was possible to be in that subordinate position and not suck ass. I wasn't sure which.

———

Winter in northern Illinois—dark and bleak and cold, the wind whistling outside frosted windows, snow piled high along driveways and carved into strange, graceful shapes at the corners of houses. Sometimes the wind blew from the northeast, blasting off the lake, and when it did the snow gathered in the divots of the dunes along the lake and narrowed to a point on crests, like windblown foam on a wave. Ice built up over the lake, and enormous chunks, translucent and hulking, blew in to shore and piled up like icebergs in a great, jumbled, icy maze on shore. I liked to go down to the beach in winter and wander through the eerie, arctic landscape, and feel like I was miles from civilization.

One afternoon in February I was on the bluff over Dyson's Beach when I saw three figures moving along the lakeshore below. That stretch of waterfront to the south was lined with magnificent houses with rolling, snow-covered lawns going down to sandy dunes where blond strands of sea grass showed above the white snow. As the three figures moved on I realized one of them was Coyle. I also noticed that they were approaching a second group of kids on a sloping lawn, huddled around a barbeque. These kids were cooking hotdogs and roasting marshmallows on the grill in the frigid dusk. They were drinking canned beers.

From that distance I could recognize a few of those kids. It was Ronny Chesil and Dennis Fink, kids from Robert's group, though I did not see Robert himself.

As Coyle and his three friends passed the barbeque area, Dennis Fink picked up a hotdog from the grill and flung it out toward Coyle and his friends, who stopped walking. After a moment Coyle walked over and reached into the snow with his bare hand and picked up the hotdog in two fingers and walked back up the beach toward the barbeque, holding that steaming hotdog in front of him. There was a moment where Coyle was on one side, a solitary figure, and there were about seven guys on the other side, faced off against him. Then Coyle flung the hotdog at Dennis and there was a moment where no one did anything and then the whole scrum collapsed on Coyle and he waded into a chaos of swinging arms, bodies thrashing, one against seven, and then Coyle broke away, and the three friends all ran off, jogging down the snowy beach, stopping to gesture defiantly, then going on, weaving among the monoliths of ice in the purple dusk.

I watched all of this from the bluff. I was too far away to help. Not that I would have, anyway. A year before I'd have been rooting for Coyle to get his ass kicked, but on that day, watching Coyle fighting all of those snarky kids in Robert's crowd, it set off a strange, uneasy feeling inside me. I knew Robert's crowd by then—their underhanded comments, their condescension—but I also knew how overbearing, violent, and intractable Coyle could be. And seeing the skirmish was like lightning in the night clouds of my soul, great forms illuminated for a moment in a flash.

Coyle never mentioned that scuffle. I never told him I'd seen it. But I knew that Coyle was watching me get closer and closer to Robert Dainty and I knew he didn't like it.

———

Three months after I'd started playing in the tennis group Robert, Tom, Liam, and I were in Robert's car. We were just turning onto Edens Expressway, all of us red-faced and sweaty after our workout, when Robert, who was in the front passenger seat, rolled his window down, reached out the window, and, grabbing the rack overhead, pulled himself onto the roof while the car was going sixty miles an hour. He clambered over our heads and dangled his hand down near me. I rolled my window down and slapped his hand. Then a moment later Robert's feet appeared again in his open window. He slid back inside the car and fell into his seat and turned to us, grinning, as if nothing had happened.

"You are insane," Liam said.

"Whatever," Robert said. "Pull over, Griggs."

"A please would be nice," Liam said.

Liam slowed and pulled over to the side.

"Get out," Robert said to me.

I had no idea what was going on, but it was normal for Robert to order us around. I got out. So did Liam, who went in the backseat where I had been sitting. Robert got in the driver's seat. The only seat left was the front passenger seat. I walked around and got in. I shut the door and the car jolted to life. Robert, who was now driving, turned to me and said, "Are you ready?"

"For what?"

"What do you think?" he said.

Robert sped up to seventy miles an hour. Tom was grinning in the backseat, waiting to see what would happen. I understood that Robert wanted me to climb out the window and onto the roof of the moving car like he had.

"I'm not doing that," I said.

"Told you," Tom said from the backseat.

"It's stupid," I said.

"I think it's a little stupid, too," Liam said.

"Shut up," Robert said. "He'll do it."

"No, I won't," I said.

"Are you afraid?" Tom said.

"Yeah," I said. "Why wouldn't I be afraid? It's completely insane. You don't climb on the roof of a car while it's going sixty miles an hour."

"I did it," Robert said. "And we were going seventy."

"Told you he wouldn't do it," Tom said again.

Office buildings and water towers went by in a blur. Robert jerked the car from one lane to another.

"All the rest of us have done it," Robert said.

"Is that true?"

"Yes," Tom said.

"Sort of," Liam said.

"What do you mean 'sort of'?"

Liam played tennis but was really a football player, and he was the guy in the group who didn't always give in to Robert.

"We sat in the window," Liam said.

"That's totally different," I said. "I'll sit in the window. I'll do it right now."

"I don't want you to sit in the window," Robert said. "If I wanted someone who'd sit in the window I'd have had Tom sit in front. The only person in this car who hasn't done anything is you. I just went on the roof."

"I don't want to do it," I said.

"Fine," Robert said. "Be a loser."

Tom snickered in the backseat.

"Told you," he said for the third time.

Robert kept looking over at me with an exasperated, indignant expression. In his mind he'd brought me into his group, let me play tennis with them, shielded me from their snarky judgment, and the least I could do was go along with his dare.

"Are you really not doing it?"

"No."

"God, loser," he said.

We usually went to Robert's house and hung out after tennis, but on that day he passed the usual exit. I understood he was taking me home and that if I didn't do what he wanted that would be the end of us hanging out together. Robert demanded obedience from his friends, particularly friends like me, who he felt owed him.

I sat looking out the window, understanding the situation. I hated it, but I understood it. After a moment, I rolled my window down.

"Hold it steady," I said.

"I don't need to hold it steady if you're not getting out," Robert said peevishly.

I looked at him. I unclipped my seatbelt.

"Just hold it steady," I said.

His manner changed instantly. He became helpful and encouraging. That's the way Robert was. He was a nice guy as long as he got his way.

"Just reach out and get a grip on the rack, Willie. You'll be fine. Get to the middle. Knock on the roof. Come back down. That's all you have to do. Then we'll both have done it. Only us and no one else."

I rolled the window down. It was about forty degrees. I felt for the rack overhead. It was cold and lumpy with rust. I pulled myself up and sat on the windowsill. The wind blasted me. I kept going. I pulled myself up and out of the window so my feet were now on the windowsill. I dragged myself over the rack so I was lying flat on the cold surface of the roof. I swung my feet over and sat up, gripping the front of the rack. I reached back and knocked on the roof like Robert had said to do. I heard him cheering inside. I had done what he'd asked. Robert had proved to the others that he could make me do what he wanted. It was a triumph for him. It was just what Coyle had said would happen. I'd been a suckass.

I sat up there on the roof of his car, the wind blasting past, a sickly, poisonous feeling in my gut. After a moment I pulled myself forward until I dangled my feet over the rack, my heels on the windshield. I lifted myself slowly over the front crossbar and slid down the windshield so I was sitting on the hood, gripping the edge near the wipers. I turned back and looked at them through the windshield. I wasn't laughing or yelling to them. I was concentrating. Robert was watching me through the windshield. He was scared now and I liked that he was scared. I wanted him to be scared.

You wanted me to do it. Ok. This is what you get, I thought.

I reached up and held the front part of the rack. Slowly, I pulled my feet up and stood on the hood of the car, but with both hands gripping the roof rack, so I was facing backward. I let go with one hand so I was sideways. Then I let go with the other hand and stood like a surfer, bent really low so I could touch the hood if I needed to. I was riding on the hood of that car and for a moment there was nothing in the world but the cold wind in my face and the cars rushing by and the feel of the engine beneath my feet. I was not fighting with Coyle or picking up balls on the tennis court or pulling up linoleum in some old office. I was right there and only there and no one could touch me.

I grabbed the rack and pulled myself on top, crawled back to the open window, and slid back inside. Robert was bouncing in his seat.

"Willie Brennan! High five! What'd I tell you? Total badass!" Robert crowed.

"Not a big deal," I said.

"You stood on the hood. You see that, Corley? Didn't I tell you he'd do it?"

I just sat casually, my heart booming inside me, pretending it was nothing, while Robert rubbed it in to the others, particularly to Tom.

Ten minutes later we pulled up at my house. Robert slapped my shoulder and called me a badass and made sure the others saw how appreciative he could be when he got his way. Then Robert screeched away and I was left standing there in the front yard, trembling. I couldn't control my hands enough to zip my jacket. It washed through me all at once. I'd stood on the hood of a car on the interstate. If we'd hit a pothole I'd have died. If a car in front had braked I'd have died.

A kind of delayed spasm of tremors passed through me

and only gradually was I able to control the tremors. I walked inside and went up to my room and lay down with the nervy fizzling rising up and then fading bit by bit.

I knew what I'd done was a kind of triumph, and that I wouldn't be asked to do something like that again for a long time, if ever. I'd proved myself. But I also knew the other kids hadn't needed to prove themselves the way I had. I guess I was used to that. We were Brennans. We had to do more than other people. It had been like that all my life.

I was proud of what I'd done. I also hated that I had to do it. But it was over, and I felt like I'd passed the test.

For the next month and a half Robert and I played together. We easily beat the other teams. And by mid-March it was settled. Robert and I would be partners during tryouts. We were pretty sure we would beat all the other challengers. It was all set.

But a week before tryouts a tennis player named Bill McCann dropped out of the junior circuit and joined the high-school team. Bill was ranked about twentieth in the country. He had not planned on playing high-school tennis, but he changed his mind in the last week, which meant the team had another top player. As all the players dropped down one slot, it meant that instead of there being two open spots on the varsity, there was only one. So Robert and I, instead of playing together as the second doubles team, would be competing with each other for the last spot.

———

On the opening day of tryouts I walked onto the Nielsen tennis courts to see that in the first match of the round-robin I was playing Robert Dainty.

"Hey, Willie," Robert said as I walked out. "I wasn't even sure you'd show up when you heard Bill came back."

"I just figured I'd try," I said. "For practice. But I know you'll get the spot."

"As long as you know it," he said in a ham-handed way. "Good luck."

"Good luck to you, though I'm sure you won't need it."

"I'm the upperclassman so I serve first," Robert said. "That's the rule."

This was not the rule. It was just something Robert made up on the spot.

We started playing. Robert had a nice, high, looping, chippy serve that was hard to return. He came into the net after his first serve. He won four points in a row. Then it was my turn. I had a flat, booming serve that I could place in either corner. I won three of the points in the first game without Robert getting the ball in play. It went on like that. For those five games we stayed on serve, so Robert was up 3–2 when we finished, but since he served first it was basically a draw.

Afterward, as we walked off the court, Robert was less complacent.

"Didn't know you were such a pusher when you played singles," he said. "Your strokes are ok, and you have a good serve, but you're a pusher. That's ok for a pro set, but it wouldn't work in a tournament. Or in doubles. They need a doubles player. You know that. Coach Schneider will see that."

Robert went on and reported the score to Schneider.

"Willie's a total pusher but I beat him three to two," he said.

Schneider said nothing to this but marked down the score.

"Who do you want me to slaughter next?" Robert said.

Schneider winced visibly.

"Go to court six. And cut the commentary, Dainty." Then, to me, in a different tone, "Court four, Brennan. Good playing. Why'd you let him serve first?"

"He said that upperclassmen always serve first."

Schneider gave me a withering look.

"Don't be a pushover, Willie."

I went on and played another five-game pro set against another player. So did Robert. At the end of the day Robert had won eighteen games and I had won sixteen. A few other kids had won eight or nine games. So I was in second place and Robert was in first.

The round-robin went on all week. I never really thought I'd win. I guess I put it out of my mind because I didn't want to think about what would happen if I beat out Robert Dainty for that last spot. I knew the rules of our friendship did not include my competing with him. I could hang out with Robert and tag along with his group, but I also had to make sure to always acknowledge that he was older and more accomplished and that I was lucky to know him, and it didn't hurt if I added in derisive commentary about Coyle. But the number-one rule was that he absolutely be the dominant one in any group. I knew that if I beat him out for the last spot on varsity tennis, it would ruin our friendship and annihilate my social life in the high school, or at least my social life with the crowd that Robert had introduced me to.

The way the round-robin worked was that everyone played one another. There were about twenty kids trying out, and after four days, Robert and I were tied for first place with seventy-two games apiece. Schneider scheduled a full match between Robert and me for the next day. That afternoon as I went to my bike Robert walked along with me.

"You know I had the seventh spot last year," he said.

"Yeah," I said.

"So it's actually fair that I'd be the one to move up this year. I mean, it's awesome that you're this close as a freshman, Willie. Just like I was. You'll definitely make the varsity next year. But I'm a sophomore. It's just fair that I make it this year. I mean, I paid my dues. I deserve to move up. You could tell Schneider that."

"And not play?"

"Just tell him that you think I should have the spot," Robert said.

"But we're playing for the spot," I said.

"Like I don't know that, Willie. And I know I'm going to win. But I shouldn't even have to play for it. I'm a sophomore and you're a freshman. It's just not that cool. You agree, right?"

"Uhm. I know you'll probably win," I said.

"And you admit that it's fair that I get that spot, right? I mean, I'm owed it. You could tell Schneider you think I'm right for the spot. Or, even better—because he's probably going to make us play anyway, as stupid as it is—you could just do the right thing when we play."

"Like let you win?"

"Yeah," he said, smiling nervously. "I mean, I'm older. I should have had that spot last year, and after all the ways I've helped you, I mean, letting you hang out and play on the court with us and never making you pay for the court, which I could have, you know, but I didn't, so you should just be cool about it. I mean, it's pretty greedy, Willie. You owe me like five hundred dollars for that court time."

"You never asked for money," I said.

"Cause I'm generous!" he shouted. "You could be grateful."

"Well, I'm sure you'll win," I said.

He let out an indignant puff of air.

"I know I'll win. I just don't want to leave anything to chance. There's no one more fair than me. But in this case it's just obvious that I should be given the spot. And particularly if I'm playing you, you should just not be uncool about it."

He walked off and I rode home and I told my father that I was playing Robert Dainty the next day for the last spot on the varsity and that news set off all kinds of conflicting emotions inside him. Dad wanted me to be friends with the children of successful people. In some magical way Dad thought that meant we were going to be successful ourselves, and also, it meant he was getting something for the misery he went through for us to live there. But he also knew Robert Dainty, and thought he was a weasel, and Dad wanted his kids to dominate in everything.

"Try your hardest and be a good sport. And no matter what, when it's over, shake his hand and tell him he played a good match."

"He won't be saying that to me if I win," I said.

"If Robert Dainty can't stand fair competition, too bad for him," Mom said from the sink. She had never liked the Daintys. She thought they led extravagant, frivolous lives. "Robert has always had an extra helping of self-esteem," she said.

"Just do your best," Dad said. "Be fair. Don't cheat. This is where you move up. Your brother has done very well. Now it's your turn."

I wasn't so sure that anything good would come of it, but I liked that Dad said it.

I walked out. Coyle was waiting in the hallway.

"Don't let him win," he said.

"Do you think I would?"

"It's been Toady Hall from you all year."

"It's not been Toady Hall."

"Good," Coyle said. "Don't be a suckass."

I got ready for bed. But no way could I sleep. The more I thought of the match, the more I knew I was in an impossible position. Robert would hold it against me if I won and Coyle would hold it against me if I lost. And the thing is, I didn't even care that much about sports. I wasn't like Coyle. I had gotten to a certain level in tennis by working diligently, but I was never going to be a great player. At best, I was going to be on the lower end of the team. I almost agreed with Robert that it was right that he got that spot. Who cares? I thought. Let him win and we can stay friends.

So there was that feeling, and then there was something else, too, some deeper order that I instinctively acknowledged. The whole current of the social world we lived in was in Robert's favor. It's something hard to define, but I had been told since I was born that the kids of the rich families would always have more than we did and that we just had to accept that, but that we'd be paid back in the end. That was our understanding of the world—that we had to put up with inconveniences that other people didn't have to put up with some magical deferred compensation. I had gotten in the habit of giving in to kids like Robert and there seemed to be something dangerous and essentially wrong in going against Robert. It felt unnatural.

All this ran through me that night. Swirls of dread. I hardly slept.

The next afternoon everyone from the team gathered to watch my match, including guys from the varsity who wanted to see who their new teammate would be. Kids stood at the chain-link fence, making bets. Jimmy and Bennie and Roscoe, my three friends, were there, too. They wanted to see if I'd have the guts to actually try to beat Robert. Mr. Dainty, who struck me as a stern, sullen man, was also there, leaning against his Mercedes. Near to him, Coyle straddled his makeshift motorcycle. He had turned sixteen recently and the first thing he'd done was get his motorcycle license. I knew that if I lost, Coyle would think I'd done it on purpose.

I walked out to the court. Robert was waiting.

"You ready to get your ass beat?" he said.

"I'm ready to play," I said in a shaky voice.

"May the best man win," he said. "Which is obviously me."

"Obviously," I said.

Robert flipped his racket to see who got to serve first.

He only spun it a few times and he didn't let go until I called it. I thought he cheated on the toss but I didn't make him do it over. He won the toss. He chose to serve. We started up.

Robert had a long, slow windup and then that fast, chippy serve. It kicked up high to the backhand and he usually followed it into the net. He won the first game in four points. I double-faulted twice to start my service and he broke me. Then he won his serve again in four more points. He was up 3–0 in about six minutes. I won my serve the second time, but then Robert won his serve easily again. He was playing effortlessly, confidently. Meanwhile, there was a jittery, churning, trembly, damp nervousness circling inside me. It wasn't exactly that I was trying to lose, just that I had been conditioned to give in to people like Robert for so long that it was hard to stop doing it. I knew Robert would go crazy if he didn't win, and it was just easier to let everything flow in its usual direction.

I went down in the first set 5–1. There must have been about forty kids out there watching, and every one of them thought I was losing either because I was letting Robert win or because I was so intimidated by Robert that I couldn't play. I hit serves off the edge of my racket. I shanked my backhands. I hit about eight passing shots into the net. I overheard the kids at the fence muttering "Toady Hall" and "tank commander." Meanwhile, Robert glided back and forth on the other side of the court, tossing the balls to me in a mincing manner that I'd started to hate. I could see how the whole thing would play out. Robert would win and then brag about his victory, lord it over me in the lunchroom, but he'd be gracious in his own way and I'd still hang out with the "cool kids" after that. Everyone would assume I lost on purpose, and this loss would be irritating for a while, but I'd get used to that.

A few times I caught a glimpse of Coyle in his jeans and white T-shirt and black hoodie, straddling his motorcycle, watching sullenly. I knew what he thought. And maybe he was right. Maybe I was losing on purpose. Regardless, I hated being humiliated in front of him, and as the set went on I felt some counterforce begin to bubble up inside me. It was something I'd felt before but could never have articulated. It was the nervy, hateful dread of waiting in my room for the beatings to start. It was the resigned resentment of our lowered position. It was the desperate feeling that I had no choice except to succeed. It was the engine of the poor, what we had instead of professional training and instruction. It wasn't a desire to win so much as a disgust with the humiliation of being forced day after day into a lowered position, and a hatred of the invisible lines of class that could easily be denied at any moment, but were inevitably used to rig the system. And slowly, the part that wanted to dominate rose up from the hidden chambers inside. I wanted not just to win, but to crush, to annihilate, to stomp Robert's face and smash his teeth in.

I broke Robert and then held my serve and it was 5–3. But then Robert held serve and took the first set 6–3. I was down a set, but by that point the fire was rising inside, turning faster and faster. It's what Coyle and everyone in the family knew about me. I was slow to action, but, once ignited, I was fiercer than anyone.

I won the first game in the second set in four points. I

won the second game in five points. I won the third game again in four points. I was up 3–0. I was smacking the balls back and forth with an effortless confidence.

As Robert walked past me he said, "You could let up a little," and nudged me, half as a joke, but not really. He was trying to rattle me.

Robert started coming to the net in the fourth game. I passed him three times in a row. He stopped coming in to the net. I drove the ball deep to his backhand.

I won the second set 6–1.

Between the second and third set Robert talked to his father, who'd stood off by himself the whole time, arms crossed, talking low.

Jimmy walked along the fence and I went over and stood near him.

"You know he's cheating, right?" Jimmy said. "He's cheated on like every close call. The only points he won that set were the ones he cheated on. You need to either cheat back or get a line judge."

Players called their own lines unless either of the players called for a judge. I didn't want to imply I thought Robert was cheating. That was just beyond everything. I couldn't do it.

"I'll win the games by so much it won't matter," I said.

Jimmy rolled his eyes. He thought I was an idiot. He walked away. A minute later Coach Schneider came out and gave me another can of balls.

"You know you can call a line judge," Schneider said.

"I will if I need one," I said.

Schneider looked off in the distance for a moment, then

turned back to watch from his hut. I walked back on the court. We started up on the third and final set.

Robert started coming in to the net again. He broke me and went up 4–1. I broke and brought it back to 4–4. We were tied at 5's, and then at 6's.

We went into a tiebreaker.

By this point we were both exhausted, and to Robert's credit, he had not given in. He got better when the match got close. He was a real competitor. He was scrambling and chipping and then hitting those high, looping forehands and coming to the net. I was basically hitting as hard as I could with my heavy topspin.

The tiebreaker started up. We were tied at two. At three. And then at four. Twice in the tiebreaker I thought I hit the line and Robert called both balls out. The second time I was sure the ball was in. There was no pretense of us being friends by that point.

"Out," he blared.

I heard someone in the crowd laughing.

I went up 5–6 in the tiebreaker. That was match point for me. Robert was serving to the add court. He hit it wide, and started for the net. I smacked the return down the line. It landed in the corner. The net pole was in my way, but I was sure the ball was going in. If it had been out I would have seen it land because I had a view of the court beyond the line, but because of the net pole I didn't actually see the ball hit the court.

"Out!" Robert called.

"Bull. Shit," a guy named Leo Dusek yelled from outside the fence. "Hook! Totally in."

Everyone started yelling the same thing—that the ball was a few feet inside the line. That it wasn't even close to being out. That I'd won the match.

Schneider was already coming out of the hut. He met Dusek at the chain-link fence.

"That ball was totally in," Dusek said. "Brennan just won the match."

I walked over. Robert lingered nearby, waiting.

"Whatta you think, Brennan?" Schneider asked me.

"I thought it was going to be way inside the line. Like two feet inside. But the pole was in the way. I didn't see it land."

"He didn't see it land!" Robert shouted.

"Every single person here saw that ball land two feet inside the line," Dusek said. "Like not even close. It was a total cheat. That's match point."

Schneider ignored the crowd and just looked at me. He seemed genuinely curious to see what I'd do. He knew I'd played on Robert's court all year. He knew Robert demanded obedience from his friends in general and me in particular.

And through all this Robert's father stood nearby, silent, but radiating displeasure.

"Do you stand by your call?" Schneider asked Robert.

"Of course I stand by it. The ball was out."

A few kids snickered.

"Do you contest the call?" Schneider asked me.

"If it went out I would have seen it. I had a view of the court beyond the line. The pole and the strip from the net were in my way. But it must have been in."

"Do you contest the call?"

Robert gave me a quick, murderous glance. By the rules of that round-robin, if multiple people saw the shot and the opposing player contested the call, the point could be replayed. Those were the rules for the team. But contesting the call could come only from one of the players actually in the match.

"Be honest, Willie," Robert said. "Does it mean that much to you? Like, are you really going to cheat me? Is that what you want?"

"Oh, whatever," Dusek said. "Come on, Willie. The ball was two feet inside the line. You won the match. We all saw it. Contest the call."

"You already admitted you didn't see it land," Robert said.

Everyone was looking at me, waiting to see what I'd do. I could see Coyle, still on his bike, watching from a distance.

"I contest the call," I said.

"Oh, God, total hook," Robert exploded. "He didn't even see it land and he contests the call. Way to be a cheater, Willie. Hope you're proud." Then, turning to Schneider, "How can you let him do it? He admitted he didn't see the ball land. I'm warning you now, if I lose, this match will be under protest."

Schneider seemed willing to accept that risk. He walked back to the court.

"Five–six. Resume play. I'll call the lines for the rest of the match."

We started up again, with Schneider standing on the sidelines. Robert bounced the ball for about twenty seconds, then smacked a serve into the backhand corner. It was a good serve. He started in to the net. I hit the ball cross-court, low and with topspin. He jabbed sideways with his racket but just missed. The ball was a foot inside the line.

"Out," Robert called, forgetting that Schneider was calling the lines.

"Ball was in," Schneider said to Robert. Then to both of us. "Seven–five. Match to Brennan. Good playing, guys."

I heard Coyle rev his engine loudly, then peel away from the court, holding a fist up in parting. I walked up to shake Robert's hand. His face was squinched and he was writhing and moving from foot to foot, as if he were being burnt.

"You are such a cheater, Willie. You know I should have won that match. And after everything I did for you. So fucking ungrateful. God. Such a fucking cheater. Don't think we're going to be hanging together anymore."

I held my hand out.

"Good match, Robert."

He just looked at my hand. He didn't shake it. After a moment I turned. I started to walk away. But then I figured if I was going to end my friendship with Robert because of a tennis match, I might as well do it in style.

I turned, holding my fingers up in a V.

"Victory is mine," I said, and walked off the court.

A few of my teammates came up and congratulated me. Some said that Robert was cheating the whole match and he had a lot of gall to say I was cheating. I didn't really care. I'd won. And even more than that, I'd resolved something inside myself. There'd been an uncertainty all year, all my life, really—a question about my orientation to the town of Seneca. Coyle's stance had always been clear. Mine had not.

When I got home, I told Dad I'd won in a tiebreaker in the third set.

"Yes!" Dad said, holding his fist up. "How'd Robert take it?"

"Not well," I said.

"He'll get over it," Dad said.

"I'm not sure about that," I said.

"Congratulations," Mom said, and came over and hugged me.

I think she understood more than any of them what that match meant to me.

I started for the stairs. Coyle waited in the hallway.

"He was cheating the whole time," Coyle said. "What'd he say afterwards?"

"He said I was cheater."

"Typical Robert. He cheats and then accuses the other person of cheating when he loses. He'll be sulking about it for the next year."

"I don't care," I said.

"That's right. It doesn't matter. You won. You beat him. Good job."

Coyle gave me a high five. It felt like the first time in my life that Coyle was actually proud of something I'd done. And I was proud of myself, though there was the expected fallout from that match. For the rest of the school year Robert avoided me, and when we did see each other he shook his head mournfully, as if I'd done something shameful. I didn't get invited to parties anymore and I wasn't welcome at his lunch table. I didn't care. What I had hidden so deeply when I started at school that year, hidden out of resentment of Coyle, and a desire to fit in, had come out during that tennis match. I hated losing as much as Coyle did. I hated being subordinate as much as Coyle did.

For the whole time that I was friends with Robert, the desire to dominate and the desire to get along had battled inside me, and in the end the desire to dominate had won out. I liked being one of the people who fit in with the popular crowd, but by the end of my freshman year I understood that was never going to happen for me. I was too stubborn, too competitive, we were too poor, and I had that Brennan predatory streak: I would rather sabotage my life than give in once I was involved in a struggle.

As it turned out, I was not a suckup. I was not a climber. I was not a user. I was a defiant, blue-collar striver, just like Coyle.

4

The Open Sea

And this is the unwritten history of man, his unseen, nega-
tive accomplishment, his power to do without gratification
for himself provided there is something great, something into
which his being, and all beings can go. He does not need
meaning as long as such intensity has scope. Because then it
is self-evident; it is meaning.

—Saul Bellow

Mid-spring of 1981—Coyle, Fergus, Maddy, and I were all in the living room watching *The Brady Bunch* on TV, jeering at it, as the program showed the Bradys in some clean house, discussing problems in a more or less civilized manner, none of them swearing or getting enraged or beating on one another. We were shouting at the TV: "Stop complaining! Stop wasting time! Do your work!" when we heard the doorbell ring. No one got up. It rang again. I slid off the couch and wandered to the front door. I thought it would be one of our neighbors complaining about the noise, but it wasn't a neighbor. It was a man in a suit with a clipboard standing on our concrete porch.

"Are your parents here?" he asked.

"Mom!" I yelled into the house.

Mom came out from the kitchen, drying her hands. She saw the man and her expression changed.

"Get inside," she said. "Go on, Willie. Why make me say it twice?"

Mom went out to the porch and shut the door. I went inside and wandered to the window to listen. The others joined me.

"What is it?" Maddy asked.

"Taxes," Coyle said. "We owe money."

"How do you know?" Fergus asked.

"Look at his car. It has a government tag. And I heard Dad talking about it. We're probably going to have to move."

"I don't want to leave school," Maddy said.

"What do you care?" Fergus said. "You don't have any friends anyway."

"Quiet," Coyle said.

We all sat on the couch, heads to the screen window, trying to listen in. Apparently, Dad hadn't paid taxes for years. Despite his many jobs, Dad still spent more than he made. Mom saved bits of string and rubber bands and tinfoil. She cut our hair herself. She patched our clothing, which we got secondhand. And with all this economizing we'd start to dig ourselves out of the economic hole we were in, but then Dad would go off and buy a car or come home with a VCR or plan a vacation we couldn't afford. I was vaguely aware of his unrealistic financial methods before I was in high school, but it was on that day that I really understood how precarious our position was. Dad owed years of taxes. And as I listened at the window I understood that the IRS guy had imagined we were rich tax evaders in swanky Seneca, but when the agent saw the house with the lilting gutter, saw the beat-up car with the rusting wheel wells, saw the four of us watching, saw the desperate look in Mom's eyes, he understood the truth. We were living in a kind of suburban poverty.

Later that night Coyle, Fergus, Maddy, and I sat together in our bedroom. We could hear Mom and Dad arguing in the kitchen below.

"Dad owes them money from taxes from before," Coyle said matter-of-factly. "But he didn't pay for a few years."

"Why not?" Maddy asked.

"He got into debt. And you know Dad. He just does what he wants. He doesn't think about it."

"He has all those jobs," Maddy said.

"Those jobs don't pay much," Coyle said. "And it's expensive here. And then there's the house. We rent it. It's being sold in the fall. Mom and Dad were saving to buy it, but you need a big lump of money to buy a house. But now they're going to have to use that money for the IRS."

Maddy looked between Coyle and me, only half understanding.

"When this house goes on the market in the fall, if we can't buy it, and someone else does, we'll get kicked out," Coyle explained. "Mrs. Dobbs, who owns the house, offered to let us buy it. But we need the down payment. It's seventeen thousand dollars. Dad had the money. But now we have to pay the IRS instead."

"Are you sure?" I said.

"They're talking about it right now," he said. "Listen."

We could hear the murmur of voices below, Dad's voice rising, getting louder.

"How long do we have?" I asked.

"Three months," Coyle said. "If not, we'll have to move. Not that I care. We probably should move anyway. We're too poor to live here."

"What's poor?" Maddy said.

"Didn't you know?" Fergus said. "Poor is us."

The next day Mom explained the situation to us as gently as possible. It was just like Coyle had said. We had been saving money for a down payment in anticipation of Mrs. Dobbs putting the house on the market, but now some of that money would have to go to the IRS. But it wasn't hopeless. We had most of the summer to make up the deficit. If we all worked and pitched in she thought it was possible that we could raise the money, but only if we saved every penny. Our plan for the summer was to have everyone work together so we could stay in our house in Seneca.

We all agreed to help, though there were varying degrees of dedication to this plan. Coyle was indifferent. He didn't really care if he went to New Trier or some other school. Wherever he was, he figured he'd play ball and get A's. I was more invested in staying. I had just made the tennis team. I had my friends. I said I'd donate all my salary from my job if we could stay. I said if Coyle didn't want to help, I would try to do double. Coyle gave me a withering look. In his mind, no matter what the situation, I always had to make it into some drama and competition.

"We're proud of your dedication," he said.

"Enough of the bickering," Mom said. "We all need to pull together. And I need you two to be on your best behavior tomorrow with your grandmother. She could alter the situation significantly."

"Will she help?" Maddy asked, and Mom got a sullen expression.

"What do you think?" she said.

Granny Bernice, my father's mother, was a tight-fisted, cautious, lonely, spiteful woman who'd inherited a small fortune from her father. That inherited money in Bernice's tight fist was a dream of future riches for our father, and at least once a month we piled into our rumbling, half-broken-down station wagon and drove across sprawling western Chicago to her yellow-brick house on Sacramento Avenue. We never felt more suburban than on those visits to the Southside, which was foreign territory for us, with its small stoops, American flags, chain-link in the backyard with dogs barking all up and down the block, all punctuated by Bernice's pointed, sarcastic Southside manner.

"My house might not be all fancy like you're used to, but at least I own it," I'd heard her say about eighteen times.

On our visits we'd mow her lawn and clean her gutters,

paint the fence, organize the garage, change storm windows, and do whatever else she wanted us to do, and at the end of the visit, if she was pleased and in a good mood, she gave Dad some money, usually two or three hundred dollars, which was a lot for us. But if she was in a bad mood, she berated my father for having four kids and for moving to the fancy suburbs with his college-educated wife and not being able to afford the life he led.

On this day, early June 1981, a week after the IRS guy showed up at our house, we drove to the Southside to do Bernice's favorite chore, which was cleaning her parents' mausoleum at the Lithuanian National Cemetery. Stukas was her maiden name. She had dumped her Irish husband after a few years, and ever since, Bernice hated the Irish. She hated that we had an Irish name. She hated that Mom's maiden name was Kelly. She hated that Mom had raised us as Catholics.

I was considered to be the one most likely to please Bernice, as I was the "best talker," and I was also not as instinctively loyal to the nuclear family, which Bernice appreciated. On that day, as soon as we arrived, everyone else was sent to rake leaves and I stayed with Bernice at the mausoleum.

"Oh, you clean in five minutes what takes me an hour," she was saying as I polished the marble. "I'd think you wouldn't know how to do it, you living in that fancy place, with all the luxuries."

"Yeah, it's all maids and butlers at our mansion in Seneca," I said. "You should come by sometime, see how fancy it is."

"Listen to you," she said. "Making fun of your granny."

"Caviar and country clubs for us in Seneca. And when

we're not playing golf we're eating oysters and brushing down our ponies."

Granny Bernice waved a hand at me.

"Oh, you're making fun, but I know the easy life you live in that fancy place. And you never come to visit Momma and Papa. Look at this marble. Dirty tree dripping sap all over it. Dirty birds flying over. And no one to clean it. I tried to cut the tree. That gardener came running. He watches me now. He knows what I'm planning."

A dark shape with a wheelbarrow near the stone office for the cemetery—the gardener did seem to be watching us.

"I try to scare the birds away, but when I come back I find shit on the steps. Shit on the sidewalk. They were in the road last week. I pretended I didn't see them as I drove up. Oh, look at you with your wide eyes. Think your granny's a saint."

"I don't think that," I said.

"Well, good for you, Willie, you're the only honest one in the family. But you won't help me. Not how I need it."

Granny Bernice's station wagon was pulled up on the curb in front of the mausoleum. The middle seats were pushed flat. The back held a bag of birdseed.

"Those dirty birds are always shitting on Momma and Papa. Always coming around here, making a nasty mess."

Furtively, Granny Bernice took a box from beneath the front seat, tore off the top, and dumped the entire contents into the birdseed. It was rat poison. She twisted the neck of the sack with the birdseed and poison and shook it.

"Papa never had a blade of grass out of place on our lawn.

Never a crack in the sidewalk. Once I painted the wood board between the bathroom and the hallway. He always stepped over that board. Never on it. Because he had respect for work. Now I got the tree, the birds, sap and shit on the marble. Papa doesn't deserve that. But I can't do it on my own. And you and your father come once a year to help."

"We come every month."

"Not to the cemetery," she said in a maudlin tone. "I try to do the right thing, but that gardener's always giving the evil eye. He's not gonna look at you, though." She nudged the sack of birdseed toward me. "Go on. You want to help your granny, give that to those dirty birds."

Coyle came up behind us with the push mower.

"What's going on?" he asked.

"I'm killing the birds," I said. "Granny Bernice put poison in the birdseed. The birds shit on Momma and Papa," I added.

Coyle thought I was kidding at first.

"Go on," Granny Bernice said. "You can help Willie."

"I'm not helping him poison birds," Coyle said. "That's just stupid."

"You're weak," she said to Coyle. "Just like your father."

"Yeah, you're weak," I said. I lifted the sack. Since Coyle said he wouldn't do it, I figured I would, particularly if Granny Bernice was going to keep calling him weak for not helping. "I don't care," I said. "I want to."

Coyle gave me a skeptical look.

"Are you really going to poison birds?"

"Sure," I said. "If she wants me to."

Coyle raised his fist like he'd hit me. I just looked at him.

"What?" he said. "You deserve to be hit. You're being an idiot."

Bernice laughed with gleeful maliciousness.

"Are you doing it or not?"

"Watch for the gardener," I said to Coyle, and walked off with the bag of poisoned seed slung over my shoulder. I went down the hill to a small pond where the geese gathered. They saw me coming and started toward me. They must have been accustomed to being fed. They were squawking and twisting their necks and flapping their wings. They jockeyed with one another and waddled closer. I put a gloved hand in the bag and ran it through the poisoned seed. I dropped a handful of seed in the grass. The geese moved to snap it up. I reached for another handful and felt someone coming. It was my father. He closed his fist around the neck of the bag.

"Is there really poison in that?"

"Yeah."

Dad got an exasperated look and swatted me.

"Have some sense, Willie."

Dad jerked the bag from my hand. He kicked at the geese so they flapped away. He dumped the seed in the trash. We walked back to the station wagon. Bernice was waiting for us with a derisive expression.

"You're weak," she said to my father. "It's always been your problem. You and all your children are weak. That's why you fail."

"Sure, Mom. Whatever," Dad said. "Thanks for the pep talk. Grandfather John wouldn't have wanted you to kill birds. You know that."

"Careless and weak," she said. "Learn how to support your family."

"Get in the car," Dad said to me.

A minute later all of us sat waiting while Dad and Bernice argued, Dad defending himself and trying not to beg for money, and then begging a little, and Bernice berating Dad for being a failure, for putting himself in the position to lose his house. Mom sat in the passenger seat, looking out the window.

After a few minutes, Dad walked back to the car.

"Did we get the money?" Maddy asked.

Coyle laughed. So did Fergus. Dad didn't answer. He put the car in drive.

"We should have poisoned the birds," I said.

"We don't poison birds for money," Dad said.

"It was us or the birds," I said. "What's more important?"

"We'll find another way. We're Brennans. We do what's right," Dad said.

As Dad drove, Mom kept looking out the window. I'm not sure she didn't think it would have been better to put the poison out and get the money for the house, but if she thought this, she didn't say it.

The next week Dad took a temporary renovation job and got the maintenance contract for a second building on Central Street in Seneca. If we finished the renovation before the end of the summer we would have enough money for the down payment, but it meant we would have to work crazy hours over the summer. There was the janitor work and the renovation work and the paper route in the morning, and Dad was also teaching tennis about fifteen hours a week and he was supposed to be writing a thesis for his teacher's certificate. He was sleeping three hours a night, at best, and the rest of us weren't sleeping much more. It was our summer of drudgery. But I have to admit that along with the endless work there was also a sense of camaraderie and accomplishment. We kept tabs on how much money we'd made. We watched the savings accumulate bit by bit. And there was a feeling of satisfaction in thinking we were all contributing. More than anyone else, I was invested in those moneymaking schemes. I bragged to my friends that I had to work to help buy our house. I walked around with ripped jeans covered in paint speckles, talking about the down payment like I knew anything about it.

"Typical Willie," Coyle said. "Always a fucking drama."

In his view I'd spent my freshman year hanging out with Robert Dainty, pretending I was a rich kid. Then suddenly I was acting like I was some street urchin out of a Dickens novel. I think I single-handedly convinced Coyle to get a haircut because he saw how ridiculous the blue-collar affectation was on me.

So the summer passed. We all worked all the time. And for a while it seemed as if we would save enough to buy the house, but in the end there were the normal setbacks that always seemed to happen to our family. The car broke down and needed a new water pump and then the IRS demanded an additional payment, and there was interest on our debt that Dad hadn't expected, and by the time school was approaching it became clear that, despite all our work, we weren't going to make it. In the last weeks of the summer there was a sense of diminishing enthusiasm as we understood that our sacrifice had come to nothing. And then one day in August, the week before school started up again, Dad drove into the driveway towing a sailboat.

"What is that thing?" Fergus said.

Coyle, Fergus, Maddy, and I had all gone out to the porch. Dad got out of the car, grinning.

"It's a boat," Dad said. "It goes in the water. Often they float."

"Apparently, not this one," Fergus said.

He walked down and put his hand through a rotted part on the hull.

"Big deal," Dad said. "That's why we could afford it. We put on a little fiberglass. Some patching. Then we have ourselves a boat. You guys worked hard all summer. We'll fix it up. We'll learn how to sail."

Coyle, Maddy, and I had followed Fergus down and were looking up at the old, battered but pleasing sailing vessel.

"I guess we bought this with all our spare cash?" Fergus said.

"Oh, don't worry about it," Dad said. "It'll work out. And you kids deserve it."

Deakins, one of our neighbors, wandered over, tugging a hose. He was a red-cheeked Irish guy, dean of a Catholic high school. He stopped to look at the boat.

"What is that? A yacht?"

"Sure. Why not?" Dad said in his most casual manner. "I just figured the kids are old enough now to appreciate something like this."

"You're getting fancy!" Deakins yelled. "We gotta get you a little captain's hat."

Dad beamed. That's exactly what he had in mind.

The front door burst open and Mom appeared. Deakins turned away, pretending to water his garden. Mom walked up.

"What have you done?" she said.

"I got a boat. For the kids. They worked hard all summer. It wasn't expensive."

"Alex," Mom said in a warning tone.

Dad made a puffing sound.

"Doesn't really matter at this point, does it?"

"It does matter."

"Come on. It was fifteen hundred dollars. It's not going to change anything. And the kids worked hard. Look at them. They're excited."

Truthfully, we were more bewildered than excited.

"We cannot afford this," she said.

"What's it matter? We're not making the deadline. And now we have a boat."

"We'll be living on it soon," she said.

"We can if we have to," he said with enthusiasm.

Mom gave him her famous withering look.

"And where did you plan on putting this monstrosity?"

"In the backyard," he said. "Until it's in the water. Which it will be soon. The kids deserve it," he said again. "And I already paid for it. You kids want a boat, right?"

"Definitely," Fergus said. "But I want one that works."

Coyle looked worried, same as Mom. He was old enough to know it was insane. "What about you, Willie? Do you want a boat?"

"Sure," I said. "But not in place of a house."

Mom turned and looked at Dad.

"See?" she said.

"It'll work out," he said. "And it's done, ok?"

Mom always made a point of not arguing with Dad in front of us, so without another word, she went inside.

"She'll get used to it," Dad said to us.

"Not sure about that," Coyle said.

All through the next month, whenever there was a nice day Dad and the rest of us clustered around that boat, fixing it up. It was a Hughes Cruiser, a sloop with a rounded rudder and a rust-colored hull and a white deck. Dad worked on the rotten part of the hull. He cut away the damaged area and applied wax remover. Then he put on the Formica, the fiber-glass fabric, and the resin. He applied the gel coat and the seal-up, and filled in cracks. Meanwhile, the rest of us repainted the deck, revarnished the exposed wood. We all understood that the house we were living in was going on the market in a month and we could be evicted at any time, and we knew that if we got kicked out of that house it was very, very unlikely that we'd find another house we could afford in Seneca or anywhere else in the New Trier school district. Our immi-nent departure from the fancy suburbs loomed on the horizon, but on the other hand, we had that boat, and that was a consolation. Mom viewed the boat as the concrete representation of Dad's impracticality, but for the rest of us, particularly for me, it was something nice that we worked on together. I became as invested in the rehabilitation of the boat as I'd been in working for the down payment on the house. I brought my friends over and talked about sailing it to Mackinac Island and taking it on a "crossing" to Europe. Other kids at school heard about it and exaggerated its size and worth. One day Robert Dainty, who hadn't talked to me for six months, walked up to me and said, "Hey, Brennan. Is it true you got a boat?"

"Yeah."

"What kind?"

"Sailboat. Hughes Cruiser."

"How big?"

"Thirty feet," I said.

I think he imagined it would be smaller, and he seemed a little deflated.

"Used, right?" he said.

I would have given a lot to say that it was new.

"Yeah, it's a junker," I said. "But it's totally cool. We're going to put it in the water this month. We might just end up living on it," I said.

"Cool," he said. "Houseboat."

A few more weeks passed. And then it was late October and our boat was ready for the open sea.

———

On the last day of October in 1981, Coyle, Fergus, and I stood on the concrete edge of Seneca Harbor, looking up at our father on the deck of our boat, which he'd just put in the water. Mom stood behind us with Maddy. She refused to get on the boat, and wouldn't let Maddy get on, either.

"Before you get overly proud of yourself," Mom said to Dad, "check the caulking. And wait twenty-four hours. We'll know then whether she is seaworthy."

"I know she is now," Dad said. "I did the work myself."

"I'm aware of that," Mom said.

Dad grinned down at us.

"You get the feeling your mother doesn't trust me? Come on, guys. Get on."

Fergus, Coyle, and I clambered onto the boat. Mom held Maddy back.

"Maddy will stay here with me," she said.

"Aw, let her come," Dad said.

"I will let her go after twenty-four hours, as is recommended by the experts."

Beyond the breakwall we could see rolling swells. Surf crashing and tumbling to shore. Gray-green water. Late fall in northern Illinois.

"Boys, you are not required to go with your father, who is determined to do something foolish."

"It's not foolish," Dad said. "It's a great day for sailing, and we're right here. We're going to the open sea."

Mom turned to all three of us on deck.

"It is a rough day and I am not certain the boat is seaworthy. I recommend waiting twenty-four hours, like the instructions said. But it is your choice."

"I'll go," Coyle said.

"I want to go, too," I said.

"Out to the open sea," Fergus said.

"I hope you've brought life preservers," Mom said to our father.

"Oh, quiet," Dad said. "Untie us, will you?"

"A 'please' would be nice," Mom said.

"Untie it, woman!" Fergus yelled.

"Sorry, Maddy. Next time," Dad said from the deck.

Mom untied the boat from the cleat. Coyle pulled in the wet rope. Dad stepped to the helm and turned the key. The engine coughed gray smoke that burbled from the water. Dad put the boat in gear and steered us slowly into the center of the harbor. Mom and Maddy stood watching us, waving, as Dad steered along the breakwall, past the pier, and out to open water. The wind was stronger away from shore. The swells lifted and gently lowered the boat. The halyards on the mast tinged. We didn't think to put the sail up. We didn't even know how to. We were just motoring out. But, still, it was lovely being out there with those powerful, steady swells, the whitecaps here or there, and that feeling of a vast, watery wilderness all around.

We motored south along the coast toward the city. Coyle, Fergus, and I lingered at the front of the boat, not saying much, but leaning against the prow and looking out at the water and mocking our father at the helm, but at the same time thinking it was pretty nice. Even Coyle, who scoffed at the pleasures of rich kids, seemed to acknowledge that the boat had turned out to be a good thing. For once we weren't arguing or fighting or plotting against each other. We were

just riding on a boat—our boat, that we'd fixed together—
and all around was the vast expanse of open water.

Dad motored down to the planetarium at Northwestern.
Then he looped it around, and once we turned back the
wind was in our faces and the air seemed cooler and the water
rougher. Spray splashed up and pattered on our jackets.

At one point we heard the roar of a motor and turned
to see a very large, sleek motorboat zoom past us, leaving
a curved white wake. It was what we called a cigar boat,
like an enormous arrowhead in the water, chugging out gray
smoke.

"Willie Brennan!" a voice called. "Coyle Brennan!"

We could see tiny figures in the boat.

"It's that suckass Robert Dainty," Fergus said.

"God, what a one-upper," Coyle said. "He heard we
were putting our boat in today, and so he had to get Liam to
come out with his father's boat and one-up us."

Fergus held a finger in the air as they roared past.

"One-up!" Fergus called.

They spun around, spraying white water, then roared past
and zoomed out far away, just a low hum on the horizon.

"You know them?" Dad called.

"Unfortunately," Coyle said.

"It's Willie's best friend," Fergus said.

"Not anymore," I said.

"Willie beat him in tennis and he goes all sourpuss," Fergus said.

The cigar boat was already out of sight, engulfed by the
swells of gray water.

We were almost back to the harbor when I felt water

slapping the hull in a way it had not before. Fergus noticed it, too. He left the prow and stepped into the small cabin.

"It's leaking," he called out.

Dad made a dismissive motion.

"The seals expand and fill in the cracks," Dad said. "It's supposed to leak a little on the first day. I'll check it when we get in."

"Yeah, all right," Fergus said. "But it's really leaking."

Coyle and I were standing at the helm. Fergus came back to us, grinning.

"Dad's an idiot. We're sinking," he said.

"We're not sinking," Dad said, overhearing.

Coyle walked back and peered into the cabin, then went over to the helm. Coyle said something to Dad and then took the wheel and Dad went down the steps into the cabin. I heard something splashing. A minute later Dad came back up. He was wet past his knees. The boat was listing.

"Turn in," Dad called to Coyle, but Coyle had already started in.

There was a hand pump down in the cabin. I heard the cough of water splattering from the bilge. As we turned broadside to the waves, I felt the boat listing even more.

"Don't turn so sharply," Dad bellowed from inside the cabin.

The boat was at a twenty-degree angle and stayed there. The engine stopped.

"Keep going!" Dad yelled from below.

"It stopped on its own," Coyle said.

We were about three hundred yards offshore. The boat listed more and more.

"Open sea!" Fergus yelled. "Out to the open sea!"

Water crept up the back of the deck, which was lower than the front, inching toward the doorway to the cabin. Dad came out of the cabin, wet to the thighs.

"There's a radio," Dad said to Coyle. "Call for help."

Coyle had been trying to start the motor. It only clicked.

"Are you not going to do anything?" Coyle said to me.

"What do you want me to do?" I said.

"Plug the hole that Dad messed up," Fergus said.

"Shut up!" Dad yelled from the cabin. "Do something!"

Everyone was panicking a little, except Fergus, who understood immediately that there was nothing to do. The hull was leaking in multiple places. Fergus was leaning against the railing, trying to make the boat tilt even more, and laughing. I worked my way over to the helm and tried the radio. It was dead. I flipped the switch a few times. Coyle made a huffing noise like I didn't know anything and reached over and flipped the switch. Again, nothing.

I heard the roar of a boat approaching and then the boat rushed past, spraying an arched curtain of water that splattered on the deck. The roar lowered to a deep, chugging idle. It was the cigar boat with Robert, Tom, and Liam. They sat, bobbing on their expensive boat, ten yards off, those three kids in their wrinkled oxfords and cutoff khakis, holding soda cans, grinning at one another as our old boat listed more and more.

"You guys need help?" Robert called.

"Yes!" Dad yelled. "Call for help!"

"Help!" Tom yelled sarcastically. "Help! I'm sinking!"

Robert said something to Tom that made him stop joking

around. Then Robert picked up the radio handset and was talking into it. He actually did call the Coast Guard. Meanwhile, Dad was running around on deck, going from the cabin to the helm.

"Help! Help!" he called to shore.

His voice was small in that vast expanse of gray-green water. He was panicking. Dad could work for days on end without any sleep. He could take on any straightforward task. But he was not good at being in a hopeless situation.

"You could pump," Coyle said to me.

"I think we're a little beyond that," I said.

Dad was desperately trying to bilge. Coyle left the wheel and found the life preservers. Fergus clung to the railing at the prow, his feet already in the water. Coyle tossed a life jacket to Fergus. He tossed one to me, too. He handed one down to Dad.

"Don't get trapped in there," Coyle said.

"I'm all right," Dad said. "We'll just work a little, get this water out."

Dad was pumping furiously, and with each pump there was a little splatter of water outside the boat from the bilge. An enormous amount of water was pouring in from the deck, way more than was being pumped out. Fergus climbed over the metal railing.

"So long, suckers," he called.

He jumped into the frigid water, surfaced, and swam to Tom's boat. Robert helped him up. He even gave him a towel.

"You should get your life jacket on," Coyle said to me.

"I'm all right," I said.

"Don't stay on too long. Make sure Dad gets off."

Coyle stepped over the railing, looked back at our father, who was still pumping, then dropped into the cold water. He swam for about twenty seconds and was then lifted into Liam's father's boat. I worked my way over to the door of the cabin.

"Dad," I said.

He was pumping.

"Dad."

"What?"

"We need to go."

After a moment Dad came out, wet to the chest. Dad balanced himself and climbed up to the helm and tried to get the faceplate off the side of the cabin.

I heard a distant roar. It was the Coast Guard's Boston Whaler speeding out of the harbor. I could see Mom and Maddy, tiny figures, watching from the end of the pier. Robert was thirty feet away, watching me. To his credit, he was not gloating as much as I would have expected. He actually seemed concerned.

"Come on, Willie. Come on, Mr. Brennan. Get off before it sinks."

"We're all right," Dad said. "Just have to pump this water out."

I heard Fergus's laughter drift over. Even at that moment Dad still thought it was possible to save the boat if he just worked harder.

I was on the lee side, which was a little higher than the rest. I tossed my life jacket out onto the water so I could grab it if I needed it. Then I leapt out, diving. I cut sharply into the cold water and submerged, I saw the graceful cut of the rudder and the curved bottom of that lovely vessel fading into the green, grainy, frigid depths, and at that moment, like a clear bell striking, I knew nothing would ever change with our family. For most of that summer I had fooled myself into thinking we were making progress, getting ahead. I'd thought we'd make a concerted effort, work really hard, and we'd get to a place where we were safe from financial ruin. But I understood then that the hard work was like Dad on that bilge. It would never be enough.

I hovered underwater, watching as the boat drifted downward, then surfaced and swam to Liam's boat, dragging my life jacket along with me. I reached the ladder. Coyle looked over the edge.

"You all right?" he said.

"Fine," I said.

"What'd you do, dive down?"

"I was watching our yacht sink," I said.

"Right. The yacht," Coyle said.

He held his hand down for me, but I didn't want his help. I ignored his hand and climbed up to see Dad clinging to the mast. Fergus yelled, "Take it out to the open sea, Dad! Out to the open sea!"

In the end, Dad understood the ridiculousness of the situation and held a mocking fist up as the boat sank. Robert and Liam and Tom looked at one another, impressed that even at that moment we could joke around. That was our defense, making jokes, turning it all into an absurd story. It was the only protection possible, and I knew I ought to have joined in with the jeering, basking in the ridiculousness of our abject situation, showing Robert and the others that it didn't touch us, but I couldn't quite do it. It was just too humiliating. That boat sinking was like hope vanishing, the last stab at normalcy submerged, a leaden weight in my gut, drifting into green depths, pulling me down.

5

The Frozen Beach

*All closely imprisoned forces rend and destroy. The air that
would be healthful to the earth, the water that would enrich
it, the heat that would ripen it, tear it when caged up.*
                                          —Charles Dickens

Room 434 at New Trier had a grand piano in one corner, a
chalkboard with lines for music notes along the south wall,
and a tiered structure so the ceiling was only six feet over the
back desks. The east-facing windows had a view of a blue slit
of Lake Michigan over the tops of far trees. It was February,
four months after our boat had sunk. I was fifteen, a sophomore, and I had started going up to room 434 instead of going
to class. I was still at New Trier. Mrs. Dobbs, the landlord,
had heard of our boat sinking and had taken mercy on us and
given my parents another six months to raise the money for
the down payment. So, in a way, that boat had saved us, but
it had also pricked a hole in my unrealistic expectations for
our family, and by the time we learned that we would not
be evicted it didn't really matter to me. That winter, Mom

and Dad would find me lying in bed with a blanket over my head, not doing anything, which was considered to be the most unpardonable sin in our family. Or I'd be at a desk with my blank homework, staring into space, my pen hovering an inch over the paper, filled with an all-encompassing lethargy, a listlessness, a leaden fog that covered more and more of my brain and heart and guts. It seemed to have started with the boat, but I think now that the boat was only the trigger. When I had fought with Coyle there had been meaning and purpose to my life, and afterward, there was nothing as vital or as all-consuming as those battles. I was learning a hard truth: Once you become accustomed to physical confrontations, nothing else matters except those confrontations for a very long time.

Bit by bit in those months after the boat sank, I stopped doing my homework. I started skipping classes. I began spending most of my time in school up in room 434, day after day, by myself, alone in this unused classroom, looking out the window with a blank feeling, the blue slit of the distant lake like some receding promise.

Dean Wilkins had said he wanted to talk to "BOTH PARENTS." He had written it in capital letters on the parental notification, and the rigid, achingly unbiased tone of the letter, the polite, cold, formal way he requested *BOTH PARENTS,* let me know that I was really in trouble.

"At New Trier we try to encourage our students to live not just by a code of conduct, but a code of honesty," Wilkins was saying to my parents as I sat outside his office, listening through a crack in the door. Mom sat with her arms furiously crossed. Dad was leaning forward with his paint-spattered hands linked, the note requesting their presence resting on the edge of Wilkins's desk.

" 'Lied' is an accusatory word. I don't mean to make this a forum on the forgery. I believe it was an act of desperation more than of dishonesty. I know there are pressures. Great pressures. Particularly"—he paused, leaning back—"in families where the children compete. I don't think it is useful or healthy to dwell on that aspect of it."

"Of course he must be held accountable," Mom said. "The first step is to let him know he has not evaded the authorities. You've talked to him?"

"More than once, which—" Wilkins glanced at Mom. "As far as the situation on our end, seemed to do little good. We thought you knew, which apparently—"

"We did not know," Mom said matter-of-factly. "If we had been alerted we would have dealt with the situation. We will now, rest assured."

Hands clasped, trying to be even-handed, Dad put in an encouraging word now and then. Dad would rip into us at home, but in front of anyone else he would protect us.

"I have a question," Dad said. "He's going to be punished. Don't worry about that. But if he gets this thing—the theme—if he gets it in, is he gonna get docked?"

"Not if he hands it in on time," Dean Wilkins said. "There is no penalty for using all the time given. We believe in intellectual freedom at New Trier. We try not to dictate work habits. We understand that students are individuals and work in different ways. But it is the biggest project he will attempt in his four years here at New Trier. For many students it is the biggest academic project of their lives. There are stages. And Willie has not met the deadline for any of those stages. Red flags were raised. We were concerned. But, as I said, often, with a child like Willie, it is not the administration that corrects the student." A vague motion across the desk. "The family does our work for us. But in this case our persuasion has not produced the results we hoped."

"We were not apprised of the situation," Mom said. "And we are fully backing any methods needed to spur him into action. We understand there is a system of warnings. Willie bypassed that system by forging our signature. Rest assured, he will be punished."

"I'm not so worried about that," Wilkins said mildly. "But you understand, if he does not get this paper in in the next three and a half weeks he will have to either take summer school or, more likely, repeat the year, as summer school is a privilege given only for extraordinary circumstances—"

"It won't be necessary," Mom said. "He will hand it in."

Dad cleared his throat and leaned even farther forward. He had been working at one of his endless series of renovation jobs before he'd been pulled out to come to that emergency meeting. He was dressed in his painting shirt and pants and boots.

"I've always believed in mind and body. But we'll concentrate on the mind for the time being. Three and a half weeks. Twenty or thirty pages. It'll get done."

"I'm glad to hear it," Wilkins said. "That's the purpose of

this meeting. To apprise you of the situation. I see no reason to belabor the point."

A minute later the door opened. Dad stood there, looking down at me.

"Go in now, Willie. Be polite."

I dropped my head and went past them and into the dean's office. I closed the door. I sat across from Wilkins, who was leaning back with his hands behind his head and his feet up on the desk. He was trying to show me I wasn't in trouble.

As I sat, Wilkins untented his hands from behind his head, reached down, and opened his drawer and took out a well-thumbed paperback copy of the New Trier students' rights and regulations. He tossed it on the desk in front of me.

"Page twenty-eight. Read the first paragraph."

I opened to page twenty-eight. There was a highlighted passage.

"All sophomores must complete the Sophomore Theme before they advance to their junior year. Those students who do not complete the assignment . . ."

I went on and read the whole paragraph.

"You understand the situation?" Wilkins said.

"I do."

"Explain it to me so there's no doubt in my mind."

"If I don't get the paper in by March tenth, I'll fail the year."

"Your parents have said you will do the work. Do you agree with their assessment of the situation?"

"Yes."

"You're sure?"

I said I was.

"If you have trouble, there's the writing center, there's Mrs. Valenta, who offers private help. But these educators will not write the theme for you. They are explicitly forbidden from doing this. Do you understand?"

"Yeah."

"Are you sure?"

"I am," I said faintly.

Exasperation slipped into Dean Wilkins's manner. I was agreeing with everything he said, but I was so listless that it was obvious his words were hardly having an effect. He pushed a document toward me. I leaned over to read it. It said that I had been informed about the consequences of failing to hand in the Sophomore Theme. There was a line at the bottom. I signed.

"Am I done?"

He tilted his head and looked at me. A pigeon on the windowsill bobbed and clucked behind him. I watched it and not him.

"Is there something wrong, Willie?"

"No."

"Are you sure?"

"Yeah."

"Nothing at home?"

"Everything's fine."

"Because you came in here a year and a half ago asking to go into the higher levels. You assured me you could do the work. And for the most part you have fulfilled your promise. Your grades have been, while not exemplary, more than adequate. But now it seems you've stalled at the exact worst moment. Did you pick the wrong subject? The Berlin Wall, right?"

"I like the subject."

"What, then?"

I just sat there, my black sweatshirt zipped to my neck, hair in my eyes, lips half parted, a dull, leaden, lethargic expression.

"I understand that sometimes there are things that you don't want your parents to know. I can set up a meeting—"

"I'm all right."

"We have Miss Womack, our social worker—"

"Everything's fine," I said. "I just need to do the work. I got behind. I'll do it."

He looked as if he'd say something more, but there was nothing to say. I'd agreed with everything. After a moment his manner became brusque.

"You know the stakes. I'm rooting for you, but I've seen this before, and it doesn't always have a good outcome. You'll write your paper?"

"I will," I said.

"Good," he said. "You can go."

I walked out of the office. Mom and Dad were waiting in the hallway. Mom was coldly furious about me forging the parental notifications. Dad seemed more philosophical about the whole thing.

"You were wrong to do it, Willie, but not a big deal. What is a big deal is that you have to start working right now."

"Immediately," Mom said. "You are grounded until you have written that paper. No TV. No friends. Nothing. Are we clear?"

"Yeah," I said.

"You have not shown good judgment. You have tried to pull one over on us and it will be a disruption in our lives because you have chosen not to do your work."

"Maggie," Dad said.

"What?"

"Just leave it for now." Mom hated it when we lied to her. She hated being embarrassed in public. She was furious. Dad turned to me. "Are you gonna do the work?"

"Yeah," I said.

"Good enough," Dad said. "We'll help how we can."

"Starting today, you are on a schedule," Mom said. "Two or three pages a day. You will finish in ten days. You will rewrite in five days. Then you will hand it in. Got it?"

I said I did.

Dad put a hand on the back of my neck and we started up, walked silently through those crowded halls, among all the self-confident students who looked askance at my father with his paint-speckled pants and his old work boots. A few months before, I would have been embarrassed to have him come to the school, particularly dressed like that. Now I couldn't care less.

We walked out to the visitors' parking lot and I told them again I would do the work. Then they got in the station wagon and started up slowly, the rumble of that old car with the dangling bumper and rusted muffler going past the kids hanging out behind the school, who all burst out laughing as it went by. I didn't care what they thought.

I walked back inside and found Jimmy waiting on the

benches in the rotunda. He knew I'd been sent to the dean's office.

"What happened?" he asked.

"Oh, some bullshit," I said.

The Sophomore Theme, which I had not started writing, was a research paper that combined history and English and was the cornerstone of the second year at New Trier. You were required to have five sources in the bibliography and it needed to be at least twenty-five pages long. The coursework for the year centered on the theme. I had actually been looking forward to it. I had chosen to write on the Berlin Crisis of 1961. I was interested in the subject. I'd read books and taken notes earlier in the year and I thought I'd enjoy working on it. Writing was the one thing that I occasionally excelled at.

But then that sickness of lassitude overwhelmed me and my dreams of writing glory faded into indifference. I stopped doing my homework. I skipped classes. I stopped working on the sophomore theme. For a while no one really noticed. I coasted. But now it had all caught up to me and I would need to make a heroic effort to finish.

When I got home that day Mom offered to edit the pages of notes that I had. She even offered to type the final draft. Dad said he could get books from his college library for me. Meanwhile, I was offered the help of the writing center. My friends said, "What the hell, Willie, write the paper." Everyone was pulling for me. If I didn't finish it would destroy my academic career. I knew this. I knew I should care, but I didn't. It was like I was outside myself, watching it all happen.

Over the next few days Mom asked to see what I'd done and I handed her some notes I'd written earlier in the year. I didn't write anything new. The machinery was frozen. The factory engines had grown cold. Inside was a wide, blank space, bones among dried ashes, the gray, windy emptiness all around.

"If he's mad, he can be mad at me. Cause I'm the one telling you to do it."

Dad had wheeled Coyle's motorcycle out to the street.

"Come on, Willie."

"I'll get on if he won't," Fergus said behind me.

"I want Willie to do it," Dad said. Then, "Coyle said it was ok."

I knew that couldn't be the whole story. Since the day I'd pushed the bike Coyle had absolutely forbidden me from even looking at it. But Dad had forced a concession from Coyle, and was now offering the bike to me.

"I don't know how to do it," I said.

"That's the point," Dad said. "You don't know, you learn. Life is not just work. We forget that sometimes. So we do fun things, too."

"Like we get a yacht," Fergus said. "And then we sink it. Fun!"

"Shut up," Dad said.

Dad was holding the helmet out to me. I took it listlessly.

I adjusted the strap, then straddled the bike. I had to stand on my toes to balance.

"Hold down on the clutch like I showed you. Give it a little gas. Not too much. Then kick it into gear. First is down. The other three are up. Ease off on the clutch slowly, feel the pull, and let it take you . . ."

I clicked the clutch into first. With my right hand I gave it a little gas. I let off the clutch and the bike ratcheted and stalled. The bike started to fall, but Dad grabbed it.

"Gotta try to hold it up, Willie."

"All right," I said.

Dad steadied me for a moment. I could see him thinking it wasn't such a great idea, him suggesting I ride that motorcycle while I was so hopelessly listless.

"A little more gas," Dad said. "And let out a little slower on the clutch. Once it gets moving it will stand on its own. But let it out slowly and smoothly. Ready, Willie? I'm letting go. Are you ready?"

"Yeah."

"You're sure?"

"I'm sure."

He let go of the bike. I did hold it up, but barely. I kept the weight of the bike on my right foot. I tried to kick-start the engine. It didn't catch. I tried again. It started that time. I settled myself, balancing, and then I gave it gas and the engine roared and vibrated. Dad hovered nearby.

"Go on," he said. "But not so much gas. Slowly."

Fergus stood to the side, anticipating a crash.

I let up on the clutch just a little. I felt the bike ease forward. My toes dragged across the pavement. I raised my feet and I was gliding over the pavement, wobbling. I picked up speed. The wind was on my face, the ground rushing by, the light flickering through bare tree branches. It was an utterly pleasing feeling. A spark of life crackled inside me.

I accelerated down the block and turned at the corner and rode up the alley hill and down the hill, then turned and sped down Washington Street, the wind blasting past. It was wonderful.

I slowed and turned again and then turned one more time and was pulling back to the house where Dad was standing in the yard. Dad grabbed the handlebars to keep the bike from falling over.

"I see you enjoyed it," Dad said.

"Badass," Fergus said.

"Do you want to keep going?" Dad asked.

"I'm all right," I said.

"Take a few more turns."

I was already getting off.

"I'm good for now. Thanks. That was fun."

I gave Fergus the helmet.

"And now for the main event," Fergus said.

Fergus got on the bike, revved it, and rode off easily. By the way he did it I knew Coyle had let him ride it when I wasn't around. Coyle and Fergus had always had an easy understanding. They got along in a way that Coyle and I never had.

"That's the way I want you to be," Dad said. "Work hard, but have fun, too. Now go write your pages."

I went inside and up to my room and sat at my desk. The

excitement and spark from the ride on the motorcycle was still inside me and I used that spark to write a few sentences, but then my pen slowed and I sat looking at the page. The signals in my brain came faintly and from far away. I closed my notebook. I was done.

I need to go back a few months now. As I was overcome by the gray fog of listlessness, Coyle had also gone through a trans-formation, one just as dramatic as mine but infinitely more entertaining. Up to that point in Coyle's life, despite looking like a hoodlum, he had been a high-achieving perfectionist. He'd gotten A's and was the star of the baseball team. He'd aced the SATs. And though he pretended not to care about anything he did, I knew he was proud of his achievements. No one gets all A's at New Trier without trying.

But that winter, at the same time as I was sinking into my gray fog of lassitude, Coyle, who had been in self-imposed social exile for three years, suddenly began talking to the kids in the old, preppy crowd that he'd once been a part of. About a month later the phone started ringing at night, and it was always for Coyle. And then one day that fall I saw Jacqueline Bagley on the back of Coyle's motorcycle. She had an arm around his waist, her long hair flying behind.

Jacqueline was a trim, athletic, lanky badminton player who lived in a gigantic house, had wealthy, permissive parents, and was known for being a wild girl. The year before she had broken her arm jumping out of a second-floor window. She'd been suspended from school for keeping a bottle of vodka in her gym locker. And now she was riding on the back of Coyle's motorcycle without a helmet.

A week later my friend Roscoe saw Coyle holding a can of beer at a party. This would have been no big deal for an ordinary student. It seemed to me that about ninety-nine percent of the students drank alcohol at New Trier. But up to that point Coyle had been the exception. There was even a story about him knocking a beer can out of a teammate's hand at a party, saying, "Don't drink on the night before a game." Coyle was the weirdo, straightedge kid in the burnout crowd.

But then Coyle was seen holding a beer can and even drinking from it. A few weeks later, he missed his curfew and didn't come home until three in the morning. Since Coyle had never missed his curfew before—not once—Mom and Dad didn't say much about it. Dad might even have been glad. I think he saw Coyle's perfection as unnatural.

A week later Coyle missed his curfew again, and this time Dad had a long talk with him. The very next night Coyle didn't come home at all, and in the morning Dad found him asleep in the bushes. There was vomit near his head.

Dad and Coyle went upstairs. I heard them yelling at each other. When Coyle came back downstairs he grinned and held a fist up.

"Busted," he said.

Coyle was grounded for three weeks. Typical Coyle, he decided to use those three weeks to do all his assignments for the entire semester.

That was in January, and as soon as those weeks were over he began to stay out late again, to miss his curfew, to show up drunk at home, and to basically act in an overly casual manner, which drove Dad absolutely bonkers.

Coyle had been perfect for eleven years of school. Dad just wanted Coyle to toe the line for three more months, until the academic year ended. Then Coyle could apply to college early decision and the last year wouldn't matter. Dad practically begged Coyle to stay the course, but Coyle was through with being the perfect kid. He actually seemed to want to do badly, to shatter his perfect record on purpose.

"I've been too good," he said. "I'm making up for it."

Like everyone else in the family, once Coyle decided to do a thing, he went all in. So, in the months after the boat sank, while I was overcome with lassitude, Coyle was infected with a corresponding swaggering indifference, and when I think back on this I believe both of these new attitudes arose for the same reason. After our physical battles with each other, nothing was as interesting or as all-encompassing or really seemed to matter as much as those fights. If Coyle saw a link between our two transformations, he didn't comment on it.

One day, a week and a half before my theme was due, I was in the writing center when the door opened and I looked up and there was Coyle. In the nine months since my tennis match with Robert there had been a thawing in our relationship. Sometimes, even, it seemed like he was on my side.

"Hey," he said.

"Hey," I said.

"Are you writing your paper?"

"I'm trying to do it," I said.

"Will you finish?"

"I don't think so," I said.

He reached in his pocket and unfolded a few sheets of lined paper.

"I wrote some things down. I thought it might help."

He tossed the papers onto the table in front of me. He'd done more than write a few ideas down. He'd written an introduction and outlined the entire essay.

"Use that if you need it. I could probably write a little more, too, if you needed me to. Let me know."

I didn't touch the pieces of paper.

"I'll be ok," I said.

"Are you sure?"

"Yeah," I said. "I'm sure."

He knew if he tried to force me to take his help I'd go the other way on purpose, even if it meant disaster for me.

"If you change your mind let me know."

"Thanks," I said again.

And that was that. I think he saw that I was never going to ask him for help. It would just be too humiliating for me. But I always remembered that he offered.

A few more days went by. I didn't write my theme. I lied to my parents about what I was doing and they were distracted by Coyle, who stayed out all night with Jacqueline, and there was a three a.m. call from Jacqueline's parents, asking where the two of them were, which mortified Mom. She hated even the appearance of being permissive. Dad got in a yelling match with Coyle in the front yard, and then spent the rest of the night digging holes in the backyard for a batting cage, hacking into the frozen soil, making grunting noises, pretty much out of his mind with frustration.

This was the situation, six days before my paper was due, which also happened to be my father's forty-second birthday.

"I tripped."

"You tripped with Coyle's fist in your face," Fergus said. "I've tripped that way myself a few times."

We were at the dining room table, gathered for a board game. We always played a board game on Dad's birthday. We were waiting for Mom to come in from the kitchen and in the meantime were talking about the boxing match that Dad and Coyle had gotten into earlier that afternoon.

"He hit you and then you just happened to 'trip'?" Fergus said.

"His hit was incidental," Dad said.

Fergus laughed loudly. Coyle threw an arm over the back of his chair.

"You 'tripped' after I hit you in the face."

"I was backing up as you hit," Dad said. "Your weak punches had nothing to do with me falling."

Coyle and Fergus both laughed. Dad laughed, too, in a pressured, unpleasant way. For his birthday Dad had jokingly said he wanted to box Coyle, which was one of the few sports he could still potentially beat Coyle in. Mom had forbidden the bout, knowing it would spiral out of control, but as soon as Mom left to go to the grocery, Coyle and Dad put the gloves on and went out to the backyard. Mom had forgotten her wallet and come back to find them bashing away at each other. She ran out to stop the bout, but Dad had already been knocked down.

"It was a tie," Dad said.

"You were on your knees in the grass. How is that a tie?" Coyle said.

"It was *incidental*," Fergus said.

Dad ignored them and turned to the kitchen, yelling, "You coming or what, Mag? What're you doing? Eating the chocolates? I can feel you stomping around in there, trembling the earth. Stop eating the chocolates."

"I'll be there in a minute," Mom said in her precise, displeased tone of voice. "Remember, all of you, make it a pleasant evening. It's your father's birthday."

"Yeah, it's my birthday. Don't aggravate me," Dad said to Fergus. Then, to me, "Whatta you think, Willie? Who won?"

"You won," I said.

I knew he hadn't won. I'd heard the yelling and walked to the back window to see Dad crawling around in the wet grass while Coyle stood over him, red boxing gloves on, stunned at what he'd done.

"Yes!" Dad gloated. "Champion."

Coyle turned on me.

"You know he didn't win."

I shrugged. It was just habit to go against Coyle. I didn't even know why I'd said it.

Dad stood from the table and started a derisive dance of glee, saying, "Victory is mine! Winner!"

"God," Coyle said. "Do you want to go out there again?"

"You think I won't?" Dad said. "We can make a little wager. If I win you stay in and study for the rest of the year."

"And if I win?" Coyle said.

"You can do whatever you want until school's out."

"He does whatever he wants anyway," Fergus said.

"If I was doing whatever I want, do you think I'd be here right now?" Coyle said.

"Good point," Fergus said.

"Coyle," Mom said, walking in. "Be nice to your father. It's his birthday."

Dad pumped his fist slowly a few times.

"The champion," he said.

"Al," Mom said. "Do not instigate any more than you already have."

"I'm not instigating. I'm stating a fact," Dad said. "I am champion."

Maddy pushed her chair back, stood, and walked out of the room. She was eleven that year, lanky and matter-of-fact. She'd started to let her hair grow longer and to dress "like a girl." Her timid phase was over. She had started spending a lot of time at friends' houses and was determined to be "normal," despite our upbringing. Whenever a fight was brewing she just walked away.

Mom turned to Dad.

"You have now driven away one member of the family."

"I didn't drive her away," Dad said. "She left. Wasn't me who did it."

"And you." Mom turned on Coyle. "Stop aggravating your father."

"How am I aggravating him? He's sitting there holding a fist in my face saying 'Champion.' If he wants to challenge me to a boxing match, lose, then act like he won, and then jeer about it, what am I supposed to do? It's maddening."

"Control your emotions."

"Do I look like I'm out of control?" Coyle said.

He was sitting with an arm casually draped over the back of his chair. He did look relaxed. Coyle turned to our father.

"Let's go back out and really see who's better."

"No problem. I'll do it," Dad said.

"Good," Coyle said. "Let's go."

Without a word Mom stood from the table and walked out of the room and came back with the cake. It had four candles in a square and two in the middle.

"If you go out there and fight with your son in the middle of your birthday celebration I am dumping this cake in the garbage. And that will just be the beginning of the consequences. Don't test me."

"Come on, Mag," Dad said. "It's my birthday."

"I am aware of that," she said icily. "And we will already be having a discussion about this later. Boxing is fighting. And there is no fighting in this house. We will enjoy our board game and cake and have a pleasant, argument-free time. I will not have your birthday marred by this backbiting. Coyle, if you have to ruin your relationship with your father, do it some other time."

"Like it's been perfect up till now," Coyle said. "Sorry to ruin my relationship with you, Dad."

"Thanks for realizing your error," Dad said.

Mom took a deep breath, and in a weary, disapproving tone said to Coyle, "Your father has had extra work caused by Willie's lack of preparation and by your newfound cavalier attitude. Despite all that, we are here together as a family and we are going to have a pleasant, argument-free evening."

Mom was determined to have at least one argument-free evening. Coyle and Dad pulled their chairs back to the table and folded their hands in a mocking manner and pretended that the bickering had ended.

"Maddy!" Mom called. "You can come back. The natives have settled. There will be no more fighting. Right?"

"I was never fighting," Dad said. "I was *crushing!*"

Maddy shuffled in, her long blond hair held back with Walkman headphones. She looked around to make sure no one was arguing. Then she took the headphones off.

"Let me know if you're going to be idiots," she said. "Because if you are I'm going to listen to music instead."

"Better keep those on," Fergus said.

"There is no need for the headphones," Mom said. "We are going to enjoy playing this board game on your father's birthday. And then we will have cake."

Dad had cleared a space in the middle of the table and was setting up the pieces for a board game called Recognition. Dad had spent weeks before his birthday going over the rules for the game and memorizing the answers to the questions, which pretty much meant he was the inevitable winner. He did it every year. It was like his birthday present to himself. He got wound up and nervy on his birthdays and he used the games as a way of establishing his supremacy over us, gloating and needling us as he won.

"Does anyone want to make a wager before we start?" Dad said.

"You mean on who's going to be *champion*," Fergus said.

"Victor in boxing and now in intellect," Dad said. "Let the games begin."

The rules to Recognition were this: You were shown a picture of a famous or historical figure, and given a question about this figure, and if you got the question right you got to roll again. If you landed on someone else you could send them back to the beginning. The first one to the end was the winner. As it was his birthday, Dad got to start.

His first question was about Plato.

"What is *The Republic*?" Dad said. "I even said it in question form. Yes!"

He'd pretty much answered before the question was even asked.

"You've memorized the cards," Fergus said.

"Might have glanced at them," Dad said. "And if you didn't shuffle the cards, whose fault is that?"

"Pure torture," Coyle said to the rest of us. "I'm glad it's only once a year."

Dad went on and answered three questions correctly, then missed his fourth question, which was about Harriet Tubman. Then it was Mom's turn. She answered one question on George Eliot then missed one on Andrew Jackson. Then Coyle rolled and answered a question about Theodore Roosevelt. He rolled again and answered a question about Caesar. By the time Coyle finished he was only two spaces behind Dad.

There was the normal roiling, bickering competition that always accompanied any game in our family. Coyle had a good memory. He read history books and biographies in his spare time. He always did well in those games. Dad needled Coyle, trying to rattle him.

"You all go to those good schools, but look who's winning," Dad gloated.

"Just get it over with," Maddy said.

The game wenr on with everyone bickering and bantering, except me. I had hardly spoken for months. I sat silently, head down.

Half an hour later Dad was four spaces from the end. Coyle was seven spaces from the end. Mom was nine spaces away. The rest of us were way behind.

Dad put the dice in his fist and held the fist in Coyle's face. "Champion!" he intoned. Coyle knocked the fist away.

"Coyle!" Mom said sharply.

"What am I supposed to do?" Coyle said.

"Do not take the bait," she said.

"He's putting his fist in my face."

"What?" Dad said. "I can't play a board game in my own house?"

"Yeah, that's what we're all complaining about. That you're playing a board game," Fergus said. "Not that you're being an idiot."

"Champion," Dad gloated. "That's what I'm being."

Dad pushed his chair back, stood, and began dancing around, waving his fist in Coyle's face. Coyle had adopted an apparently casual attitude, which is what he usually looked like just before he snapped.

Dad sat back down. He had to roll a four or greater and answer one question to win. As it turned out, Dad rolled a three and it was a question about the assassination of Abraham

Lincoln. Coyle took the card. He read, "What is the name of
the theater where this political figure was assassinated?"

We all waited. By the way Dad sat there I could tell he
didn't know the answer.

"The Grand Theater?" he guessed.

Coyle made a derisive, hissing noise.

"The kind of car you drive," Coyle said without looking
at the card. "If you'd known that, you'd have won. But you
didn't. So maybe I get to be . . . *The Champion.*"

Coyle picked up the dice. He was six spaces behind Dad
and seven from the winner's circle. Coyle could win with a
good roll and a question answered correctly. Dad watched
intently. He desperately wanted to win. We could all feel it.
Dad worked too hard. His life was basically a series of hum-
bling moments. But he was still king in the house. Or he had
been. But now Coyle was challenging him. Coyle had been
baiting my father for months with his new offhand manner.
Now he could stick it to my father by winning the birthday
board game.

Coyle shook the dice for a long time, taunting. Then
he rolled and the dice came up a six and a one. That meant
either Coyle could go seven spaces to the final spot and
answer a question right to win the game or he could move
six spaces, the number on one die, land on Dad, lose his turn,
but send Dad back to the beginning. Basically, he could benefit himself or screw Dad. Coyle didn't say which he would
do. He simply reached for his piece and counted out the
spaces slowly, raising the piece really high as it jumped from
space to space—one, two, three, four, five, six—then, instead
of moving the seventh space, to win, Coyle pulled his hand

away, and said, "Back to square one, Dad, where you're most comfortable."

"Those aren't the rules," Dad said, flustered. "Where does it say you can send someone back?"

"I got sent back earlier in the game," Fergus said, laughing. "By you."

"This is my house. I do what I want," Dad said. "I'm not going back."

We were all silent. Bantering and baiting was one thing. But he was refusing to obey the rules.

"That's a total cheat," I murmured.

Everyone turned and looked at me. I'd said little for the entire game. I'd hardly spoken unless I had to for months.

"The mute speaks," Fergus said.

"You can't cheat like that," I said, louder this time. Probably for the first time in my life I was sticking up for Coyle. "You have to go back to the beginning. Those are the rules."

"You be quiet. You didn't even write your paper," Dad said.

I didn't bother responding. I just leaned forward, pulled my finger back, and tweaked Dad's piece so it sailed across the room and pinged against a glass lampshade.

"Back to the beginning," I said.

Fergus began to laugh mockingly when Dad raised a fist high and smashed it on the table, sending the pieces flying.

"Poor sportsmanship!" Dad bellowed. He grabbed my shirt in his fist and dragged me over the table. "If you weren't my son I'd pound you."

"Like that stopped you before," Fergus said.

Dad's eyes had gone crazy. He had me in his arms. Coyle

grabbed my legs and was pulling back, like it was a tug-of-war with me as the rope. Maddy got up and walked out of the room, holding her hands over her ears. "Stop stop stop!" she was shouting.

Suddenly I felt Dad's hands loosen. I was sprawled halfway across the table. I looked up at my father. He was pale and still. He sat back down. He opened his mouth. Then his eyes went flat and his face turned ashen. Coyle jumped up at the same time Dad slumped and fell straight forward. He smacked the tabletop with his face. Blood splattered across the board. Coyle pushed the table away and Dad flopped and thumped the floor. He was lying there, ashen-blue, vomit oozing from his lips.

"Call an ambulance," Mom said to Fergus.

Fergus didn't do anything. He just stood there, looking at our father.

"Do you hear me? Call nine-one-one."

Coyle was already kneeling to Dad, feeling for a pulse, but it was awhile before the rest of us took it in. Our lives would never be the same.

Three days later Coyle, Fergus, Maddy, and I were sitting on the couch in the living room eating Neapolitan ice cream from the carton, each of us holding our own spoon. Clean laundry was dumped in a pile in the middle of the floor. We'd just been taking clothes from the pile when we needed them. I could see the vomit and bloodstain on the carpet where Dad had slumped. No one had cleaned it. The sink was full of dishes. There were dirty plates and fast-food bags lying on all the surfaces. Mom, who was normally a vigorous housekeeper, had basically stopped cleaning. For three days Mom had been in the hospital. At first the doctors had told Mom that Dad had a heart attack, then that he hadn't had a heart attack but had an arrhythmia that made him pass out. Then they told her that he was totally fine and it had simply been fatigue. They said he needed a bypass, that he didn't need a bypass but an angiogram and a stent, then that he didn't need either of those but a pacemaker. There were about four different doctors, all with different diagnoses. It was bewildering. The only thing that everyone agreed on was that he'd passed out and had woken up in the ambulance. No one knew why.

Now, on the third night after his collapse, Coyle, Fergus, Maddy, and I were passing the ice cream back and forth, arguing about who got the last of the chocolate, when a black Mercedes pulled up in front of the house.

"Who's that?" Fergus said. "The undertaker?"

But it wasn't an undertaker. It was Mr. Dainty, and Robert was in the backseat. Mr. Dainty waved for Robert to stay in the car, then started up our driveway, past our rusting station wagon and the broken handrail of the porch that was lying in the shrubs.

"What's this suckass want?" Coyle said.

"Probably here to evict us," Fergus said.

"Mom," I called.

"What is it?"

"Someone's here for you."

"Who?"

"Mr. Dainty."

"Who?" she asked again.

"The little weasel Robert Dainty's father," Fergus said.

"What's he doing here?"

"No idea," I said.

The doorbell rang. I heard the water turn off at the sink. Mom passed the opening to the living room and was hastily trying to fix her hair. The door creaked open.

"Hello," we heard Mom say.

"Hello, I'm Jack Dainty. Our sons are friends."

"Like you're friends with that suckass," Fergus whispered. Coyle elbowed him to be quiet.

"Yes. I believe they are," Mom said in a wavering tone.

"I heard about your recent trouble. I came to see if there's anything I can do."

"Oh, that is very kind," Mom said faintly.

Mom and Dad were so busy that they had few close friends. And Mom was deathly afraid of asking for any help and being a bother. She hadn't told anyone what had happened.

"Can I ask how he is?" Mr. Dainty said.

"He is awake and not in pain, but the doctors have not been able to agree on a diagnosis. They scheduled a bypass but then postponed it. It has not been efficient."

"Have you heard of a cardiologist named Dr. Murphy?" Mr. Dainty asked.

"Of course. He's where we started," Mom said.

Dr. Murphy was the most famous cardiologist in Chicago. He lived in Seneca.

"Unfortunately, Dr. Murphy is in high demand and was

unavailable and we had to go to someone further down the list."

"Of course he's busy," Mr. Dainty said. "But I know him personally. We play squash together. Would you let me call him for you?"

"Oh, I don't want to be a bother," Mom said.

"It's not a bother," Mr. Dainty said. "He's a friend and would be glad to help. And it would be a favor to me. My son Robert is not always as gracious as he could be. I'd like to set an example of how we can be of service to others."

Mom hated asking for a favor from anyone, but particularly from someone like the Daintys, who she saw as being wealthy, frivolous people. But she had spent three days in limbo in the hospital and Mr. Dainty put it cleverly, making it as if he was asking a favor from her to set an example for Robert.

After a moment, she said, "Of course you can try. But I don't want to take up your time. But if you could make that call, when you had the time . . ."

"I have the time now," Mr. Dainty said. "It's why I've come."

He stepped inside without being asked. He passed by the opening to the living room, nodding to us.

"Hello, boys," he said.

He went on to the telephone in the kitchen.

"Hello, boys," Fergus said to Maddy. "He called you a boy, man-woman."

Maddy swatted Fergus, but didn't put much effort into it. We were all trying to hear what was going on in the kitchen.

We heard the phone dialing. A moment later Mr. Dainty

was talking to a secretary, then a nurse, and then, after a five-minute wait, to Dr. Murphy himself.

"Hello, Thomas. This is Jack Dainty . . ."

Very quickly, Mr. Dainty was giving our father's name, and his doctor's name, and the wing he was in at Evanston Hospital.

Afterward, Mr. Dainty said, "We're in luck. He has another patient on that floor. He can see Alex tomorrow morning between eight and ten. If you would like to meet him, be there at that time."

"Of course I will be there. I don't know how to thank you."

"Then don't," Mr. Dainty said. "Your sons have known my son for years. They have had a good effect on Robert."

"Oh, I hardly know about that," Mom said, flustered.

"They are an example of hard work, diligence, and honesty. Robert needs a little help in those areas."

Something moved inside me. I had always assumed the Daintys looked down on us. I had assumed that, like all of Seneca, they watched our struggles with discomfort and distaste and wished we'd go away. Even when I was friends with Robert, I assumed his father thought our family was ridiculous. My certainty of their dislike was a pillar of my understanding of the world we inhabited.

Mr. Dainty stepped into the hallway and looked into the small living room with the frayed carpet where the floorboards were visible through holes and the four kids sat on the worn couch that was patched in places with tape. We looked at him silently.

"I grew up in a house very much like this one," he said.

"How are you, Willie? You keeping up with your school-work?"

"Yes," I said, though it wasn't true.

"The doctors will take care of your father. You keep on with your work." He turned to Coyle. "Congratulations on all of your accomplishments."

"Thanks," Coyle said.

Mr. Dainty turned to Mom.

"I'll have Gretchen bring some food. Good luck."

He walked out and Mom stood there, stunned. She had bad-mouthed the Daintys many times. Now they were the first people who'd helped.

The next morning Dr. Murphy examined my father and reviewed everything that had been done up till that point. He canceled the bypass and scheduled a stress test. The EKG was found to have been abnormal beforehand, and so was not necessarily caused by a cardiac event. The enlarged heart was a sign of high blood pressure, but also a sign of physical conditioning. Dr. Murphy wanted to do an angiogram, and an angioplasty, if necessary, and said he'd go from there. All that was scheduled for the following day, when we were let out of school so we could see my father before his procedure.

I was lying out in the cold sand along the winter beach a few hours before my father's surgery. I was listening to the crisp tearing of the icy waves and looking up at the tree branches overhead. There was a very clear awareness of what was at stake. I knew that Dr. Murphy might find something terrible in Dad's heart. I knew it was possible he would die during the procedure. And lying there, on the frozen beach, I realized I desperately wanted our father to live. There were times growing up when I had wished if not that he would die, at least that he wasn't around, times when I just wanted to be a normal kid with summer camp and video games and not have all the extra work and extra sports and be involved every day in his self-improvement schemes and his menial drudgery. But at that moment I didn't care about our struggles. I was proud of my father, who was attempting to remake his life, and had gone through all sorts of humiliations for us. He had not done it without his periods of anger, but he had done it with boisterousness and swagger and usually with good humor, and I knew that despite the insane regimen Dad had put us through, despite his nitpicking, perfectionist personality and his impracticality about money, our lives would be much worse without him. I lay there listening to the surf and hoping, praying, that he would be ok, and at the same time there was the physical, sensory pleasure of being out there in the crisp, winter morning. Lassitude weighed me down—it had taken a long time to build up and there's no way it would dissipate instantly—but there, on the beach, I was aware for the first time in months of the beauty of the expanse of water and the curve of the shore and of the soft hiss of waves tumbling in, and it was like those waves were cleaning my insides moment by moment. Dad's collapse had pierced through the fog of my lassitude and I could feel that fog dissipating. I took deep breaths of cold air, fearful about my father's surgery, but also alert and awake and feeling alive for the first time in months, lying there on the frozen beach, looking up through dark, tangled branches.

"You're the one who tweaked his piece," Coyle said.

"You're the one who boxed with him," I said.

The four of us were sitting outside the SICU. We were supposed to go in and talk to our father, but we'd been waiting fifteen minutes and Mom hadn't come out yet. We thought maybe we'd missed it.

"Don't argue in front of Mom," Maddy said. She was sniffling. "Mom actually cares that Dad could die."

"I care, too," Fergus said. "If Dad doesn't die it means he's coming back home."

"Quiet," Maddy said. "Here she comes."

Mom was hurrying from the surgical rooms, glassy-eyed. She stood in front of the brown plastic couch where we all sat. Maddy got up to hug her.

"The nurses were shilly-shallying, so we only have a few minutes," Mom said. "Fergus, you go in first. Maddy, you go second. Coyle and Willie, stay here."

"Why do I have to go in first?" Fergus said.

"It's sort of like eating your vegetables first," Coyle said.

Mom turned on Fergus.

"Do not argue with me. Go in there. Be nice to your father. Do you hear me?"

"Be hard not to," Fergus said, which made Coyle bite his lip.

Fergus walked in. Maddy looked like she might cry.

"Is Dad ok?"

"He is prepared for whatever happens," Mom said. "You can come with me. Coyle and Willie, I'll call for you."

Mom walked Maddy to the SICU. Coyle and I were left alone in the hallway, both of us slumped, acting overly casual. Coyle tossed a tennis ball against the far wall and caught it as it bounced back.

"Do you know what he's going to say?" I said.

"He's probably going to tell us we're grounded for life. And to outline the next five years of study and workouts."

A doctor passed us, shaking a finger at Coyle for his ball tossing. After he passed, Coyle tossed the ball to me. I caught it.

"If he dies maybe they'll let you write your sophomore theme in summer school," Coyle said. "Student hardship and all that."

"Something to hope for," I said.

"Did you write any more of it?" Coyle asked.

"Not really," I said.

"What does that mean?"

"It means no."

"Why not?"

"Didn't feel like it," I said.

Coyle just shook his head at me. Idiot, he was thinking. It was due in three days.

"You better hope Dad dies," he said. "If not, he's going to kill you."

"If he doesn't kill you first," I said.

The SICU doors whooshed open and Mom stood there.

"Coyle," she called.

He stood jauntily and walked off to the SICU and I was

left out there alone in the hallway, holding that tennis ball. I set the ball on a windowsill. It rolled a little. I decided if it fell off that Dad would die, but if it stayed up he would live. It drifted a little but stayed on top. I thought that was a good sign. But then I thought that was stupid. I had no idea what would happen. And whatever happened, I'd just have to deal with it. A minute passed. Then the door clicked open.

"Willie. Come on. You have a minute."

I walked into the SICU and saw Fergus standing behind Mom, eating a chocolate pudding. He waved a plastic spoon.

"Free pudding," he said. "Thanks, Dad. You should have a surgery every day."

"You're doing your best to make that possible," I heard Dad say, then laugh loudly at his own joke. I could tell by his laugh that he was scared.

I walked around the corner and found our father on a stretcher, in a hospital gown, holding on to a bar on the wall to stop the transporter from wheeling him away.

"He's right here," Dad said, pointing at me.

"You have one minute," the transporter said. "They're already waiting."

"Shut the door," Dad said after the transporter walked out.

I shut the door and was suddenly alone with my father. He already had the IV in his left arm. He was grinning openly in a way that was not normal for him. They had given him a relaxant of some sort.

"Just wanted to talk to you before I go in," he said in a forced, ham-handed tone. "I'll be fine. So don't worry about me."

"I'm not," I said.

It was supposed to be a joke, but it came out sounding like I meant it.

"Good," Dad said. "I don't want you kids to think about me at all. I've had a good life, and whatever happens to me, you have to go on with what you're doing, which is more important. Your lives are all going to be better than mine. You'll do great things. Your mom and I are both very proud of you."

This was not how I had expected the conversation to go at all. I thought he would talk about not moping around and writing my sophomore theme.

"I'm not doing that great," I said. "I know that."

"You're getting A's in the 4 levels. You made the varsity tennis team."

"I'm not getting A's now. And I've hardly played for months."

"You will make the team when you start to play again. You may have a speed bump here or there, but you are moving beyond what I ever did. Your mother and I are both very proud of you."

I thought he must be loopy from the drugs to be complimenting me so extravagantly. In our family we bickered and criticized one another. Compliments were considered bad form.

The transporter appeared again and tapped his wrist. Then shut the door.

"I've been hard on you kids. I know that. I thought it was for the best so you would be prepared to compete in that tough school. I was never great in school or anything, so I thought what I could teach you was to work hard. I thought that was what I could give you. But I want you to know that both your mother and I love you kids like nothing else and we see that you'll do great things. And you, in particular, Willie, you have a bright future. You're smart and everyone likes you. Not a grunt like me. Whatever happens, you should know you're the good part of my life."

He reached out and for a moment his big arms surrounded me, not to thrash me but to hug me. A warmth flowed into me, but a strangeness, too. It felt unnatural to be hugged by my father, particularly at that moment. I thought he was going to yell at me or tell me to do my work, but he was saying nice things, things I'd never heard him say before. After a moment he pulled away and said, "Be nice to your brother, ok?"

I knew he meant Coyle.

"I am nice to him," I said.

"Then keep being nice," he said. "He really cares for you."

I started to make some sarcastic comment about that, but the door opened.

"Gotta go," Dad said.

Dad was wheeled out and I just stood there in the room by myself. My eyes were glassy and I was embarrassed. Crying was for babies. I stood there for at least a minute, getting ahold of myself, feeling a strange, soft glimmering inside.

When I walked out, Coyle was in the hallway.

"Did you talk to him?" he said.

"Yeah."

"What'd he say to you?"

"Nothing," I said. "What'd he say to you?"

"Nothing, really," Coyle said, and by the way he said it, I knew Dad had said the same sort of thing to Coyle.

"Maddy and Fergus are with Mom. We're supposed to go home and wait."

"Wait for what?" I said.

"To hear what happens."

"Oh," I said. "All right. Are you ready?"

We walked back out past where I'd put the tennis ball. I thought I needed to leave it there on the ledge for good luck.

Coyle and I drove home in silence. As soon as we were home Coyle went into the den to watch basketball. I went upstairs to the bedroom and lay looking at the ceiling and thinking about what Dad had said. For half my childhood I had dreamed about what it would be like without the exercises, without having to work adult jobs on the weekend, and without having to be constantly afraid Dad would lose his temper, but now that it was really possible that he wouldn't be around I saw the other side of it.

I lay in bed for an hour. Then I went downstairs and made a bologna sandwich, and while I was in the kitchen the phone rang. Coyle answered it in the den.

"Uh-huh. Uh-huh," I heard him saying. "All right."

He hung up. I walked into the den. Coyle was looking at the TV. He didn't turn from the screen when he spoke.

"That was Mom. Dad's fine. They didn't even do the angioplasty. There's nothing wrong with his heart. He had an arrhythmia. From stress."

"Stress from you beating on him," I said.

"And you tweaking his piece," he said.

Neither of us said anything more for a while. Coyle was glad. So was I. But we weren't going to show that, particularly to each other. The TV flickered basketball.

"Anyway, he's fine," Coyle said.

"Good," I said.

"Yeah, it's good," he said.

I was embarrassed about being happy, so I left Coyle and went outside and walked around the neighborhood for a while. When I got home Mom was at the sink doing dishes. She came out and hugged me and told me what I already knew. That Dad was ok and he'd be home in a few days. I walked upstairs and found my notebook still resting on the little desk between the beds where I'd left it days before. I shut the door behind me and without thinking about it I started writing my sophomore theme. Something had sprung loose inside me. It was because of the crisis with our father, and also because of what had happened with Mr. Dainty. I had thought the attitude in Seneca toward us was entirely disapproving, but I was wrong. I wrote all that night. I slept for a few hours and wrote for another twenty hours the next day. I did it straight, without stopping or even rereading.

My sophomore theme was supposedly on the Berlin Airlift, but in my version of the assignment it was not really about the political event at all, but about the effect on the residents of being cut off from the rest of the country. It was about solitude and perseverance. It was about hunger and hardships. It was about the problems of the world played out in a single isolated population and how they coped with it. It was about endurance. I filled the paper with anecdotes from those who had lived through the crisis. I finished at five in the morning on the day it needed to be turned in. I didn't proofread, so I got a D on grammar, but I got an A on content, which came out to a B- on the total paper, which I accepted as a minor miracle.

The day after I handed in the sophomore theme Dad was released from the hospital, and when he got back we all saw that something had changed in him. It was like there had always been a cloud of charged particles around him, a tense, nervy, energy radiating off of him. But now, suddenly, that cloud had mostly dissipated. After his hospital stay his posture became more relaxed, his manner more casual. Dad still had a temper at times. He could still fill a room with his displeasure, but his temper flared less and less.

When I look back on that springtime it seems a miracle that we all made it out without a total and permanent disaster. It was family chaos that brought on that crisis and it was family chaos that saved us from it. I don't pretend to understand this or to present it as a reasonable cure. I am only saying what is true. I was knocked out of the gray fog by my father's collapse. It happened at the last possible moment to avert ruin. It was like some deity reached down and saved me, though he almost had to kill my father to do it.

6

The Trip

Any disciple who has entered any kind of practice must begin with seemingly unnecessary, futile things. But of course these things are part of the discipline. Without such seemingly trifling things there can be no perfecting of the practice.

—Reverend Kanero,
quoted in Thomas Merton's *Asian Journal*

I was riding my bike on a highway in eastern Iowa. I could hear the crank of the gears, the drone of crickets, tires on pavement. All around were the endless cornfields. If I peered out into the waves of heat I could see Coyle on his bicycle somewhere far ahead, a gray smudge. Fergus and Dad were somewhere miles behind me. It was summertime, three months after Dad had gotten out of the hospital, and we were riding west across the great plains. I was fifteen years old.

Earlier that spring, just after getting out of the hospital, our father, exuberant after getting his clean bill of health, and wanting to do something excessive and dramatic, began thinking about taking a long vacation. Other families went on extravagant trips to Europe, to Japan. Dad wanted the same for us, but of course we didn't have the money for a family vacation, particularly after his hospital stay. But Dad didn't care. He wanted to do something enormous, something magnificent, arduous, impressive, mind-blowing, and needlessly extreme. He wanted it to be something everyone would remember. He was doing what he always did. He was being our father.

"What do you guys think about going on a big trip this summer?" Dad had asked. "We'll see the country. Do something none of your friends have ever done, or even think is possible. How's that sound?"

We were all quiet, and then Fergus said, "It sounds like a trick question."

Dad kept his hands on the table. He paused for dramatic effect.

"How about we ride our bicycles to California?"

We just looked at him blankly. None of us had ever ridden our bikes more than ten miles. It seemed completely farfetched and more like an ordeal than a vacation.

"That's going to suck," Fergus said.

"Well, you better change that attitude, cause we're doing it."

Two months later Coyle, Fergus, Dad, and I had panniers on either side of our bikes, tents and soft pads strapped to the racks, and with the loaded bikes, we started west from our house in Seneca. It was just the boys on that trip. Maddy stayed home with our mother.

Dad had estimated we needed to ride sixty miles a day to make it to California over the summer. That was our goal.

Sixty miles. Every day. We didn't know anything about long-distance bike riding. We didn't have very good bikes. We didn't even know that when you rode west you rode against the wind every day.

On the first day, starting early, and riding for seven hours, we rode forty miles, and by the end of the day I was so tired I could not pick up my bike. I weighed a hundred and ten pounds at the time. My bike and the packs weighed around forty-five pounds. If the bike fell I needed someone else to lift it. Fergus, who was thirteen years old, could hardly stand upright, and at a gas station west of Aurora, Illinois, Fergus left his bike unlocked and walked out into a field, hoping someone would steal his bike and he wouldn't have to ride it anymore.

On the second day we rode all day and when we were finished we'd gone thirty-five miles. By that point we were on Route 30, heading west among cornfields that stretched for a thousand miles. The towns were spaced eight or ten miles apart. From the edge of one town we could see the grain elevator of the next town far in the distance. Mile markers were small green placards on the right. You could see the tiny dot of green a mile away. And every mile was difficult. Our legs were often so tired we stopped between towns because we couldn't go on. And we were still in Illinois, more than two thousand miles from the coast. California seemed a crazy goal.

On that third day Fergus made up a song, a simple song that he sang for, oh, about six hours straight as we struggled with our loaded bikes.

"We're not going to make it, do-dah, do-dah . . ."

This song enraged our father, and because it did, Fergus kept singing it.

Fergus, with his mop of brown hair and his loaded bike, weaving on the flat, straight, mostly empty highways between the cornfields.

"We're not going to make it . . ."

We rode thirty miles on that third day. We were falling far behind our schedule and we were bickering and in bad moods. It was going to be a humiliating failure when we didn't even make it out of Illinois. Coyle started to ride far ahead just to get away from us. I was a little behind Coyle. Fergus went excruciatingly slow, hoping Dad would see what a crazy folly that trip was and give it up. For hours I was alone between Coyle and Fergus, the cornfields on either side, just me on Highway 30, no one else in sight.

On the fourth day we rode forty miles, but we were stronger at the end of the day. I was actually able to lift my bike myself. We even felt we could have gone farther. On the fifth day we rode fifty-five miles. On the sixth day we rode sixty. That was the first day we had made our quota. We were far behind our schedule, but still, we all felt pretty good. It was an easy sixty miles. We thought we could even have gone farther.

On that day, the sixth, I first noticed that our bodies were changing. We were all getting stronger. We were also getting more confident. I saw that it was not any one thing that was hard. It was just getting up and riding day after day, over and over. That was the trick. The bike trip, if nothing else, was a lesson in the surprising, cumulative effect of consistent effort.

On the seventh day we rode more than seventy miles. On the eighth day we rode seventy-five miles. We weren't even that tired at the end of it. We started to think it might be possible to ride to California. Sixty miles a day wasn't that hard.

I don't want to give the wrong idea. That bike trip was not a wholesome family vacation. It was not some Brennan brother lovefest. I don't think that was ever possible for us. Fergus resisted every minute of that trip. Coyle thought we were weak and slow and would rather have been home with his friends. We bickered with one another endlessly. But Dad had decided we were going to ride our bikes across the country and we were driven on by the force of his will and the threat of his fists. We threw rocks as we rode. We tried to drive one another off the highway. When we were not fighting or arguing or racing, we mooed at the cows as we passed, trying to get them to stampede. We let the air out of one another's tires. But we kept moving west. At least three times I overheard adults telling my father that we were too young to be out there on the highway on our own. I never even considered that these people might have a point. They were soft, weak, spineless people who couldn't understand us. It might be too young for other kids, but we were Brennans. We had a different kind of training. We did whatever we wanted to do.

In Cedar Rapids a woman pulled a shotgun on us when we stopped at the edge of her property. In western Iowa we were chased by a Doberman, the dog snapping at our heels and biting the backs of our tires. Outside Lincoln we rode through a sea of grasshoppers that crunched beneath our wheels and got caught in the spokes. In eastern Colorado a pig farmer showed us how you could hold a weed to an electrical fence and feel the electricity pulse through the fence and into your wrist, the muscles twitching in your arm as the current ran through the body and into the ground. The next day we saw the Rocky Mountains, seventy miles away, a black, jagged silhouette on the horizon. Two days later we were in the mountains, struggling up Trail Ridge Road, which rises from the plains to more than twelve thousand feet, the highest continuous highway in the United States. Our father had chosen the most difficult route over the mountains on purpose. He wanted us to get the full effect. We pedaled twenty-six miles uphill. I fainted when we got to the summit. Dad sat me up afterward, gave me a water bottle, and put some nuts in my palm and said, "Eat some peanuts. You'll be fine. You did it."

An hour later we were gliding downhill, our brakes smoking from constant use.

A few days after that we were out in the Great Salt Desert, which we crossed in a single day: one hundred thirty miles, the four of us wearing white hotel towels beneath our hats, looking like sheiks, the ground as flat as the surface of an ocean.

A few days later, in eastern Nevada, we got caught in a dust storm. Huddling beneath a viaduct, heads in our jackets, we breathed through our shirts as the storm passed. Afterwards, Coyle and I walked out from beneath the viaduct to see a monochrome world of gray, like being on the moon, the area around our eyes and the inside of our mouths the only color in all that vast, gray, dusty world.

A few days after that we crested the ridge near Lake Tahoe and crossed into California, and that was that. We had made it. We had ridden our bikes to California from our house in

Seneca, Illinois. It had taken five weeks and we had fought the whole way but we had done it, and it was something we all talked about later and that became representative of our family. We might have less money than other families. We might have epic battles and be an embarrassment in the neighborhood. But we had ridden our bikes to California together. It was really something.

Near the end of the trip Mom and Maddy drove out. We had a few days' vacation at Lake Tahoe. Then we drove back across the country with the bikes on the roof of the car, and later, no matter how much we complained about our father, no matter how much we said he was crazy, called him a slave driver, said he was impractical and foolish, we knew that he had also brought us on a bike trip across the country. What we had done was unusual and we were proud of it.

I bring this up now because I feel that with the stories I have chosen to tell I have half misrepresented my childhood. Everything I've said is more or less true. The upbringing was arduous. The fights were real. But there was also something beyond the fighting and struggles. My childhood was sometimes brutal, but it wasn't unhappy. At least it was not all unhappy. We did work hard, but there was compensation in the independence we had, and in the feeling of accomplishment when we mastered something other kids our age couldn't conceive of doing. And though we fought bitterly with one another, there was also an unspoken loyalty and the recognition of ourselves as a single unit, a distinct species, separate from other people. We were Brennans, which meant we were poor and we were violent and we were extreme in our views, but it also meant we were hard workers, and we never complained. We had grown up around kids we thought of as being coddled and complacent, and we took a perverse pride in the hardships we'd endured.

In those weeks after we got back from our trip to California, some of the happier memories from our childhood began to come back to me, memories that were a counter-pull to the ice inside, the resentment that I still carried from those battles with Coyle, which was undeniably the worst part of my childhood. Our rivalry never flagged, the ice never melted completely, and I suppose that's not surprising, as we were both strong personalities. But there was another side to it. No matter how much we'd fought, or how much I resented Coyle, we had been forged in the same fires, and I knew no one was more like me than he was.

7

Philanthropists

An old joke has an Oxford professor meeting an American former graduate student and asking him what he's working on these days. "My thesis is on the survival of the class system in the United States." "Oh really, that's interesting: one didn't think there was a class system in the United States." "Nobody does. That's how it survives."

—Christopher Hitchens

Every spring at New Trier there was a coupon book sale. The money raised by the sale went to the Chandler Fund, which paid for uniforms and sports equipment and scholarships. The sale was basically a way to get students to raise money for a good cause and to teach the benefits of community service. Students could organize into teams of five, and at the end of the selling period there was an award ceremony for the team that sold the most books. The winning team got free tickets to the prom, their own page in the yearbook, and were made Chandler Fund Knights, which could be put on a college résumé. For as long as anyone could remember, the winning team was connected to either Indian Hills Country Club or the Kenilworth Club. It was a rich-kid thing. The teams for the clubs sold to their parents and their parents' wealthy friends. No one in our family had ever been involved in the coupon book sale. Our family was more likely to receive charity than give it. But that fall, when Coyle was a senior and I was a junior, I walked out to the soccer field during a free period to see the destruction from a tornado. There was a brown swath up the middle of the field, with debris littered everywhere and a chain-link fence tossed up in trees and a house along the far side of the field with a torn-off façade. I was basking in this glorious destruction when I saw Robert walking across the field toward me. Robert wasn't playing tennis that year and we didn't talk that much in the hallways, and though there'd been a softening of relations between us, it's not like we went out of our way to interact, either. So, by the purposeful way he approached I could tell he wanted something.

"Did you see it?" Robert asked when he reached me.

"Are you kidding? I was crammed down in the field house with everyone else."

"Same for me," Robert said. "Barb Jamison saw it, the ditz. She thought the alarm was just a drill. Then she looks out the window and saw a funnel cloud going by. She said it peeled off the side of the house like wrapping paper and turned silver when it sucked up the water over the lake."

"Cool," I said.

"Totally cool. Anyway, we gotta talk. You know the coupon book contest."

"I know it exists. I've never been in it."

"Well, I have."

"Congratulations."

"Yes. It's the thing I'm most proud of. My mom makes me do it. Anyway, the team I'm on has always won."

"That's great, Robert," I said.

"You can stop with the sarcasm," he said. "I'm not saying that to brag. I'm trying to tell you something. Liam and Tom are always the captains, which is annoying, because I do all the work. But their fathers buy the most coupon books, so they get to be captains, and I don't get recognition."

"That's rough," I said.

"I sense your heartfelt sympathy. But it sucks. If I'm going to work harder than anyone else I want everyone to know. I thought of making my own team, but everyone I know is already on a team. But you're not on a team, right?"

It took me a moment to understand what he was asking.

"On a team to sell coupon books?"

"Yeah."

"No, I'm not on any team and I didn't plan on being on a team. That's working for free. I already have a job. I get paid for it."

"Well, think about it. We could do it together. You're a hard worker. And I know your brother is, too. I could be captain. We could get some of Coyle's friends. It would be great to beat Liam and Tom. They're so smug."

I thought it was interesting that Robert talked as if he were essentially different from Liam and Tom, but I didn't mention this.

"So, would you do it?" he asked. "You, me, and your brother."

"I doubt Coyle would do it," I said. "And even if he did do it, in what version of reality do you imagine Coyle volunteering to let you be his boss?"

"How about co-captains? Me and Coyle. And if we win you can put it on your transcript. That will be good for you. And it would be a way to stick it to Liam and Tom. Coyle's gotta like that. Just ask him. Will you at least do that?"

I hesitated, but in the end said I would ask him, though I was pretty sure Coyle would say no. After Robert started off, he said, "How's your dad?"

"Good," I said.

"Glad to hear it," he said.

He walked on and that was that. He didn't mention that his dad had helped mine, but that was what he was saying when he asked about him. Robert couldn't help bringing that up.

I figured I'd talk to Coyle, he'd refuse, and that would make it easy for me to refuse as well. But that night when I asked him, Coyle surprised me.

"Yeah, I don't care, I'll do the coupon thing," Coyle said. "I'm not the one who has a problem with Robert."

I just looked at Coyle like he was crazy.

"You slapped him in the face and refused to apologize to him."

"That doesn't mean I have a problem with him," Coyle said. "That just means he pissed me off so I hit him. I beat on him and then got over it. I don't hold grudges," he said. "You should try it sometime."

I didn't know how to respond to that.

"Robert's father helped Dad. We can help him. And we can put it on our transcripts."

"So you'll do it?"

"I'm not going to take orders from that suckass," he said. "But, yeah, I can get Farrelly and Ron Toll to work with us. You can be the fifth member."

I said nothing at first. I didn't want to do the coupon book sale. Coyle gave me a disparaging look.

"Stop being so lazy, Willie. Robert's father really did help us. So, yeah, tell him I'll do it. And tell him you'll do it, too."

"It'll be weird being on Robert's side," I said.

"We'll just have to suck it up. It's only like two weeks."

So that was that. We registered our team the next day. The sales would begin the following month.

A few days after that Dad called a family meeting, our first in almost half a year. We were all so busy and involved in so many disparate activities that it was unusual for the whole family to be together, and definitely unusual for us all to be paying attention to any one thing at the same time.

On this afternoon Coyle, Fergus, Maddy, and I were all sitting side by side on the long couch. Dad sat back on the easy chair, seeming pleased about something. Mom came in from the kitchen, drying her hands.

"Your father and I feel that sometimes all we're doing is what we need to do, and not taking time to smell the roses."

"All stick, no carrot," Fergus said. "Welcome to the family."

"Will you shut up," Maddy said. "I don't want this to take all day."

"Your father and I want you to have fun and not just be working all the time," Mom said. "And so, with that in mind, your father has an announcement."

Our father cleared his throat and leaned forward and tried to look benevolent. He obviously thought he had something momentous to tell us.

"As a treat for everyone, I have a surprise."

"Are you going back into the hospital?" Fergus said.

Dad put his fist into his palm.

"If anyone's going into the hospital it's you. Now shut it." He turned to the rest of us. "I have gotten five tickets to the Bob Seger concert, which is in two weeks. Me and all of you will be going to this concert together."

Dad waited for a reaction. There was complete silence.

"You mean we're going to a concert with you?" Fergus said after a moment.

"I can arrange for you to renovate instead."

"I'd almost rather," Fergus said. "Why doesn't Mom have to go?"

"Oh, be quiet," Mom said. "Your father has gone out of his way and spent a lot of time and money and gotten you tickets for a concert. Are you all that ungrateful? What do you say?"

There was a long silence, then Coyle said, "Thanks."

———

I haven't mentioned Bob Seger yet, but he was a deity in our house. Dad loved Bob Seger with the unalloyed force of his relentless personality. He loved the anthems. He loved the slow ballads. He loved the blue-collar rockers. You basically couldn't ever say anything bad about Bob Seger unless you wanted to call down the full wrath of my father's fury. For all our childhood, whenever we worked in the office buildings, or exercised in the basement, or went on road trips, it was always Bob Seger in the tape deck, particularly *Night Moves,* which was my father's favorite album.

And so when Dad heard that Bob Seger was coming to the Chicago area that fall he didn't ask us if we wanted to go. Like everything else, he just assumed that we'd all go along gladly, and if we didn't, too bad. It was a "family obligation."

That family meeting about the concert was in late October. In mid-November, we all climbed into the car on a Saturday afternoon and Dad drove us to Fanny May's, where we got three boxes of chocolates. We then rode to Big Al's Beef, where we each got a foot-long sandwich. Then he drove on to the Rosemont Horizon. I think we arrived at around five o'clock, four and a half hours early. They hadn't started to collect for parking yet. The concession people were just starting to arrive. We were insanely early. Dad got out of the car and looked around the empty lot.

"Number-one fans," he said.

Coyle, Fergus, Maddy, and I got out of the car and looked at Dad sullenly.

"What?" Dad said. "We'll get good seats."

"It's not general admission," Fergus said.

"We're five hours early," Coyle said.

"Let's just check it out," Dad said. "Stop complaining."

Dad started toward the stadium, bustling and swaggering, which was the way he acted when he knew he'd messed up and felt self-conscious. We arrived on the west side of the stadium and saw the ushers walking into a double-doored entrance, which was propped wide open. Dad motioned furtively for us to follow him, all cloak and dagger. Maddy, who was eleven years old, stopped outside the doors. She knew we weren't supposed to go in without them taking our tickets. Fergus grabbed her and dragged her in, and by that point Dad had cut to the right while the guards turned left. We met him at the base of a series of concrete ramps.

"Yes!" Dad said. "First ones in."

"We'll be the first kicked out," Coyle said. "We're not supposed to be in here."

"They didn't take our tickets," Maddy said.

"Didn't you ever sneak into a movie?" Dad said.

"No," Fergus said. "Did you?"

"All the time," Dad said.

This was news to us. Dad turned to Maddy.

"Don't worry. We have tickets. We're not doing anything wrong."

"I actually think we're trespassing," Coyle said.

Dad began to reply, but then music echoed through the empty walkways. It was the muffled first notes of "Turn the Page" coming from inside the stadium.

"Yes!" Dad said, holding a fist up. "Sound check. Let's go."

"We'll get kicked out," Coyle said.

Dad gave Coyle a derisive look.

"Are you a wuss?"

"Wuss," Fergus said to Coyle.

"We're missing it!" Dad said.

Dad hurried up the ramp and disappeared somewhere above us.

"Should we go after him?" Coyle said to me.

"How should I know?" I said.

"We snuck in," Maddy said. "We'll get in trouble."

"We'll just say we were following our father," Coyle said. "It'll be him who gets in trouble."

Dad was above us somewhere, sprinting up the concrete ramps. Being that close to the great man overrode all sense of caution. Seger was doing his sound check!

We were left alone with Coyle. Since Dad's medical scare, our father had become less insanely concerned about our every action, but strangely, Coyle had become more attentive to us, as if our father and Coyle had switched places. We waited for Coyle to tell us what to do.

After a moment, he said, "Dad's being an idiot, but we better follow him."

We walked up the ramps after our father. We entered a concrete hallway that opened up into the vast, gloomy stadium. Far away we saw the lit figures of the band wandering around onstage. Dad was already halfway down to the ground floor when we arrived in the open area of the stadium. Dad waved to us furtively and kept on going down into the gloom. Coyle, Fergus, Maddy, and I muttered about how we weren't supposed to be there and we'd definitely get kicked out and how we should be hiding, not walking right up to the stage, but we followed him.

Dad walked to around the twentieth row and then cut into the aisle and we came up and sat next to him, the five of us slumped in the unlit stadium, while onstage, twenty yards away, Bob Seger, Dad's favorite musician of all time, was talking with a soundman. Dad motioned to us, making sure we were taking it in. There he was. The rock god! Bob Seger! And we were there for the sound check. Yes!

The soundman walked off and Seger turned to his band— one, two, three—and kicked into "Against the Wind," and at that moment Dad just about lost his mind. He was bouncing up and down and shaking his fist and smiling from ear to ear.

I was not a fan of Bob Seger. By the age of sixteen I had put classic rock behind me. I liked REM and U2 and Elvis Costello. I thought Seger was cheesy and for old people. And even if I had liked him, which I didn't, Dad's unbridled enthusiasm would have turned me against him.

But I have to admit, despite my skepticism, Seger sounded pretty good. Even in the sound check he seemed like he was having a good time. He seemed like he got along with the guys in the band. He put his heart into it.

So Seger played "Against the Wind" and Dad was rocking back and forth in his seat, utterly pleased with himself, checking us every few moments to make sure we understood that we were getting our own special concert. Seger went on to play "Mainstreet" and "The Fire Down Below" and the first chords of "Rock and Roll Never Forgets." Soundmen and musicians were talking over the songs, giving instructions, but the band went on playing and got through the entirety of "Mary Lou" and then started in on "Night Moves." Despite myself, I thought "Night Moves" was a pretty good song, and for about six minutes the five of us sat there, transfixed. As much as we liked to mock our father, to say that he was crazy, that he had no common sense, we had to admit that he had led us on some unique adventures and had thrown himself into his duties as a father wholeheartedly, and for that moment, listening to "Night Moves," we all felt pretty good about being together there at that concert. For our entire lives we'd been told that other kids got special things but we didn't because our situation was different. We had to accept what we could get. But now Bob Seger was playing a concert just for us. And it was pretty nice.

The song ended. Seger jumped off the stage and started toward the open doors, where daylight filtered in. His bus waited just outside.

"Stay here," Dad said, and started down the aisle.

"Where's he going?" Coyle said.

"To be an idiot," Fergus said.

"Let's go," Maddy whispered.

"I'm not missing this," Fergus said.

Dad walked up to the stage and stepped right in front of Bob Seger as he went toward his bus. Dad held his hand out.

"Just wanted to shake your hand. I love your music," Dad said.

It was so quiet in there we could hear every word.

"Cool, man," Seger said.

They shook hands.

"Good music," Dad said with all the force he could muster. "Really good music."

"Thanks. Glad you like it."

Dad pumped his hand some more, then Bob Seger said

thanks again and pulled his hand away and walked on. A security guard was already approaching Dad from behind. He took him by the elbow and began to lead him out.

"Busted," Fergus said.

"Let's go," Maddy said.

The four of us walked back along the aisle in the direction we'd come. We made our way up the steps and then down the ramps and when we walked back out into the parking lot we found Dad standing near our car.

"I shook Bob Seger's hand! The guy looks like a lowlife, but he makes good music."

"You hear that?" Fergus said. "He looks like a lowlife."

"But we'll forgive him," I said. "He makes good music."

"He sort of looks like your friends," Dad said to Coyle.

"Imagine that," Coyle said.

About four hours later the real concert started and our seats were so far away that the guys in the band were just dots in the distance. But all the time we were watching the concert we knew that we'd had our own special performance beforehand.

On the way home that night Dad talked about the sound check and how it was a special thing just for us, and at first I liked that he mentioned it. It was true. It was a good moment. But over the following days Dad kept going on and on about the sound check and the more he talked about it the more it started to bug me. I could see that it wasn't just a memory at a good moment. He wanted that concert to be this legendary thing that we'd all remember, something that would be a barrier between us and our childhood difficulties. And I guess

I can understand his wanting to draw a line in the sand, to have a fresh start, but the thing is, I didn't want our past struggles to be forgotten, either. For me it was a question of being truthful. The fights had happened. I wasn't going to deny them. If anything, I wanted to remember them vividly, even to exaggerate them, to accept them as part of our story. I told myself that if my parents were going to try to make this fantasy version of our childhood, then I was going to hold even tighter to my version of events. I was going to be the one in the family who remembered.

The winning team in the coupon book competition usually sold somewhere between five and seven hundred books, which meant five thousand to seven thousand dollars raised. A team could get receipts from only five people, but the easiest way to fudge on this was to get coupon books from other kids and pool them together on a single team. That was considered normal and even essential to be a contender for the award. Most people didn't want to work without recognition, so human nature kept this method in check, but, as it turned out, Coyle's friends didn't care if they got credit for their sales. They just wanted to stick it to Liam and Tom, whom they'd never liked. It didn't help that Liam and Tom called their team the Gladiators—a name we mocked relentlessly. Our team was the Choppers, after the bikes Coyle and his friends rode.

The sales went on for four weeks, and I found that I was

better at selling than Coyle, who would just hold a book up and say, "You want one or not?"

Selling seemed like begging to Coyle. He just couldn't do it.

I, on the other hand, had no problem begging. I would wheedle, cajole, banter, and make deals. I wasn't above making myself look pathetic. I was articulate and looked like I was about twelve years old and I came in with more sales than anyone else, except Robert, who hadn't been lying when he said he was a good salesman.

Coyle managed the crews, took in the sales slips, and tallied them. He ran the business end and made sure the salespeople showed up to work. Robert ran the sales crew and for four weeks we all worked together, and by the end, as far as we could tell, we were beating the Gladiators by at least a hundred coupon books, probably more.

One afternoon in the last week of sales after we'd all gotten used to working with one another, we were in the backyard and Robert walked out to where Coyle's bike was parked. It was a warm day and Robert was wearing his cutoff khaki pants and a pastel tennis shirt and high-top sneakers. He glanced back at Coyle as he reached the bike, to see if it was ok, and Coyle nodded that it was ok. Three and a half years before they'd fought because Coyle would not let Robert touch the bike. Now Coyle agreed offhandedly.

Robert threw a leg over the bike. He kick-started the engine and put the bike into gear and gave it a little gas. The bike eased forward and Robert rode slowly around the backyard once, and then a second time, then brought the bike back to the spot where he'd gotten on it.

"Take it out on the road if you want," Coyle called. "I don't care."

"That's all right. Thanks."

Robert turned the bike off and walked back, holding a fist up, saying, "I finally got to ride your bike."

"Only took you four years to get permission," Fergus said.

Coyle saw me watching all of this. He knew what I was thinking. He had let Robert ride it but he still didn't want me touching it. There had been a warming between us over the last years, but a part of me resisted this warming of relations, and I think part of Coyle resisted it as well.

"When you match Robert in sales you can ride it, too," Coyle called.

He said it as a joke, but I knew the prohibition against touching his bike wasn't a joke. I'd only ridden it that one time with my father. Coyle had never said it was ok. The bike was still a sore spot between us. I guess I didn't blame him after I'd hit him with the gun, but it bugged me. Everyone could ride it—even Robert—but not me.

On the last week of the sales period, the only neighborhood we had left to cover was the richest one in Indian Hills, a private development that lined the golf course. We had saved that neighborhood for last because many of the houses had gates so you could not get to the front doors, and the houses were so far apart that it wasn't efficient to walk between them. Robert, Coyle, Fergus, and I were going one way on the Ring Road when we saw Liam and Tom and Doug walking the other way. They were three of the five members of the Gladiators, and as we passed Liam called out, "This is private property."

"Just ignore them," Robert said, but Fergus yelled out, "Private for you, too."

"I live here," Liam said complacently.

"Do you really?" Fergus said with mock admiration.

Robert and Coyle snickered.

"Come on over here and say that," Liam said.

"I don't care," Fergus said. "I'll come over."

Fergus handed his backpack to Coyle and started across the street toward Liam and Tom and Doug, who were standing along some clipped hedges. Fergus was a stocky fourteen-year-old at that time, with his straight brown hair, a loose-limbed, rolling, athletic way of walking, and a cheerful, sarcastic, joking manner. Liam, who was eighteen, had droopy eyes, shaggy blond hair, and a thuggish demeanor. He played defensive line on the football team and had broken a quarterback's arm that year. I'd also heard he'd choked his girlfriend in the hallway. He was not a nice kid.

As Fergus crossed the narrow, empty road Liam said something low to Tom and Doug. Robert tapped my side.

"He's going to grab him."

Coyle tensed, ready to sprint across the street to help. Fergus was almost to Liam when he held his hands up like he'd apologize.

"I was just saying you don't own the neighborhood—"

Then two things happened quickly. Liam reached to grab Fergus's shoulder and Fergus ducked beneath his arms and, pivoting, hit him hard in the kidney. Fergus had spent years sparring with Coyle. He knew how to box. He really nailed him. Liam jerked to the side and let out an uff sound and fell on one knee. Fergus leapt away and skipped across the street.

"I'm too fast, can't catch me," he called.

Liam sat down in the road and then fell, holding his side. Fergus started prancing back and forth on the other side of the road.

"Down in three! Down in three! I am the greatest!"

Robert turned to Coyle.

"I love your family," he said.

"Idiot," Coyle said to Fergus.

"What?" Fergus said. "I am the greatest!"

A car had stopped across the street.

"Are you ok?" the driver said to Liam, who was lying on his side.

"We better get going," Robert said.

We hurried away and got in Robert's car and drove back to our house and half an hour later Coyle, Robert, and I were standing in our driveway when a green Jaguar pulled up and stopped in front of the house. Liam was in the passenger seat. In the driver's seat was a very complacent-looking guy wearing a camel-colored coat. He stepped out of the car and Robert waved to him.

"Hey, Mr. Griggs," Robert called.

"Hello, Robert," he said.

"Is Liam ok?"

"He will be. No thanks to you."

Robert held his hands up.

"Not me who hit him. I come in peace, Mr. Griggs. You know that."

"Cut it, Robert" was all he said.

The screen door creaked open and Dad appeared in the doorway. He came down the porch steps. Mr. Griggs motioned to Liam to get out of the car.

"Your son got in a fight with my son. Hit him in the kidney. Cheap shot."

Dad turned on Coyle, who held his hands up.

"Wasn't me," Coyle said.

Dad looked at me.

"Not me, either. It was Fergus," I said.

Dad's expression changed. He glanced at Liam, who was six-foot-two and weighed at least two hundred pounds. Fergus was about a foot shorter.

"Fergus!" Dad yelled.

A moment later the door opened. Fergus came out, grinning, then saw Liam and his father at the bottom of the driveway.

"Get over here," Dad said.

Fergus walked down the steps slowly.

Mr. Griggs saw Fergus and seemed bewildered. Robert turned away, holding laughter.

"Is this the kid?" Mr. Griggs asked Liam.

Liam kept his eyes down.

"He hit me before I could do anything," Liam said.

"He was grabbing for me," Fergus said. "So, yeah, I fought back."

Liam's father turned to Liam, who shrugged a little.

"Well, tell him you're sorry," Dad said. "Can't go around hitting people."

"Sorry," Fergus said. "Didn't mean to hurt you."

Liam's father looked like his head would explode.

"Get in the car," Mr. Griggs said to Liam.

Mr. Griggs looked back at my dad.

"Won't happen again," Dad said.

Mr. Griggs nodded, and as he was getting back in the car, Dad said to Fergus, loud enough that Mr. Griggs could hear, "Next time, pick on someone your own size."

Robert, Coyle, and I burst out laughing. Liam's father gunned the engine.

That was the second-to-last day of the coupon book sales.

By the morning of the last day we calculated that we had sold more than eight hundred coupon books, which was a record. Liam's team had sold less than six hundred, so we were pretty confident that we had won, but on the last day of the contest Robert, Coyle, and I walked over to the administrative offices to check the tallies and saw that the Gladiators were now winning.

"Impossible," Robert said. "Must be a misprint."

Robert went into the administrative offices, and when he came back out he told us that it wasn't a mistake. Tom's and Liam's fathers had each bought two hundred and fifty coupon books that morning. That was five thousand dollars. There was no way we could make up the deficit in the time we had left. Even in the administrative offices there was some grumbling that it wasn't exactly in the spirit of the thing to have the parents buy the victory for their kids, but it was all for charity, anyway, and an escalating competition was exactly what the Chandler Foundation wanted.

"Maybe we get everyone together and make one last push," Robert said, but we all knew there was no way. If it was fifty or a hundred coupon books, maybe we could have sold them. But we were now behind by three hundred coupon books, and to sell three hundred books in a day would be impossible.

After school we were all out at the bike racks. Robert paced back and forth, cursing. Coyle stared off with a fixed expression. If you didn't know him you might think he didn't care. But it was the opposite. He cared too much.

"Doesn't it bug you?" Robert said.

"Whatever," Coyle said.

Coyle was sinking into himself, like he did when he was disappointed.

"Hello, boys." It was Robert's father, pulling up in his car. "Are you basking in your victory?"

"Nope," Robert said. "Stewing in our defeat."

Robert's father got out and Robert told his father what had happened. Mr. Dainty went over the numbers carefully. I could tell he was suspicious that Robert was making an excuse for losing. He saw he wasn't.

Just then our father walked up. He had also come to pick us up.

"Come here a minute," Mr. Dainty said to our father. "We gotta talk."

Mr. Dainty and my dad walked off, and when they came back Mr. Dainty said, "Al and I have decided to make a joint donation to the Chandler Foundation. We'd like to buy five hundred books, just like the Corleys and the Griggses."

"Yes!" Robert shouted.

A shadow passed over Coyle's face.

"You don't have to," he said to our father.

"We want to. It's all for a good cause," Mr. Dainty said quickly. "And I wouldn't be doing it if you hadn't already put in the work and were beaten by some underhand maneuverings. Both me and Al want to contribute."

Coyle knew that Dad couldn't have put in much, if anything.

"Thanks, Dad," Robert said. "Thanks, Mr. Brennan."

"Agh. Not a big deal," Dad said, looking a little sheepish.

Mr. Dainty went to his car and wrote out something and then he took my dad aside and after a while they shook hands. Then Mr. Dainty walked back to us.

"I have the check right here," Mr. Dainty said. "It's from both of us."

"Yes!" Robert said again.

He snatched the check and went in and registered this final sale and that was it. An hour later the contest ended, we won, and Mr. Dainty, along with our father, were made Knights of the Chandler Foundation, which we mocked for the next ten years. Our father, patron of the arts, philanthropist, Chandler Foundation Knight.

A few weeks later they had the Chandler Foundation award ceremony, and after the ceremony the parents and family members lingered. Coyle stood among the crowd, pleased with himself but trying not to show it. When he was younger,

Coyle had always been the captain of his teams, the president of the student council, at the center table in the cafeteria. He had been cast out of these positions of esteem around the time he turned eleven. It was because we were poor and our lives were harder than the other kids and we acted differently than them. That had mattered for a while and then, slowly, it had stopped mattering. That year Coyle had been invited back into the same group he'd been cast out of years before. I saw all this clearly that day at the banquet. Coyle had rejoined the mainstream.

Robert, of course, was in his element at the banquet. He paraded back and forth. He rubbed it in in front of the Corleys and the Griggses. He basked in our triumph.

At one point Robert walked over and shook my parents' hands and said congratulations and Mom and Dad said congratulations to him and for a moment it felt like we all belonged there in Seneca and at that fancy school. At the time I decided it was an artificial feeling brought on by the money that Mr. Dainty had spent, but I'm not sure this is true. I think now that the family probably fit in more than we realized. We didn't have the house or the cars or the clothes that other families around us had, but we'd grown up in that world and we more or less knew what was expected of us. By the age of sixteen I knew for a fact that in the upper-class world there was shame in poverty and casual ridicule of anyone who appeared not to have money, but I also knew there were methods of defusing this snobbery, and to some extent, it had power only if you let it have power. Coyle had proved that. In my heart I would always be on the blue-collar side of things. I would always be aware of the kids who had grown up

with privilege and how kids who had a lot of money immediately gravitated to other kids who did, and that bugged me.
But I wasn't completely inept socially. Almost despite myself,
I had learned how to operate in that rich-kid world, and that
was a valuable skill. I was a New Trier student, and I would
be marked by it for the rest of my life.

The Chandler Foundation award ceremony was my last
real interaction with Robert. I saw him in school afterward
a few times, but we didn't talk much and half a year later
he left for college. I hardly considered his departure at the
time—he wasn't a close friend—but since then he's grown in
my memory. Robert was both a competitor and a collabora-
tor with our family and was the closest thing I ever had to
a friend on the other side of that class line. And I don't just
mean kids from families with money, because there were lots
of kids with money at New Trier, but I mean that group of
kids who let you know they had money, whose every action
was saturated with that world of privilege. Through Robert
I had begun to understand how to act around people who
knew that they were privileged and expected others to know
it. Even more, I began to understand that all these well-to-do
kids weren't against us, that the doors might be open if we
tried them. That was a useful lesson for me and one I'm not
sure I would have learned if it weren't for Robert.

Years later, when I considered New Trier and our place in
it, I thought of Robert Dainty as the epitome of the New Trier
student: competent, driven, self-satisfied, crafty, and entitled.
After we moved on from New Trier I didn't know whether
I resented him or felt indebted to him. I never talked to him
again. I think about him all the time.

8

Departure

Any life, no matter how long and complex, is made up of a single moment; the moment when a man finds out, once and for all, who he is.

—Jorge Luis Borges

All through February and March of that year when I was a junior and Coyle was a senior, I was aware of the mail. We didn't talk about it that much, but when I came into the house my eyes always went to the newel post where the mail was put, and I scanned the letters and envelopes to see if there was anything from universities. It was college acceptance and rejection time, and Coyle was waiting.

Up until his junior year I thought Coyle would go to Harvard. But then Coyle had spiraled and gotten a few B's. He'd ditched school a few times and had disciplinary reports. No one seemed to know what this meant for his chances, but we were pretty sure it meant he would not be getting into the very top schools. There were enough kids with perfect transcripts that if you did not have a perfect record you had to settle for something other than the best.

Coyle had applied to Harvard, Princeton, Stanford, Brown, Virginia, Cornell, and the University of Illinois. Coyle figured he'd at least get into U of I, but his college counselor wasn't so sure.

"The recent grades are weighted more heavily. You did not end well," he said.

This comment freaked my parents out. My attitude was more complicated. A part of me wanted Coyle to do well, as it was a harbinger of how I would do myself. But it was also a competition, and I knew that if Coyle got accepted everywhere it would annoy me, because there was no way I was getting into an Ivy League school or anything close to that. I'd almost flunked out my sophomore year.

So I waited along with Coyle, twisted inside, half fearing, half eager. And then one day in late March I walked in to see a letter from Harvard on the newel post. The envelope was pretty thin.

Coyle came in right after me. He picked up the envelope. Mom was in the kitchen. She pretended she didn't know what was going on, but of course she did. She was the one who'd taken the mail and put it on the newel post.

Coyle glanced at me, annoyed that I was hovering nearby. I think he considered going to his room to open it in private, but that would have meant admitting that he cared. Coyle tore the letter open casually, glanced at it, and tossed it onto the table in the hallway.

"Rejection," he said. He walked past me and into the kitchen, "Shot down by Harvard."

"Oh, forget them," Mom said. "It's only the first. You'll get in somewhere."

"Sure," he said, and went on down the stairs.

I stood holding my mouth shut tightly, trying not to smile. I realized I was relieved. It would just be too annoying if Coyle got into Harvard.

Princeton came the next day. Again I got home before Coyle. I saw the envelope on the newel post. It was another skinny letter. I was filled with a combination of vindictive glee, guilt, and uncertainty. I didn't want Coyle to have an undiluted success, but if he didn't get in anywhere that meant it would be hopeless for me.

An hour later Coyle walked in with his baseball glove. He saw the letter from Princeton. He opened it.

"Rejection from Princeton," he called out.

He tossed the letter aside. Mom looked like she wanted to hug him, but he just dropped his head and walked past her and went on down to his room.

That night at dinner everyone was careful not to talk about it, but I woke in the night and saw Dad's light was on and heard him huffing as he did push-ups and sit-ups at two-thirty in the morning. Mom made an extra-large breakfast the next morning, with bacon and coffee cake. Fergus said he wished Coyle got rejected every day. Coyle himself didn't talk about the rejection. He pretended he didn't care.

Later that day the four kids all had to clean out the basement of a building Dad was renovating. We worked all afternoon carrying bricks from a collapsed wall to an out-side Dumpster. Later, on the way home, we stopped by the

lakeshore. It was mid-March and about twenty-five degrees
out and the wind was blasting off the water. Coyle had not
talked about the rejections, but he had been distracted all day.
Our whole upbringing was on trial. It all depended on the
results of Coyle's applications, and I knew he felt that pressure. Coyle got out of the car and without a word walked out
to the bluff where we could see waves crashing and tumbling
in toward shore. There was ice built up onshore and over
the pier. Water frothed and churned around the pier. Waves
struck the barrier rocks at the end of the pier, exploding in
glittering cascades. There was a red light on a pole at the end
of the pier.

"Let's go," Coyle said.

"Go where?" Fergus said.

"Out onto the pier," Coyle said. "We'll make it out to
the red light."

I looked doubtfully at the crashing waves and rocking
swells. The pier was not the kind that is on stilts. It was a concrete slab that went straight out into the water and was only a
few feet above the level of the water. There were no railings.
The largest waves broke across the surface of the pier, which
was covered with a skin of ice. There were icicles hanging off
the underlip of the pier.

"If a wave comes over we'll get swept in and die," I said.

"So, we'll avoid the waves," Coyle said. "Big deal."

"Why are we doing this?" Fergus said.

"Who else is going to do it?"

Fergus was pleased by that logic.

"Do I have to go?" Maddy asked.

"No," I said, and Coyle wheeled on me, furious.

"Willie!" he hissed. "She does have to go."

That was all he said, but I understood that the walk on the pier was more than just a dare. It was what Coyle was doing instead of talking about colleges. He wanted us all with him. After a moment, I relented.

"We're all doing it," I told Maddy.

So, I gave in to Coyle, that one time, when he wanted to walk on the icy pier during the college acceptance season.

"Yes!" we all said at the same time.

Coyle started down the bluff, not even looking back to see if we were following. Fergus, Maddy, and I all looked at one another, waiting to see if anyone would resist, but none of us did. Fergus followed Coyle and then I followed him and Maddy followed me and we all walked down and reached the beach, where frigid gusts blasted off the water. Spray stung our faces. We stood together at the base of the pier, on the wet, slick, icy surface.

"Maddy will hold on to me," Coyle said. "If I turn back, follow me. If I go forward, you keep going. If anyone falls in, swim to shore. We'll try to help."

I looked at the swirling, slushy, ice-filled water around the pier. Enormous ice chunks were grinding and knocking against one another in the waves. There was no way we could swim in that water if we fell in.

"We fall, we die," I said.

"Incentive not to fall," Coyle said.

And with that, Coyle took Maddy's hand and started out onto the pier. Fergus and I followed, inching our way out over the wet, icy surface, with the churning, ice-filled water on either side. I will remember the walk over that pier for the rest of my life. I'll remember that we were out there in the first place because for the only time in our adolescence I'd given in to Coyle. And I'll remember, in the end, the way we clung to one another, imagining that would protect us if a wave rose up and swept across. I'll remember the frigid water rocking and sloshing on either side of us as we went out. I'll remember that feeling of relief and exhilaration as we made it past the halfway point and were protected by the rocks piled up at the end of the pier. Coyle anchored himself on the pole with the red light and we anchored ourselves to him. From that vantage point I could see lights from the large houses that lined the shore. Mansions, all of them, set back from the water, wedged in trees. We let out cries as the waves smashed into the barrier rocks and sent water up in glittering sheets that were blown back and pattered on our jackets, whooping and hollering as the glittering water blew past us. Coyle never talked about the rejections. He never complained. He just walked out on the ice-covered pier to prove that he could do it. And we all did it with him.

Two days later I arrived home and saw that Coyle had gotten envelopes from Brown and Cornell and the University of Illinois. I thought a few of the envelopes were thicker than the ones before, but it was hard to tell. If he got rejected from Illinois he would likely not get in anywhere else. Mom and Dad knew this, too. It was the moment of truth for them. They had bet their whole lives, years of drudgery, on the idea that living in Seneca would increase our chances of moving up in the world. Dad believed intrinsically that his plans had worked, that we were "superior human beings." But if Coyle didn't get into college it would be a clear indication that his methods had been flawed.

Over the next few hours Maddy and I lingered in the living room, waiting for Coyle to get back. Even Fergus, who was watching TV in the den, seemed to understand that something big was going to happen, either good or bad. We were not, in general, a very tactful family, but during that time no one talked about what was happening. Everyone knew that Coyle's fate, and in some way our own, would be decided that night.

Coyle had a baseball game and Dad was working late so it was just me and Mom and Fergus and Maddy at the dinner table. We ate without mentioning the envelopes that were waiting but I knew we were all thinking about them. Finally, at nine o'clock, a car pulled up in front and Coyle got out in his baseball uniform with tan dirt on the knees and his mitt hanging off his bat. He walked in, holding his muddy cleats in one hand, his bat in the other. He saw the three envelopes on the newel post. He leaned his bat against the wall and set his cleats down. I heard Fergus in the den turn down the sound on the basketball game.

Coyle opened the first envelope from Illinois. He glanced at it. He paged through a few sheets of paper. He tossed them onto the table.

"Hey," he said offhandedly. "I got into U of I."

Mom came into the doorway, wiping her hands.

"Congratulations. I thought you would."

She hugged him.

"I know it's not your first choice. But congratulations. What about the others?"

Coyle opened the next letter from Brown and let out a little huff.

"Got into Brown. No scholarship. But I got in."

"Oh, congratulations."

She started crying.

"Not like we can afford it," Coyle said.

"We'll apply for aid."

"We better get a lot," Coyle said. "It's really expensive."

"Oh, Coyle, I am so proud of you."

He opened the last envelope. He held it up.

"Triple crown. I'm in at Cornell."

Mom let out a little shriek.

"Oh my God, I'm so proud." She just kept saying this. "I am so proud. Oh, Coyle. Oh, Coyle. I'm so proud."

And she was wringing her hands and crying and wanting to hug him but she'd already done that and so she was stepping from foot to foot and wrapping a dish towel around her hands. Fergus walked in and held his hand up.

"So you're getting out of this place. Congratulations."

Coyle slapped his hand and went on to the freezer for ice cream, leaving the letters on the entranceway table for us all to see.

When Dad came home an hour later Mom couldn't wait for him to get in to give him the news. She walked out to the driveway and told him what happened and Dad let out a whoop that could probably have been heard three blocks away. It was ten at night. I saw a light go on in our neighbor's house. A dog down the block started barking. That's how loud he yelled.

"Yes!" he shouted, holding a fist up, standing in the driveway in his paint-spattered clothing. "Yes! My son's in two Ivy League schools! Yes!"

A minute later Dad burst in carrying the white bucket with the scrapers and paintbrushes and cleaning supplies. He sat at the kitchen table and read each letter about four times and then paraded around the house with them in his fist. "Illinois, Cornell, and Brown! You see, kids. This is what happens. You work hard, you get rewarded. You're all going to be able to do whatever you want. Yes!"

Coyle acted like he didn't care.

"Doesn't really mean anything until I get aid."

"Don't worry about that," Dad said. "We'll find a way to pay for it."

"How?"

"I'll get another job," Dad said.

Fergus laughed loudly.

"It will work out," Mom said, and started crying again.

A day later Coyle was waitlisted at Stanford. Then the day after that he got an acceptance and full-ride offer from the University of Virginia. The baseball coach actually called Coyle, explaining he was being offered an academic scholarship, but he wanted him to play baseball. And that was it for Coyle. He accepted the Virginia offer on the spot. The coach said that he needed to talk to his parents, but Coyle already knew.

That night Dad tried to convince Coyle to wait to see if he could get aid from Brown or to hold out for Stanford, but Coyle said, "I don't want to go to those suckass rich-kid schools. Virginia gave me a full ride. And I can play ball."

"School is more important than baseball."

"But UVA's a good school. And I got a full ride. You

won't have to pay at all. It's my decision. It's over." He held a fist up. "Go Cavs!"

I never knew whether Coyle accepted Virginia's offer because he really didn't want to go to an Ivy League school, or because he wanted to play baseball, or because it was cheaper and was the right thing for the family. Regardless, Coyle accepted UVA's offer. For a few days Dad grumbled about it. I think he'd been blinded by the idea of saying his son was going to the Ivy League. But after a few days the sense of it sunk in and he swung the other way entirely.

"In at UVA! Full ride! Yes!"

For the next three months whenever anyone asked where Coyle was going to college, Dad got this silly, annoying grin on his face, and said. "My son got into University of Virginia. Academic scholarship. Full ride!"

He always had to add that at the end: "Full ride!"

I found all this unspeakably irksome and I think now what happened in those last months before Coyle left for school was at least partially because of my father's gloating. Coyle had won, and Dad wouldn't let anyone forget it, and it got under my skin.

Then, one night at the dinner table Mom held her hand up and said, "I need to make an announcement. Coyle is leaving at the end of the summer and on the night before he leaves we are all going to be here and we're going to have a goodbye dinner. We're going to exchange gifts. And we'll celebrate Coyle's achievement."

"That's like six months from now," Fergus said.

"It's three months away."

"Whatever. It's not next week. Why are you telling us now?"

"I'm bringing this up now, far in advance, because I want you to know that we are establishing a family tradition. When one of us leaves the house for the first time you are all required to be at the last dinner and to exchange gifts. This is a family obligation. We will be together one more time. And then part amicably."

"I think 'eagerly' is the word you're looking for," Fergus said.

"Amicably. Regretfully. Those are the words I mean," Mom said.

She had a quaver in her voice just thinking about it, which I found ridiculous. Despite her steely manner, Mom was sentimental when it came to the family.

"Coyle has worked very hard," she said. "We will send him off in a fitting manner. On that night Coyle will have his choice of food."

"Tacos," Coyle said. "I'm telling you right now. I want tacos."

"Tacos it is," Mom said. "At that dinner each of you will give Coyle a present. And Coyle will give a present in return."

"How much do we need to spend?" Maddy asked.

"It's the thought that counts," Mom said. "It does not even have to be something bought. It could be something personal. A letter or a poem."

"I'm definitely writing Coyle a poem," Fergus said.

"I'm sure your brother would appreciate it," Mom said. "I want you all to understand, you are all going to be here on that last night, and with a present. Got it?"

So Coyle was also getting some overblown goodbye party. It was irritating.

That night I lay in bed, not sleeping, hating the idea of that party. It was overkill. It was like we were trying to pretend we were a mushy, loving family, which I thought was a total lie. I decided I wasn't going to get a present. I would go to the dinner. I would sit there at the table and listen to everyone go on about how sad they were that Coyle was leaving and how great he was and all that. But I wasn't going to pretend his departure was anything other than a relief to me. And I wasn't going to get a present. That was just beyond everything. I kept this to myself for a few days, mulling it over. Then I was passing Coyle in the stairway and I said, "I've been thinking about that last supper that Mom's going so crazy about. I don't want to exchange presents. It's stupid. I'm not doing it. And you don't need to get me a present, either."

"I don't care. Whatever," he said. "Fine with me."

And that was that. Neither of us mentioned it again.

By the time I was sixteen I felt I was comfortable with myself and my role in the world. I wasn't winning any awards but I was ok with that. In school I was pretty much known as a helper. I would always give a ride or clean up after a party. I volunteered to make floats or set up for homecoming. But at home I resisted all work and I held a grudge against Coyle and all the family if I was forced to do anything for them. And this was strange, because, by all measures, conditions in the family had gotten better. Dad had finally saved the money for the down payment and bought the house we'd been renting. He'd gotten his teaching certificate and found a job for the fall, which would be an enormous relief for us, as it would allow our father to quit most of his other jobs. Dad's temper wasn't as bad as it had been. And it was clear that for all Dad's quirks, his methods had more or less worked. Coyle was going to college on a scholarship and we were living in the fancy North Shore. We'd moved up in the world. And more than anything else, Coyle and I had actually started to get along.

I could have acknowledged the improvement, but I didn't want to. Part of it was just that Coyle had won so completely. He'd gotten his "full ride." But it wasn't only envy. In some deep part of myself I was accustomed to resenting my family, and I think I felt I'd lose myself entirely if I let go of that dark impulse.

As spring slipped into summer Coyle's departure loomed enormously in my mind. I told everyone who would listen that I was looking forward to his leaving. I said it was going to be the best day of my life. I told stories about our father's explosive temper and Coyle lashing out and our epic battles. Chaos and violence and mismanagement were the pillars of those stories. I reveled in anything that highlighted the ridiculous, abject circumstances in the house, but particularly anything bad about Coyle. As everyone else leaned into the whitewashed version of our upbringing, I went the other way entirely. And I was absolutely determined not to get Coyle a present.

———

A few weeks before Coyle was supposed to leave Fergus came into the bedroom with a shopping bag from a sports store. I was at the desk. Maddy was on her bed. Fergus reached into the bag and tossed a new White Sox baseball cap at me, the tags still on it.

"What's that for?" I said.

"Present."

"Thanks," I said.

"Not for you, idiot. For the farewell dinner."

I tossed it back to him.

"I'm not getting him a present. And he's not getting me one."

"He's not getting you one because you said you weren't getting him one. Surprise him, Willie. Just give him something."

"I don't want to."

"Why not?"

"It's stupid."

Fergus was not someone who cared at all about sentimentality, but he understood the present wasn't a sentimental thing. Our parents would freak if I didn't get a present, and it would cause trouble. He was trying to avoid a last blowout.

"Be smart for once."

He tossed the hat to me. I tossed it back to him.

"Do you know what's going to happen at the dinner when Mom and Dad find out you decided not to get Coyle a present?" he said.

"They'll see I'm the only honest one in the family?"

"That's not going to be the reaction."

"I don't care."

"You're going to care when you're at the dinner and you don't have a present. It doesn't matter to me, but you're being an idiot."

"I want to be an idiot."

"Good," Fergus said. "Mission accomplished."

Maddy, who'd been listening to all of this, made an impatient sound, shut her book with a snap, and shouted, "Willie!"

"What?"

"Fergus is right. Just take the present. Be nice."

"Exactly," Fergus said. "What does it cost you?"

"I just don't want to do it," I said. "I'm glad he's leaving. It's like a lie."

"Who cares if it's a lie?" Maddy said. "You'll get in trouble if you don't do it."

"I'm not giving a present," I said. "And if that causes trouble . . . good."

Fergus knew me well enough not to try to push it. He just snickered in that way he did when one of us was doing something stupid.

"Your funeral," he said.

He put the hat on himself and walked out of the room.

Maddy went back to her book. They both thought I was being ridiculous. I didn't care what they thought. I said I wasn't getting a present. I was determined not to do it.

Faint swirls in the flat, gray water. Fog over the water. It was a very still, cool afternoon in mid-summer, the day before the farewell dinner. Jimmy and I had brought his canoe out to Lake Michigan and we were paddling away from shore through the dense, shifting veils of fog.

"It's just so annoying," I was saying. "They're all acting like they're so sad that Coyle's leaving, but it's obvious that it's going to be better for everyone when he's gone. All we do is fight. The house is too small. And we never liked each other anyway."

Jimmy had heard about the party all summer. It was practically the only thing I talked about. He just listened, as I talked, and we paddled into a gray, seamless world, the silvery shimmering sheet of water all around us. There was the occasional slap of water on the side of the canoe, but that was the only sound.

"I'll get my own room," I was saying. "I won't have him judging me all the time. I won't be compared to him. Coyle leaving will be the best day of my life."

"You could still give him a present," Jimmy said.

"But I don't want to get him a present," I said. "That's the whole point. I want to show what I really think. They can't make me do it," I said. "And Coyle doesn't care."

Jimmy had lived next door to me since I was born. He knew how brutal our fights had been on both sides. But he also knew Coyle, and I could tell he didn't believe that Coyle didn't care about the gift giving. Coyle could be brutal, but he could also be sentimental. And there had undeniably been a thawing between us since the fight with the gun. In the last weeks I'd felt Coyle lingering, wanting to clear the air, and it was me who'd resisted it. I see now that I'd purposefully stretched out our feud, wanting it to last until he left. I hated the idea of giving him a last-minute reprieve.

The Brother Years

So I'd avoided him on purpose and planned to stick it to him. And it wasn't true he didn't care. He did care, and that's why I didn't want to do it. It was a last blow in our struggle against each other.

Jimmy stopped paddling. I set my paddle down and I lay in the bottom of the canoe looking up into the fog. The canoe drifted to a stop and was absolutely still on the smooth, placid, foggy lake. I knew there was no way they could make me give in. I was thinking with pleasure of my steely resolve, when suddenly Jimmy sat up.

"Which way's shore?" he said.

I sat up. I looked one way and then the other. I pointed off into the fog.

"I thought it was that way. Which way did you think it was?"

Jimmy pointed in the exact opposite direction. We both realized at the same time that we had no way to tell direction. We looked off into the mist. We listened for sounds from shore. We didn't hear anything. We were pretty far out.

"Let's wait," I said. "Maybe we'll hear something. Then we'll know."

We waited. We listened. The mists parted and curled around us. Every once in a while there was a lapping sound as the canoe shifted with our weight and a rounded, diminishing ripple was sent out into the silent, gray sheet surrounding us. Once we thought we heard a car horn, but when we heard it again we realized it was a Canada goose calling in the mist.

It was past seven o'clock. It would be dark in an hour. The darkness didn't matter in itself, but if a storm came up without the fog lifting it could be dangerous. The water was in the low sixties. If we tipped there was no way we'd make it to shore.

"Which way did you think it was again?" I asked.

Jimmy pointed off into the fog.

"Let's wait a little longer," I said. "It can't stay foggy forever."

"But it might until the wind builds and a storm comes up."

I hadn't thought of that. A canoe wouldn't be much good if the waves built up.

Silence, white mists turning gray. It was getting dark. And then, for a moment, it grew a little brighter, and the flat, perfectly round outline of the sun showed through the shifting veils of mist, low on the horizon, and in the exact opposite direction I'd expected. It looked like a nickel.

"If that's west or southwest, then the shore must be this way," Jimmy said.

We turned the canoe around and started paddling in the direction he'd pointed, going quickly, trying to get our bearings. The sun vanished after a minute, but we kept on paddling in what we hoped was a straight line. We'd stop, listen, and then paddle again. After twenty minutes, faintly, we heard the white noise of cars and traffic. Another twenty minutes went by and then the shore, suddenly, came into view. I saw the line of the harbor breakwall. We were farther south than we should have been. We paddled alongshore in the shallow, still water with the sandy, ridged bottom passing beneath us.

At the swimming beach we slid by three park workers in green hip waders walking waist deep, picking trash out of the sand with pointed spikes. I held the wet paddle up as we passed by and they each waved silently in the fog and we went on until we saw the looming bluff of Dyson's Beach. We paddled in hard until the nose ran up and crunched to a halt on the soft, brown sand. An expanding, rippled path spread out behind us. Jimmy got out of the canoe and then I did. For an hour, while we'd been lost, I hadn't thought of my brother or the party. We hauled the canoe onshore and stood looking out at the misty lake.

"That was kind of weird out there," Jimmy said.

"Yeah. Kind of weird," I said.

I took one end of the canoe. Jimmy took the other. On top of the bluff the sound of traffic became loud and intrusive and there was a feeling of coming back to the ordinary world. Jimmy and I looked out over the lake from the bluff. I had thought the water was completely flat, but it wasn't. The water was coming out of the mist in lines of rounded, silvery undulations that moved toward shore slowly and broke with one-inch waves that, from the bluff, splashed on the wet sand, flattened out, and receded silently.

Cloth napkins and candles lit and flickering, all of us crammed together at the small table. It was Coyle's last night, and I was sitting at the dreaded goodbye dinner. We had just finished dessert and I knew what was coming.

Dad leaned forward and put his hands on either side of his plate.

"Who knows how long it will be before we all sit around this table again? I just want to say a few words before Coyle goes on to further successes. Coyle, you are a great kid. You have worked harder than any of your friends. And because of the hard work you've put in, you are going to succeed at college and have an active, productive life. And it will be the same for everyone here. You'll all do just as well."

I rolled my eyes.

"Do you really imagine we're all going to get full rides like Coyle?" I said.

"Try not to ruin things," Mom said.

"I'm not ruining them," I said. "I'm being truthful. A little lowering of expectations is not going to hurt anyone."

"You'll all do just as well in your own way," Dad said. He was beaming and glassy-eyed. I could see he really believed this. "All of you are going to be superior human beings, and will have the opportunity to do whatever you choose."

Coyle had given everyone else presents except me. He said he was going to give mine later. Now it was our turn to give presents back. Dad reached beneath the table and handed a wrapped package to Coyle.

"This is just a little thing. I hope you like it."

Coyle took the package. Dad had written a note in his small, neat script. Coyle read it silently and nodded to Dad.

"Thanks," he said.

He didn't tell us what it said. He folded the note and put it in his pocket.

Then he unwrapped the present. It was an electric razor.

"A razor?" Fergus jeered. "That's a present?"

"I like it," Coyle said. "Thanks."

"See," Dad said to Fergus. "He can shave wherever he wants."

"Or not shave at all," Fergus said. "He'll come back looking like ZZ Top."

"He better not," Mom said.

Then she reached beneath the table and held out a gift bag. Coyle took the bag and pulled out a hoodie sweatshirt with a big "V" on the front.

"Well, I like this," Coyle said.

Fergus was momentarily silenced.

"You don't have anything to say?" Dad said to Fergus.

"Nothing except Mom gave the better present," Fergus said. "Not as good as mine, but way better than yours."

"As usual," Mom said, and Dad grumbled amiably. He wasn't going to lose his temper, not at the family's last supper.

Fergus reached beneath his chair and held out a large glass mug. He hadn't even bothered wrapping it. There was a card in the mug that read: *Good luck, Dude.*

"That's for all the beer you'll be drinking. Probably the only present you'll use."

"I'll definitely use it," Coyle said.

"I hope not too much," Dad said.

"You should use it tonight," Fergus said, and Dad scowled at him.

"Eighteen-year-olds don't drink," Dad said, and Fergus made a scoffing sound, and Dad just laughed and no one said anything else.

Coyle's eyes went to the clock. He was supposed to meet his friends in a few minutes. He knew he wasn't supposed to rush the dinner, but he really wanted to get going. It was his last night.

Mom turned to Maddy, who reached beneath the table and held out her gift. It was flat and rectangular and wrapped perfectly. There were tears in her eyes.

"I'm sure you won't like it," she said.

Coyle took off the wrapping. Inside was a framed picture of the family.

"You can put that on your wall," she said hesitantly.

"I'll put it up. Thanks," Coyle said.

"As a dartboard," Fergus said.

"What a nice present," Mom said.

"Thanks," Coyle said again. "I will put it up."

Maddy lowered her head. Now she was crying. Fergus gave her a look like she was insane. I sat looking at the table without moving. I had bragged about how I was being honest by not getting a gift, but I understood now that Fergus was right. It just looked small-minded not to join in the celebration. I was desperately trying to think of some lie that would make it seem like I wasn't just a wound-up freak.

"Where's your present?" Dad asked me.

"I haven't wrapped it yet," I said.

Fergus laughed.

"Go get it," Dad said.

"I'll give it later," I said.

"He's leaving tomorrow," Dad said.

"I'll give it in the morning."

Dad's eyes narrowed. A spark of annoyance.

"Just go get it."

"I know about it already," Coyle said quickly. "I can get it later."

Mom looked away and said nothing. She knew what was going on. Everyone at the table understood except Dad. He worked so much and had such a rosy view of the family that he never really understood the depths of the rift between Coyle and me.

"Just go get it," Dad said. "He's your brother. Give him the present and don't be an idiot and try to ruin things."

I hesitated, trembling. I opened my mouth. I was going to say I hadn't gotten him a present, that I wasn't giving him one. I was going to say that Coyle and I had agreed not to exchange presents because we didn't like each other and never had and they just needed to accept that. In my nervousness I was going to blast the whole party with some misplaced supposed truth-telling, but before I could speak Fergus stood up, holding a scoop of ice cream on his spoon, as if on display.

"Watch this superior training," he said. Everyone looked up at him, and Fergus turned the spoon upside down. The ice cream fell to the floor with a plop. Fergus lifted his foot, held it above the ice cream, and stomped down. The ice cream splatted across the floor.

"Squash that fly!" Fergus said. He stomped on the ice cream. "Squash that fly!"

"Fergus!" Mom shouted.

Maddy was cracking up. It was not so much what Fergus said. It was his ridiculous manner, that bright-eyed look.

"Have you lost your mind?" Dad said.

"I thought I saw a fly," Fergus said.

Fergus made as if he were following a fly. He was doing what he did best, playing the jester, distracting us from our squabbles. He started out of the kitchen, going out to the carpet in the living room with his ice cream–covered sneaker.

"Fergus!" Mom screamed.

"Gotcha," Fergus said.

He took his sneaker off, turned it upside down, and held it beneath the faucet in the sink. He washed the ice cream off the sole of the sneaker, then put the sneaker in the dishwasher, shut the dishwasher, and turned it on.

"Good God," Dad said.

Mom reached for the dishwasher. She turned it off. Fergus took his shoe out.

"See. All clean," he said.

He put the wet shoe back on and began to clean the ice cream on the floor. The whole thing was meant to divert their attention and it absolutely worked. Coyle looked at the clock and stood up.

"All right. That's it. I gotta go. I'm meeting friends. Later," he said. "Thanks, everyone. I'll see you in the morning."

Dad looked like he'd try to hold him there for another moment, our last dinner as a single unit, but Coyle was already walking out. We heard Coyle downstairs. Then there was a honking outside and Coyle ran out to the waiting car.

"Bye, thanks," he called again.

And that was it. After the months of silent resistance, the party was over in less than an hour. And nothing had happened. I'd slipped past the party without getting in trouble. It would have ruined the party to explain why I hadn't gotten a present. We would have had one last blowout. But Fergus had saved me from a confrontation.

As I started to the bedroom Fergus walked behind me.

"You should have just gotten him a fucking present," he said.

That night I had strange, twisting, vivid dreams of sailing out on the lake with ice-clogged water on either side. Then we were on a very long pier, the waves coming in, the dark water stretching out for as far as I could see, me slipping on the ice on the pier, getting closer to the icy water, falling beneath the surface.

I woke in the night with a single thought: Get Coyle a present.

I stood and got dressed and walked out of the bedroom and downstairs. I thought I could go to the White Hen, the twenty-four-hour store, and get some trinket, but there was no way I could do that without getting caught. Dad was a light sleeper and the bikes were just below his bedroom. I'd wake him. He'd ask where I was going. I'd have to tell him what was going on. That wasn't an option.

So I thought I'd write out a letter to Coyle. That wouldn't be as good as a present, but at least it would be something. It would be the gesture that counted. He would remember that I had at least done something. Mom had even said a letter or a poem was as good as a present.

I got a pen and a sheet of paper and sat there over the blank page but bit by bit I realized I couldn't do it. My thoughts were too jumbled. And, anyway, something in me resisted putting any conciliatory thoughts into writing. It felt overblown.

So then I thought of going downstairs and waking Coyle and saying what I had to say right to him. I'd apologize for not getting a present and tell him I wished him luck and say that I'd miss him. I'd make me not getting him a present more of an afterthought than something I had planned. I'd make him understand that I wished him well.

But even as I had these thoughts I knew there was no way I would wake him up to say these things or even write them down. For one thing, I was still pissed off about those years of beatings when Coyle took his frustration out on me. I had probably deserved some of it, but not all of it. I didn't want to apologize for things that weren't my fault. And even if I could have parsed the good and the bad, I still didn't want to forgive him. And I thought maybe he didn't want me to. Not really. If I'd had to encapsulate Coyle's attitude it would be that he thought I'd made a big deal about small transgressions and blamed him for things in the family that weren't his fault. Coyle had the same hardships and the same punishments as I'd had, but he hadn't made a big drama about it the way I had. We fought. So what? he thought. Everyone fought. Making a big deal about it was stupid.

But another part of me thought it was easy for him to say that. He'd had me to beat on whenever he felt like it. I thought some of his success was based on taking his frustration out on me. And he'd never had to get absolutely thrashed day after day the way I had. He didn't know what it was like. I'd been beaten hundreds of times. I resented it.

And so, though I had some generous feelings toward Coyle, though some of the ice had melted, not all of it had. I half regretted pulling a gun on him, but I wasn't ready to go back on it, either. Pulling the gun had worked. It ended the beatings. Our childhood had been arduous. Maybe our father's methods had worked, but they'd also been excessive and extreme and difficult, and Coyle had made it more difficult for me. That was undeniable. I resented it.

Maybe if we'd had more time to come to some reconciliation things would have been different. But it was useless to think that way. He was leaving in the morning. And I was pretty sure there wasn't going to be any resolution later on. We'd never come to terms as we got older. At least I didn't think so. It would be a dwindling and fading. If I wanted to end things well, I thought I ought to do it right then, when I had the chance.

But I couldn't make myself do it.

I walked back upstairs. I lay in bed. I told myself I could always say something later, but I knew that wasn't really an option. Once Coyle was gone everything would be different and all those battles that seemed so important—the fight with the ice ball, all the stolen and destroyed items, the incident with the gun—all that would fade into insignificance. The time to smooth things over was right then, and I knew I ought to, but I couldn't make myself do it.

I lay awake most of the night thinking about what I could say, but I never went down to say it, and around dawn I fell asleep. I did not wake until ten o'clock, which was the latest I had slept in my entire life.

———

I was half awake, feeling like something strange had happened. I opened my eyes. The light was at a weird angle. I sat up. The clock read ten o'clock but I thought it must be some mistake. When I realized it was actually ten in the morning and that Coyle might already have left, I leapt out of bed with a terrible booming in my chest. I went to the window and saw Coyle's duffel in the driveway. Relief flooded through me. I realized I didn't want him to leave without saying anything to him. I got dressed hurriedly and walked down.

"Hey, Sleeping Beauty," Dad said as I came out the front door.

"We thought you were faking so you didn't have to say goodbye," Fergus said.

"Like Coyle cares if I say goodbye," I said.

Coyle was bent over, tying his shoe.

"I care deeply," he said.

Maddy came out carrying another duffel full of clothes.

"Go help your sister," Dad said. "Seeing how you haven't done anything else all morning while the rest of us have been working."

"My plan has succeeded," I said.

"Typical Willie," Coyle said.

I walked back inside and went down to Coyle's room, which was the converted, concrete-walled shed off the main room in the basement. I would get that room as soon as he left.

That converted storage room had pipes running along the ceiling and a concrete floor with a drain in the middle and one little window up near the ceiling. There was a desk to the right of the door and then his cot. There was a vacant feeling to it. Most of his things were in the car already, but there was a trunk on its side near the door. I lifted it and walked up the stairs and Coyle edged past me in the stairway. I heard him rummaging around in the drawers, getting his last things. I brought the trunk to Dad, who had meticulously arranged the back of the station wagon.

"Watch and learn," Dad said.

He slid the trunk into a slot in which it fit perfectly.

"You kids go to those good schools but I can still teach you something. That's planning and precision right there."

The screen door slammed. Coyle came back out.

"Is that it?" Dad asked.

"That's it," he said.

"You don't have any last little things like your mother would have. Always going back in the house."

"I got it all," Coyle said. "I'm ready."

Coyle tossed a small backpack in the front seat.

Maddy, Fergus, and I were standing there. Dad was grinning, his eyes glassy.

"Well, we better get going," he said in a gruff tone.

"Say goodbye to your brother," Mom said.

"Later," Fergus said, and made as if to punch Coyle.

Coyle gave him a high five.

Maddy, imitating Fergus, held her hand up. Coyle gave her a high five. He turned to me.

"Bye," he said.

"Bye," I said.

We shook hands. It was awkward. With the others the goodbye was jaunty and affectionate. With me it was constricted and formal. They got a high five. I got a handshake. Mom and Dad noticed this, but pretended they didn't.

Mrs. Chambers, our neighbor, was driving by and saw us standing around the parked car. She slowed and rolled her window down and said hopefully, "Are you going somewhere?"

"Hell, yes, he's going somewhere!" Dad shouted. "He's leaving for school. University of Virginia. Full ride!"

"Full ride!" Fergus mocked at the same time.

"Congratulations," Mrs. Chambers said. "Good for you. Good luck."

She said it nicely and drove away. Mom turned to us.

"Your father is very proud of our accomplishments."

"Not like he did anything," Fergus said.

"I think someday you will have a different opinion," Mom said.

Coyle went to the car and started arranging his army duffel into a pillow in the middle seat. He shut the back door and walked to the passenger side.

"You're not giving me a hug?" Mom said.

"I thought I already did," Coyle said.

"That was awhile ago. Now you're saying goodbye."

Mom hugged Coyle for about fifteen seconds. Coyle rolled his eyes over her shoulder. Dad opened the driver's-side door.

"Enough," he said.

Coyle held a hand on the door and, looking away, said to me, "So, I got you a present, Willie. I left it in my room. You'll see it."

"Where's your present for him?" Dad said. "You didn't give it last night. I remembered after Coyle left."

My eyes slid to Coyle.

"He already gave it to me," Coyle said.

"When did he do that?"

"He left it for me."

"Good," Dad said. "That's what I want to hear."

Fergus made a snorting sound.

"Yours is in the room," Coyle said again.

He held his hand up. I slapped it. So in the end I got a high five, too, just like Fergus and Maddy. That felt better.

Coyle got in the car. He took Dad's keys, which were on the seat, put them in, and turned up the music. Dad got in the driver's seat and turned off the music and said, "You're not a college student yet. Don't touch the radio."

"It's going to be Bob Seger all the way to Virginia," Fergus said.

Dad got out and kissed Mom, then got back in the driver's seat. I just stood there, heart pounding. I told myself I was glad he was leaving and after this I would get my own room and would not have anyone to answer to and not have anyone watching my every move. But I also knew that I'd botched the goodbye. He thought I was sticking it to him in the end and that wasn't really how I felt. Truly, I didn't know how I felt, but it wasn't resentful, and even at that moment I thought I could yell something that would make everything all right and would change the tenor of the goodbye. I could go up to the window and tell him I was sorry. I could apologize for our battles and for pretending I didn't care he was leaving, and I wanted to say I knew I'd messed up, and I did care, but another part of me knew I wouldn't say any of this. Not with everyone standing there. And not even if they weren't standing there, either. There was a counter-pull inside me, and it would be years before I worked it out, and I knew by that point it wouldn't really matter. The time for a good ending was right then, before the car pulled out of the drive-way, while the family and our positions in it were still intact. I ought to have been gracious. We ought to have had an ending fitting for our family, but I'd botched it, and what-ever understanding we had arrived at between us, whatever patched-up truce we'd made, that was it. That was all we had.

The engine had started. Coyle was adjusting the volume, not looking up.

"Back in three days," Dad said out the window.

The car was pulling into the street now. A fluttering panic filled me.

"So long, suckers," Coyle called.

I tried to yell goodbye or good luck, something that would show my good intentions at the very end, but it got caught in my throat and came out a stupid gargled cry. Dad held a fist out the window. The car slipped away. They were gone.

"Awesome," Fergus said. "One more year and I get my own room."

Mom turned abruptly from us and walked back into the house, hiding tears. Maddy sat on the porch with her head leaned forward and her long blond hair hanging straight down, hiding her face. I knew she was crying, too.

"What do you care?" Fergus said. "Just one less person to beat on you."

"Quiet," she choked.

"If you want, I can beat on you double," Fergus said. "If you miss it so much."

Fergus went on to the backyard, swinging a baseball bat. None of us wanted to be around one another. We were always ashamed of any emotion, but particularly sentimentality.

I went inside. I started upstairs, then remembered that my room was now downstairs. I was getting Coyle's room. I was now the oldest.

I walked through the basement to the concrete-walled cell. I stood in the doorway, looking it over. The baseball posters on the wall. The neatly made bed. The bookshelf. The old bats in the corner. I noticed there was an envelope on the pillow and I remembered Coyle had said he'd gotten me a present. I realized he must have put it there when he'd gone back down after I'd brought the trunk up. On the outside of the envelope was the word "WILLIE." I got nervous seeing my name in Coyle's handwriting. I thought of all our battles and I figured he'd written a letter to get the last word in. It's hate mail, I thought. I knew I deserved whatever last thing he'd written. He'd wanted to make it up in the end, to show that the fights and the competition didn't matter, but I hadn't been able to go along with the reconciliation and I hadn't even gotten him a stupid present for his goodbye dinner. So I knew I deserved whatever he wrote. Still, if it was malicious I felt like the framework of my soul would crack. I was exposed and I knew if he slipped the knife in I would close up and not open again for a long time, if ever. The letter will say, So long, idiot. It will say, Fuck off. It will say, Goodbye, loser.

I stood holding the envelope. I didn't have the courage to open it. I thought I'd just toss it. But then I'd torn the edge a little. Then a little more. Then I opened it and the keys to Coyle's motorcycle fell onto the table. The letter read:

> *Take care of it. Good luck,*
> *your brother Coyle*

Later that rivalry with my brother and the disagreements inside the family would seem small in comparison to the turmoil of early adulthood. I look back on those battles now not with bitterness but with the indulgence one gives to a family eccentricity. With every year my fondness for my family has grown and though I do not forget the early hardships, they seem less important as they are viewed from adulthood. We had our battles, but we were a close family. Not some half-hearted, polite, bloodless thing, but a real family with feuds, hatreds, battles, and love running underneath. We survived and stayed together in our own way. We became ourselves in the fire of our conflicts.

Epilogue

All of childhood's unanswered questions must finally be passed back to the town and answered there. Heroes and bogey men, values and dislikes, are first encountered and labeled in that early environment. In later years they change faces, places and maybe races, tactics, intensities and goals, but beneath those penetrable masks they wear forever the stocking-capped faces of childhood.

—Maya Angelou

In a series of developmental studies on the neural cortex a group of kittens were raised entirely in darkness except for an hour every day when they were bound, could not move their heads so they could not see their own bodies, and were shown only vertical lines. This confinement went on for the first twelve weeks of the kittens' lives, which is the sensitive period for the development of eyesight in felines. After that the cats were let loose on the world and the researchers noticed a strange thing. The cats that had been shown only vertical lines in their youths could see only vertical lines as adults.

They'd actually run into the cross-struts of chairs. What they found was that if the cats were not exposed to something while they were young, it was impossible for them to learn or even acknowledge its existence later. I believe that something similar happens on an emotional level in close families. For better and for worse, life afterward is always a version of the family. It becomes the framework for our personality and it is how we are oriented to the world and everything in it. There is no getting away from the family, but to see the pattern, to understand it, to come to terms with it, often the individual has to get outside of it, and leave the family behind.

Mid-July, I was nineteen years old, and I was in a patch of shade on sloped land overlooking a rock quarry in Central Indiana. I had grown six inches my senior year of high school and I was now a lanky, bookish college student. I listened to indie rock. I self-consciously denied interest in anything except literature. I feigned indifference to all physical activities, particularly sports.

It was the hottest part of the afternoon and I was lying back with Conrad's *Lord Jim* propped open on my chest, the white beach spread out beneath me, colored towels laid out near the water and cars parked near the line of trees.

"Will!" I heard a voice call.

It was Fergus, far below.

"Rise and shine. Get up."

I sat up to see Fergus at the water's edge, waving his fist, imitating our father. Maddy had come partway up the path.

"We're starting," she said.

She was fourteen now and had just finished her freshman year at New Trier. She was a self-assured teenager with a laconic streak, a swimmer, almost six feet tall, with long, chlorine-bleached blond hair. We had called her man-woman and cro-magwoman all her life, but other people actually thought she was attractive.

"Are you doing it?" I asked.

"Someone has to," she said. "All his friends backed out. And you know what Coyle will do if it's canceled. He'll ruin the day for everyone. You'll do it, right?"

"I'm here to please," I said.

I brushed dirt from my pants and started down the path toward where the others were waiting on the rock-chip beach. About fifteen of us had driven out to the quarry for the afternoon. Coyle had arranged a competition, but his friends, when they understood what the competition consisted of, had all dropped out. It was up to us, his siblings, to be his challengers and victims in the contest.

"He's been talking about it all week," Maddy said, walking alongside me. "He wanted it to be this big thing, but no one else will do it."

"Cause it's too high," I said.

"Of course it's too high. We just need to pretend to try."

On the rock-chip beach there were coolers and blankets and the tinny sound of a radio. Coyle leaned against a pickup truck with his old baseball hat on. He was talking to his summer girlfriend, a matter-of-fact pre-law student. He motioned to me with his beer can.

"You're doing it, right?" he called out.

"I don't want to," I said.

"I love the enthusiasm," he said. He held a fist up. "If you don't compete, you have no chance of being . . . The Champion."

Maddy had waded ankle-deep into the water. She was counting the stone sections of the quarry wall with the end of a twig.

"Ten, eleven, twelve," she was saying. "Thirteen slabs. Each slab is eight feet."

"A hundred and four feet, to be exact," Fergus said.

"Too high," Jimmy said from where he was sitting on a beach towel with his arms around his knees. "Don't do it."

"But if I win I get a prize," Fergus said in that wide-eyed manner.

"What's the prize?" Jimmy said.

"Probably like a gigantic cash bonanza," Fergus said.

Maddy walked from the water and put her shoes on. A few girls we knew from high school sat on their beach towels, watching us. They had heard there was a race to the highest part of the quarry and over the edge.

"Are you really doing it?" one of the girls asked me.

She had long, straight hair that went all the way down her back.

"Apparently, one of us is," I said.

"Someone broke his neck jumping from up there last summer," she said.

"They must not have been tough like us," Fergus said.

The girl whispered to her friend and they both watched us. They knew of our family. Our reputation had grown as we'd gotten older. We were Brennans. We did crazy shit.

I walked over and put my hand in the water. It was warm on top, but colder when I stirred it. I stepped back, wiping my hand on my pants leg. Fergus took a beer from the cooler and shook the water off. I walked over to where Fergus waited at a line that Jimmy had drawn in the rock chips with his heel. Coyle put on a T-shirt. He was still in good shape, but he didn't seem to care that much about sports anymore. Coyle was majoring in business and was talking about getting a job in finance. He said if he was going to have to work he might as well make a lot of money. I thought he was becoming just like Dad.

We stood there, the four of us, lined up on the rock-chip beach.

"Anyone else want to race?" Coyle yelled.

A few dim shapes shifted beneath the trees.

"No one else is stupid enough to do it," Maddy said.

Jimmy walked over.

"Don't jump," he said to me.

"Not like I'll get the chance to," I said.

Coyle's friends lingered at the edge of the clearing. Some of them still had long hair, but others looked like the kids they'd mocked when they were younger. One of the long-haired guys held up a bottle of Maker's Mark.

"Extra bonus prize to whoever wins."

"Oh, great," Maddy said. "Just what I always wanted. A bottle of bourbon."

"There's another prize," Coyle told her. "Something good."

"What is it?" Jimmy asked.

"A surprise," Coyle said. He turned to me. "Are you ready?"

"I'm as ready as I'm going to be," I said.

The four of us stood at the starting line. Coyle was to my left side. Fergus was next to him. Maddy was on the far end from me. I was still holding my book. I folded my page over and put it on a beach towel and walked back.

Coyle handed Jimmy an empty green Heineken bottle. Jimmy held it up in the air.

"This is for Brennan bragging rights," Jimmy said. "When the bottle drops, that's the start. On your marks. Get set—"

Coyle, Fergus, Maddy, and I were all bent down, poised, ready to race up the steeply sloping side of the quarry. Jimmy dropped the bottle.

"Go!"

As he said the word, Fergus pushed Coyle, who fell into me. Coyle grabbed Fergus and all three of us—Coyle, Fergus, and I—ended up on the ground, tangled with one another. Maddy bolted ahead, running free. She had been in training all school year. She was in good shape. She left us all on the white dusty beach.

Fergus was the first to get up. Coyle tripped him. I held on to Coyle. Fergus wriggled free and was up and running, and then we were all up, the three of us, sprinting across the white beach after Maddy, who had at least a ten-second head start. She reached the steeply sloped hill and started up, clawing her way, entering the pines on a braided dirt path. Fergus reached the path and started after her. Coyle and I, at the same time, broke from the path and started straight up the slope, pulling on tree branches, on shrubs, on weeds, elbowing each other when we got close. I hadn't cared about the race until it started, but once I started I wanted to win.

Fergus was a little ahead of us, and when the traversing path crossed in front, Fergus was right there. Coyle reached out and tripped him and climbed over him. Fergus grabbed his leg and Coyle had to shake him off. I scrambled past the two of them and then all three of us were together in a scrum, getting scratched and bruised, pulling one another down, clawing and writhing, making our way through shrubs, thorny bushes, over rocks, going up the steep slope. Maddy had taken the path, which was easier but slower, and as she passed us, her route crossing ours at an angle, Fergus tripped her and pulled himself up and over her. Maddy grabbed his foot as he went over. Coyle ran past both of them. He dodged a stick thrown by Fergus, then was pulling himself up the last incline, clawing his way to the top. Maddy was panting, slowing, disgusted. She had never beaten us in anything, and for a moment she had thought she could win. But once Coyle was ahead she knew none of us would catch him. Fergus and I were clambering up the last bit. Coyle disappeared over the edge.

"Winner and still champion!" we heard Coyle yell.

"Shit," Fergus said.

"That sums it up," I said.

I was bleeding in about six places.

Fergus and I crested to see Coyle in some dusty flats. He jogged to the edge of the dropoff like he'd jump out but stopped at the last moment, skidding. A puff of white dust drifted out over the dark water.

"No way!" he said, laughing.

Fergus ran up ahead of me and peered over the edge. He made as if he'd push Coyle. The two wrestled around, getting close, then backed off.

"Bonus prize for whoever wants to jump," Coyle said.

He reached into his pocket and took out a beer can that he'd brought with him. He hurled the can far out over the quarry. The can arched up high and far, glinting in the light, then fell and kept falling. Far below it made a small white splash in the dark water. A delayed plunking sound rose up. Ripples spread out slowly, the can bobbing in the water.

"Go fetch," Coyle said.

Jimmy and the others down below waited, but none of us jumped. And as I stood there, I realized that Coyle wasn't going to do it. Something had changed in him, and in all of us, really. We'd lived through the hard years, but they were now permanently and irretrievably behind us. The scars were fading and in time would be almost invisible, and all the weapons we'd used to survive in our house would become our most useful tools. Competition would turn into ambition, stubbornness into resilience. Ten years later Coyle would be in finance. Fergus would be a computer programmer. Maddy would be a teacher. We were trained to be warriors, to be explorers, to throw ourselves into arduous and extreme tasks, but the world was not designed for poet warriors. It was a place for ordinary people, and in a few years my siblings would enter normal jobs and normal lives, with just the memory of our excessive childhood inside us, fading bit by bit. It was an affirmation of my father's methods, but it was also a disappointment. I was accustomed to us being Brennans. We were supposed to be different.

The four of us eased from the edge of the cliff and started back into the pines, taking the path. I could imagine the others down below, waiting for one of us to jump, and then seeing the four of us walking back together, shoulder to shoulder. It would be a relief and a letdown. They knew it was stupid to jump from up there, but they expected stupid things from us.

I stopped to look up the slope. I had always wanted to beat Coyle in something, and I could feel that desire still lingering inside me. Walking past, Coyle saw what I was thinking and nudged me forward.

"Come on, Willie," he said.

"Don't touch me," I said.

Fergus looked back.

"Never changes," he said.

"Don't fight," Maddy said.

"We're not fighting," Coyle said. "We're communicating."

Coyle held his hands up to show it was a joke, then motioned for me to follow as the three of them, Coyle, Fergus, and Maddy, went on down the dirt path. I started after them but stopped after a moment. The familiar, ever-present wheels of competition were turning inside me. I wanted to win. I had always wanted to win. And as they went on down I turned and started back up the slope. Coyle realized what I was doing and called my name and then came after me but I was already over the lip of the ridge and crossing the flats. I was too far ahead for him to stop me. I arrived at the rocky edge of the quarry, sprinting, and it was that great moment in adolescence where you throw off what you think you ought to be and start imposing your true personality on the world, a moment of grace and strength and beauty and danger. I was leaping out as high and as far as I could. I was more than a hundred feet over the water, hovering, and then I began to fall, quickly, straight down, turning in air, head thrown back, arms spread wide. I do not remember shouting or making any noise. The entire descent was silent, solemn, and a part of me was outside of everything, watching it. It was finally happening—a tiny white figure plummeting among the enormous gray rock into the dark, still water.

Acknowledgments

This book, like all my books, was not written in isolation. I sent it out to friends and family who let me know what worked and what didn't. That advice was particularly useful on this project which was so close to me personally. I'd like to thank John Zomchick and Michael Knight, who were early readers and encouraged me when I wasn't sure I'd finish. I'd like to thank Terry Shaw who gave me a critical piece of advice at a crucial juncture. And Susan Falls who gave a close, perceptive read. And Tom Garrigus who helped me with ideas for essential pieces in the back end of the book. And Theresa Profant who lived through many versions of the book and was, as always, a force of optimism and strength. I'd like to thank David McCormick, my agent, and Deb Garrison, my editor, for taking on the book and persevering through the long, long editing process. And lastly, I'd like to thank my family, Mike, Ian, Erin, Mom, and Dad, for putting up with my intrusions and public scribbling.

A NOTE ON THE TYPE

This book was set in a version of the well-known Monotype face Bembo. This letter was cut for the celebrated Venetian printer Aldus Manutius by Francesco Griffo, and first used in Pietro Cardinal Bembo's *De Aetna* of 1495.

Typeset by Scribe,
Philadelphia, Pennsylvania

Printed and bound by
Berryville Graphics, Berryville, Virginia

Designed by Nicholas Alguire